HELEN COX

Death Awaits in Durham

Quercus

First published in Great Britain in 2020 by

Quercus Editions Ltd
Carmelite House
50 Victoria Embankment
London EC4Y 0DZ

An Hachette UK company

A CIP catalogue record for this book is available
from the British Library

HB ISBN 978 1 52941 034 1

10 9 8 7 6 5 4 3 2 1

Typeset by Jouve (UK), Milton Keynes

Printed and bound in Great Britain by Clays Ltd, Elcograf S.p.A.

Papers used by Quercus are from well-managed forests
and other responsible sources.

Death Awaits in Durham

ONE

A desperate scream echoed out over the scratchy laptop speakers. The shriek was abruptly muffled and then there was silence.

Slowly, Grace looked over at Kitt. She was perched on the end of the bed in Grace's dorm room, allocated by the administrative powers at Venerable Bede's Vocational Academy in Durham. Secretly, Grace was revelling in the juxtaposition of the strait-laced Kitt and the kitsch-cool Powerpuff Girls duvet cover she'd brought up from Leeds. If she let on about it, however, Kitt would move seats and this somewhat comical view was the only thing distracting her from the morbid story of what happened to Jodie Perkins the year before. After just four weeks at the academy.

'All right, that scream's enough to give anyone nightmares. How did you find out about this?' Kitt asked, frowning.

'I'd have to be deaf and blind not to know owt about it.

1

It's been all the first years can talk about. They never caught her attacker so everyone's wondering who's next? If one of us is going to get picked off, disappear, just like she did.'

Kitt stared for a moment at her ex-assistant who had worked with her at the Vale of York University library before starting on the library studies course here at Venerable Bede's. 'And this recording was just, lying around, I suppose?'

'Not exactly,' Grace said, tucking a brown curl behind her ear. 'The academy has a student radio station. It was in their recording archive.'

'Tell me you didn't hack in,' Kitt said, closing her eyes as if that might shield her from the inevitability of Grace's answer.

'Their password was VENERABLEBEDE2020. Come on, you can't really classify that as hacking. I've seen pub Wi-Fi passwords harder to crack than that.'

Kitt opened her eyes and gave a vague shake of her head. 'Just so long as you know, I'm not paying your bail money when you get caught.'

A look passed between the two women. They both knew that when Grace's rambunctious streak at last put her behind bars Kitt would definitely be the person footing the bail charges. After all, it wasn't as though Grace could call her parents, especially not after what had happened over the summer.

'Play it again,' Kitt said.

Grace took a deep breath and prepared to listen to the somewhat unnerving audio clip once more. It wasn't exactly what you would call Sunday night easy listening. Assuming Kitt had her reasons for asking for the encore, Grace obliged and clicked the mouse over the play button.

'You're listening to Castle Rock FM, a radio station for the students by the students, and I'm Randy Hobbs.' The presenter's voice was sickly smooth, almost cloying enough to make Grace cringe. She'd listened to this clip five times already and the DJ's voice hadn't got any less annoying for it. 'Now, any first years out there might be familiar with our next caller, mechanics student Jodie Perkins. She got in touch with the show because she claims she's uncovered a secret that's going to rock the entire Venerable Bede's community. Quite a big claim just four weeks into her study here. We've got her live on the line now. Hello, Jodie?'

'Randy?' Jodie part-screeched the DJ's name and there was a rustling sound as though she was running and the phone was moving up and down as she did so.

'Yes, Jodie, we can hear you. Everything all right at your end of the line? I understand you've got something to tell us about someone pretty important here at Venerable Bede's.'

'Yeah,' said Jodie. The rustling sound slowed and then stopped. Given how she was breathing into the receiver she seemed to be trying to catch her breath. 'The way things are at Venerable Bede's, this probably won't be a surprise to some

3

but I've been doing some digging and now I've got proof that . . . that . . . what? No . . . What are *you* doing here?'

'Jodie, everything all right?' Randy pushed.

'No! It's . . . Ssssss . . .' was all Jodie managed to say, before there was a scuffling sound and then that all too familiar ear-splitting scream rattled out.

There was a moment's pause before Kitt spoke again.

'What was that sound at the end there? She seemed to be hissing through her teeth.'

'I don't know,' said Grace. 'She seemed to be trying to say something. A name maybe?'

'And the police never found Jodie, or a body?'

'Nothing. The police could never be sure a murder had even taken place. No body. No forensic evidence of a struggle.'

'What about witnesses?' asked Kitt.

'Nobody ever stepped forward. Randy Hobbs works the graveyard shift. This all took place in the early hours of the morning on a Wednesday. Not many people about at that time.'

'But she was clearly talking to someone at the end of that clip, likely an assailant. That in itself is at least some evidence of a struggle.'

'I don't know all the ins and outs but we don't hear the other person's voice so we don't know what was going on at her end of the phone. She screams out, but she might have done that as she was running away from whoever was there, and maybe she got away and disappeared. We don't know if whoever she were talking to got hold of her or did anything physical to her at all.'

'We don't know it, but her disappearance might suggest it,' said Kitt. 'It is tragic, Grace, especially given how young the lass was, but I'm not really sure what I can do to help at this stage.'

Grace stared hard at Kitt. 'Don't give me that. You're the most qualified person I know to sort this out.'

'I wouldn't let Mal hear you say that if I were you,' Kitt said with a funny little smirk.

'DI Halloran's gang have already had their go at solving this one. It's our turn now.'

'Investigations don't exactly work in turns. And I'm not sure referring to the police as "Halloran's gang" is entirely appropriate either . . .'

Grace folded her arms. 'I thought you did that private-investigation qualification to help people?'

'I did, but PIs help their clients. Paying clients.'

'So, what? You won't work this case because you can't turn a profit?'

Kitt let out a sigh almost too quiet to be heard. Almost. 'It's not about profits. It's about costs. Forgive me for not wanting to throw money away on a Grace Edwards-coordinated goose chase. Setting up any kind of operation takes some funding. I'm just starting out and only have the basic apparatus. Speaking of which, is this why you asked me to bring my kit with me? I thought you just wanted to have a play with it.'

'Well, nobody can judge a girl for wanting to have a go with a coffee cup holder that's really a camera, but the opportunity to play with spy gear is a secondary consideration when a young girl is missing, possibly dead.'

'It's a terrible business, just terrible, but it would take a lot more than the resources I have to dig into a trail that went cold a year ago. In cases like these, where someone so young has gone missing, there's a responsibility to be sensitive to those who lost the victim. You can't go charging in and dredging up memories like that lightly.'

'I'm not suggesting we do, but surely there's somewhere we could start. The limited resources only make this case more of a creative challenge, don't they? And anyroad, I thought you wanted to set up your own agency?'

'I still do.'

'Well, you're never going to be able to go part time at the library *and* fund your book habit if you haven't built a reputation as a hard-boiled detective, and the odds of you doing that by following a couple of cheating spouses around the centre of York are low.'

'Oh really,' said Kitt, with a knowing look. 'And you have a better plan, I suppose?'

'Solving a cold case like Jodie Perkins' disappearance would definitely put you on the map.'

Kitt's nose crinkled; her expression dubious.

'Don't make me play you the YouTube video of Jodie's parents appealing for information. It's heartbreaking,' said

Grace. She kept to herself the fact that she'd cried over the footage for a good ten minutes after it had finished. *'We know you're out there somewhere, Jodie, love,'* Jodie's mother had said. *'We will not let you become just another lost girl who's never found. We will never give up.'*

A parent appealing so lovingly to bring their daughter home to them would have drawn a tear or two on any ordinary day, but right now it hit a particularly raw nerve. It had been six weeks since she'd even spoken to her own mother on the phone. She'd tried to convince herself this was a good thing. That maybe some time apart would finally help her mother get used to the idea she was never going to show the level of obedience traditionally expected from a young woman of Indian heritage. All that said, she didn't believe there was anyone out there who wouldn't pine for family after watching the Perkins' TV plea.

Life in Durham had felt more insulated than expected. She was isolated from her friends back in York and Leeds, FaceTiming wasn't quite the same as meeting down the pub or going out to some local dive for a dance, and she hadn't really connected to anyone here yet. The fact that Durham was essentially its own little peninsula cut off by the River Wear didn't help with the sense of separation. A TV news plea from parents trying to find their missing daughter had well and truly knocked down the last of Grace's defences.

'There's no need for that,' said Kitt, interrupting Grace's

musings. 'I can only imagine what her parents went through, which is why I'm reluctant to open up old wounds. At any rate, haven't you got enough going on without diving into a private investigation? Usually, you want in on these things because you're low on excitement levels but you've just started a new course in a new institution in a new city. I can't think that you're short of things to do with your time.'

'Yes, I'm busy enough with the academy but when I heard what happened to this lass, it . . . well, it preyed on me.'

Kitt's frown deepened.

'I know I made a crack about everyone thinking they were going to be picked off next but the truth is, I'm genuinely worried that somebody took this girl and did something to her and that the same thing might happen to someone else. I know you're saying we shouldn't reopen old wounds, and I hear you. But when a parent doesn't know what happened to their kid, do you really think a wound like that ever heals?'

'I suppose not,' Kitt admitted.

'We don't actually have to involve Jodie's parents until we're sure we've got something real to go on. If we do find something that offers them some closure, isn't it worth having a go?'

'Yes, you're right, it is. And if it's causing you genuine concern that also puts a different complexion on the situation.'

'I'm sorry, did you just say I was right? Can I get that in writing?'

'Oooh, give over!' said Kitt. 'Maybe I'm just appeasing you so you don't run off and start your own investigation – which without my guidance you'd no doubt make a real hash of. Besides, it's true that cheating spouse cases, though my bread and butter so far, can hardly be considered stimulating work.'

'So, you'll help?'

'If it will bring you some peace of mind, I'll look into it. But I can't make any promises about solving it. Don't get me wrong, I am skilled. And my encyclopaedic knowledge has served me well during similar investigations.'

Grace tried not to smirk at Kitt's bragging. She recognized the sight of her former boss getting into the spirit of an investigation and wasn't going to do anything to derail her enthusiasm.

'I don't want to get your hopes up though. I'm only in town until Wednesday which gives me three short days before I'm due back at the library. I can continue to look into it over subsequent weeks but it's likely that momentum will slow after that. Work tends to overtake.'

'I'm sure three days is more than enough time to find a pertinent clue for Kitt Hartley, super-sleuth!'

'If you call me that again I'm going home right now,' Kitt said, though a small smile betrayed the fact that she might get used to the name given half a chance. 'I had enough grief getting out here in the first place without you adding to it with silly nicknames.'

'Oh yeah. You're not supposed to take annual leave in October because it's so busy. Did Michelle play war with you?'

'Of course she did. But I tuned out most of it by replaying the 2006 *Jane Eyre* mini-series in my head. Took the edge off. Even if I had a month, though, you've got to understand that the trail's gone cold now and . . . and . . . Grace!'

'What?' Grace said, but on seeing the direction in which Kitt was looking she had to put a hand over her mouth to stifle a chuckle.

'Why have you got that silly picture of me on your bed-side table?' Kitt pointed over to a photo Grace had framed. She'd taken it yonks ago, not long after she'd started working as Kitt's assistant. In the photograph, Kitt was biting into a large slice of her home-made ginger cake. Grace had placed the frame on her bedside table as a prank ahead of Kitt's arrival and – truth be told – was a little put out Kitt hadn't noticed it sooner. She'd arrived some thirty minutes ago and Grace wasn't a fan of delayed gratification.

'I don't know what you're taking that tone for. I don't get to see you every day now and I miss that. You should be flattered.'

Kitt shot Grace a sharp look in response. But if Grace was really honest with herself, that wasn't so much a lie as it was a mild embellishment. She had missed Kitt, a lot more than she was letting on. Excited as she was about her place on the library studies course here at Venerable Bede's – at the same institution Kitt had taken Library Studies herself, no less – it had meant leaving behind the only family she had after her own flesh and blood had made it clear they wanted nothing more to do with her.

'If you were hoping I'd be flattered, you should have chosen a more flattering photograph,' said Kitt. 'I'm starting to reconsider that recommendation letter I wrote to win you your place here, I can tell you.'

Grace responded with a long, rich chuckle.

'You can redeem yourself by telling me you at least have a starting point for us on this investigation.'

Grace, still smiling, tapped the mouse a couple of times. 'Where better to start than with the people who never stopped looking for her?'

Grace watched as Kitt skimmed the webpage she'd brought up that appealed for information on Jodie's disappearance. The page header was comprised of a large photograph of Jodie. Her big green eyes had seemed to plead with Grace the moment she saw them and Grace had made a silent promise that she would do everything in her power to find her. As a young woman suddenly in unfamiliar environs, fending for herself, Grace had developed a heightened awareness of the number of young girls who were lost and never found. Grace had no hope of finding her way anytime soon, but, with Kitt's help, she believed she had the power to help find Jodie.

'Who's this guy?' said Kitt. She was pointing at a picture of a man who looked about the same age as Grace. He had short black hair that was gelled back. Grace had viewed this website a number of times before Kitt arrived and on closer inspection she had noticed that his deep brown eyes had a naturally wounded look about them.

'That's Patrick Howard. He's a third-year Community Justice student here. He's probably our best contact in the first instance if we want to wait before contacting Jodie's parents. He was seeing Jodie when she disappeared.'

'Puppy love? Or something more serious?' said Kitt.

'They were engaged, and according to the rumours he's never forgiven himself for her disappearance.'

Kitt leaned forward to take a closer look at Patrick's photograph. She looked his face up and down a number of times, examining every feature. 'I wonder,' she said at last, 'if he never got over Jodie's disappearance because he had something to do with what happened to her.'

TWO

'We're going to be late if we don't stop faffing about,' said Grace, glancing at her watch.

'I know, I know, just give me one more minute to look at her,' said Kitt.

Grace stifled a sigh. On any other given day, it would be she who was holding up the painfully punctual Kitt – she wasn't much enjoying the taste of her own medicine.

Late last night, just before Kitt departed for her guest house in the centre of Durham, it had been agreed that Grace would organize a meeting with Patrick Howard to discuss Jodie's disappearance further. Patrick had got back to her right away so in no time whatsoever she'd been able to schedule a meeting at noon – right after her morning lectures. Subsequently, she and Kitt had arranged to touch base at quarter to twelve, outside Venerable Bede's Academy library. Grace wasn't surprised by Kitt's choice of meeting place but she hadn't expected Kitt to stand outside in the gathering October chill, mooning up at the building in a similar manner to how Grace had – on occasion – seen her look at her boyfriend, DI Halloran.

Grace studied Kitt in profile for a moment. Her maroon trilby was perched on her head, as it always was in the autumn and winter months, and her red hair billowed in the sharp breeze. Focusing on the wide, almost searching expression in her ice blue eyes, Grace wondered what Kitt would do if ever she had to choose between her love for books and her love for Halloran. Luckily for Halloran, that was a dilemma unlikely to present itself.

Despite Grace's nudging, Kitt continued to gaze with admiration at the Victorian lines of the old library rendered in red brick. Looking up at the building itself, Grace agreed with Kitt that the library was a beauty. Students scurried in through a grand arch, held aloft by two tall columns. As the eye travelled upward, it was greeted with four large bay windows, one for each floor of the library, which was topped with a row of ornate gables. Perhaps the most striking element of the building, however, was the tower, which was located at the rear and stood proud of the roof by some margin.

The architects of Venerable Bede's had obviously recognized that the library was the jewel in the institution's crown as it was situated at the very heart of the campus, next to the student union and a lake that, the academy brochure had crowed, was the widest artificial lake in Europe to be lined with recycled plastic. The department buildings and lecture halls, also built of red brick, had been constructed in a large square around the library, and beyond them stood the halls and a small campus shopping complex.

'Hard to believe it's been more than ten years since I sat here and studied everything there was to know about cataloguing and organising the written word, just as you will,' said Kitt with a dreamy look on her face. 'Since I started work at the Vale of York University, it's been my mission to ensure my section of the library rivalled the overall grandeur of this one.'

'Well, the sooner we get inside, the sooner you can see if you've managed it,' said Grace. It was five past twelve. They really were late for meeting Patrick Howard now, and she was concerned he might leave if they didn't show their faces soon. Grace had waited a long time to be at the forefront of one of Kitt's investigations and she wasn't about to let the chance to close a case for herself slip through her fingers because of Kitt's obsession with all things library-related. Especially given her private, silent promise to the victim.

'Oh all right, come on then,' said Kitt. But it transpired that getting Kitt up to the top level of the library, where they were due to meet Patrick, wouldn't prove any easier than getting her over the threshold. Seemingly high on the smell of old books, Kitt at once started to roam the stacks, take photos of particular volumes on her phone and skim read almost every journal that caught her eye.

Only after Grace had assured her that there would be plenty of time for all that after the meeting with Patrick, did Kitt acquiesce and follow Grace up the staircase to the top floor.

'That's him there, I think,' Grace said. She waved at the man sitting at a bank of desks near the window, through which the spires and battlements of the medieval city beyond could be glimpsed in the distance.

Patrick waved back and stood while Grace and Kitt navigated some low bookshelves and another row of desks to get to him.

Grace's first thought was that Patrick looked taller than she had expected. Which, of course, was a silly thing to think because it was almost impossible to tell a person's height from a selfie. His hair was longer than it had been in the photograph and fell in waves about his ears. He was wearing a pair of glasses that hadn't been evident in the photograph either; they were perched on a nose that some might say was a little bit too big and sharp for his face.

'Patrick?'

'Grace?'

'Yes, and this is the friend I mentioned, Kitt Hartley.'

Patrick reached out and shook hands with them both. There was a tenderness about the gesture that made Grace's smile widen.

'I saved these seats for you,' Patrick said, gesturing to a couple of chairs. Grace and Kitt obliged. 'I'm so glad you showed up. I – I thought you might have had second thoughts.'

'Yes, sorry for the slight delay,' Grace said, trying not to make it sound too pointed whilst simultaneously wishing there was a way of letting Patrick know the lateness wasn't her fault. The guy had been put through the wringer enough without having to wait around, wondering if some strangers who promised to help him were going to show up or not. 'But we do have some experience in this area and would like to help if we can.'

Patrick smiled. 'I was . . . pleased to get your message. Most people we've hired to look into this, and most of the people who volunteered out of the goodness of their hearts, have given up now. Written Jodie off as a lost cause.' His smile faded and a pained look crossed his face. At this, Grace felt a hard tug somewhere inside. She'd never had a long-term relationship herself – she reasoned she hadn't really been alive long enough to get that serious about another person – but in that moment she found herself trying to imagine the horror of your first love disappearing like Jodie had. How did you live with the idea that the last thing you might ever hear from them was a desperate scream recorded live over the student radio station? For some reason, she couldn't quite make her brain go there. But the look on Patrick's face gave her a small hint about how much grief was involved.

'Out of the people who volunteered, is there anyone left

who's willing to work with us?' asked Kitt, following Patrick's lead of getting straight down to business. 'The more hands on deck with these kinds of things, the better.'

'My mother is the only one still as committed as I am, so we can always call in a favour with her if we need it. She feels sorry for me, I think. That I can't let it go. Move on, you know?'

'Yes,' said Kitt. 'I know what it's like to hold onto something you feel you can't let go. I wouldn't wish it on anyone and I'm sorry you've been through it.'

Patrick nodded slowly, sombrely, but then seemed to make a conscious effort to offer a smile. 'On the plus side, Mum is pretty comfortably off. Thanks to a divorce settlement a few years back she was able to retire early and can pay you for your time and expenses – Grace mentioned that you're a trained PI. I've already had a word with Mum and she's more than happy to pay for professional services.'

Kitt's face visibly brightened at this. 'I completed my training a couple of months back and have taken on a few modest cases since.'

Grace narrowed her eyes. Modest cases? That seemed a bit of an understatement considering they had once brought a serial killer to justice. It wasn't like Kitt to underplay her role in solving the crimes she'd worked on with Halloran and Banks but then, Grace remembered, her friend's reserve was likely due to the fact that she wasn't really supposed to talk about working on those cases in any detail. If Halloran's superiors ever found out quite how much case information he had shared with Kitt, it would likely cost him his badge.

'I'm not interested in profiteering in this instance,' Kitt continued, 'but with a budget I could set up a proper investigation for you. I'll need to do some initial research before anything else, mind. I won't string you along. Given it's a cold case, I can't make you any firm promises.'

'I understand that, but you'll have another go? Look into it, I mean? See if you can find her or, at least, what happened to her?'

Kitt nodded. 'If there's anything left to be found out about what happened that night, I'll do my very best to uncover it.'

'I really appreciate it. Any hope is welcome right now. The anniversary of Jodie's disappearance was . . . hard.' Patrick looked down at the desk for a moment. Some student, bored of whatever book they'd been looking at, had scratched the name 'Gemma' into the wood and etched a heart around it. Grace prayed it was a detail Patrick wouldn't notice. By the cut of him, the last thing this guy needed was more reminders of all he had lost.

'I'm so sorry for all you've been through,' said Grace.

Kitt, as if sensing she had already raised Patrick's hopes too far, added: 'This time of year must be very difficult for you but again I have to underline that it may be a little too soon for hope.'

'Don't worry,' Patrick said. 'Though I've been praying for

19

the best, I'm all too aware of the kind of things you might uncover. Right now, no matter what you find, I just want to get to the truth.' Though the loss of his fiancée was clearly still raw, Grace noticed Patrick straightened his posture when he said this and it gave her a little faith that he could handle whatever they discovered – which of course could be almost anything.

Kitt removed a notebook and pen from her coat pocket. 'I'm afraid there's no way of me getting to the bottom of this without asking you to recount some things you'd probably rather not.'

'I understand,' Patrick said, his voice gentle. 'Like I say, I'm willing to do whatever it takes to do right by Jodie.'

'That's the spirit,' Kitt said with a small, encouraging smile. 'I need to start first with Jodie's disappearance. I've heard the radio clip and can see the time and date stamp on it is 3.32 a.m. on Wednesday the ninth of October of last year. Is there anything else you can tell me? Anything the police dug up about the nature of her disappearance that might be helpful? Please, spare no detail.'

'From what the police said not long after Jodie disappeared, and what was reported in the local press, they triangulated her mobile phone just before the time of the radio call. At 3.25 she took the cut through down Moatside Lane and then headed down to the riverside path in the direction of campus, walking along the cathedral side of the river.'

'From the clip of the recording I heard,' said Kitt, 'I'm not sure if she was walking at all. She was out of breath. Sounded to me like she'd been running.'

'Yes . . . you're right. I haven't listened to that clip in a long time. Too painful, you know? But I remember she was out of breath. I assumed it was nerves or something, about what she was going to say on the radio show. But you think perhaps she knew she was being followed? And was running away from someone?' said Patrick.

'I think it's quite likely, given . . . well, given what happened at the end of the recording,' said Kitt. 'But don't let me interrupt you. Tell us what else you know about the police's findings.'

'There's not too much more to tell. By 3.33, the signal on her phone was lost. The police found it washed up at the weir a little way downstream a few hours later and took it in for analysis. One of their theories was that Jodie's attacker threw it into the river so that – wherever he was planning on taking her next – they couldn't be tracked.'

'Seems a sensible assumption, and tells us something about our attacker,' said Kitt, making a few notes, while Grace tried not to imagine what might have happened to Jodie directly after that. 'They were savvy enough to get rid of the phone, which suggests some calculation. Somebody who attacks impulsively might not think of that, so it was premeditated. Either that or this wasn't the attacker's first offence. They had some kind of plan. I take it there were no fingerprints on the device?'

'If they threw the phone in the river would there be any fingerprints left on it?' asked Grace.

'It makes it less likely,' Kitt conceded. 'But there's always a chance that some latent fingerprints were left behind. They're not visible to the naked eye but certain chemicals can make them show up in a lab setting.'

'We didn't have any such luck in Jodie's case,' said Patrick. 'If we had, the prints would be on the police database and they might have found a match while investigating some other crime. But the only fingerprints on the device were partials that matched Jodie's. Which lent weight to one of their other theories – that Jodie wasn't abducted at all. That she had some kind of altercation down at the river that night and threw her phone in the river because she wanted to disappear of her own free will.'

'Do you believe that?' asked Grace.

'Not for a second,' said Patrick. 'Even if for some reason Jodie couldn't cope, she wouldn't just leave. Leave me and her parents wondering what happened to her, or if she was even alive. It just wasn't in her to hurt us like that.'

Kitt raised her eyebrows and made a few more notes in such a way that Grace suspected she still wasn't ruling out the possibility that Jodie was a runaway. Though it would be a bitter pill to swallow if someone you loved put you through all that, at least Jodie would still be alive. Which would surely be the best-case scenario?

'The scene of Jodie's disappearance didn't offer any other

clues then?' said Kitt. 'I take it the police searched the stretch of the river they tracked Jodie to while she was on the phone to the radio station?'

'Yes, the students at the radio station called the police as soon as it all happened. They tracked her phone down to the river and from what they said they were on the scene in just over an hour.' Tears formed in Patrick's eyes for a moment but he blinked them back. 'Despite what the police or anyone else say, I know she didn't just run off. She even tried to come to me that night, before she disappeared.'

'She came to your house?' said Kitt, while Grace acknowledged privately that Jodie's appearance at Patrick's house that night didn't mean she hadn't disappeared of her own accord. Perhaps she went to say goodbye to him, for good.

'According to the phone-tracking the police did, she was outside my house for several minutes around the quarter to three mark – which is weird in itself. We'd arranged to see each other much earlier than that – the plan was for her to come around about nine o'clock. But I fell asleep well before nine and didn't hear her when she knocked. We'd had so much fun going out together during Freshers Fortnight we didn't want it to end so we'd been out every night the week before and a couple of nights that week too. I was wiped.'

'I didn't know second years were interested in Freshers Fortnight activities,' said Kitt.

'We're encouraged to go out and meet the new arrivals. And, of course, a lot of the second years go out in those weeks hoping to hook up with someone new. But I would've been out anyway because it was Jodie's first year and I wanted to celebrate her first couple of weeks here. I'd not got back before four a.m. for the first three weeks of term and it must have caught up with me.' Patrick paused and his features tightened. 'Early the next morning, when the police came to the house, I woke up to so many missed calls from her and several cryptic voicemails that just said she wanted me to meet her but didn't say where or when. When I didn't respond to any of her calls, she must have come round to find me in person. I try not to think about it, you know. That she was stood outside the house, probably banging on the front door trying to get to me. If only I'd stayed awake, I'd have known when she didn't show up at nine that something was wrong. Or I'd have picked up one of her calls. I'd have been able to help her.'

'If something did befall Jodie, then the only person responsible for it is the person who hurt her,' said Kitt.

'I know. It's just the idea of me being sound asleep, peaceful, oblivious, while she . . .' Patrick shook his head. 'Well, who knows what happened? They didn't find any blood by the river. They didn't find any trace of Jodie at all, in fact, except her phone.'

'Not even a footprint that matched hers?' said Kitt.

'Nothing,' said Patrick. 'The night Jodie disappeared we had heavy rain and it gets muddy down by the river.'

'So clear footprints, or even partials, would be unlikely

and any other evidence might have been washed away, even in the space of an hour – especially if there wasn't much of a struggle,' Kitt said with a small sigh.

'The police got a break when Jodie phoned into the station. They knew straight away that something was happening but the weather put them at a disadvantage before they even started. Not that I've ever been convinced they tried as hard as they could have,' said Patrick.

'Why would you say that?' asked Grace. 'You think the police investigation wasn't thorough, for some reason?'

'I don't want to cast the police in a bad light,' said Patrick. 'Jodie was eighteen when she disappeared. Old enough to do her own thing. And there were circumstances to Jodie's disappearance. It's not just the lack of forensic evidence that led them to believe that Jodie ran away rather than properly investigate the possibility she was taken.'

'What circumstances were those?' said Kitt, pausing her note-taking and staring hard at Patrick.

'The day she disappeared, Jodie was in a right state.'

'How come?' asked Grace.

'She had a place at the academy on a scholarship programme. The morning she disappeared she received a letter from our dean, Regina Berkeley, saying her scholarship had been revoked and that she was being expelled.'

'Why?' asked Kitt.

'The story was that a random locker search had turned up a sizeable bag of pot in Jodie's locker.'

'Who conducted the search?' said Kitt, her pen poised.

'It's academy policy to carry them out sporadically. It will have been someone who works here, somebody in a custodial role more than likely, but we never got a name. The whole thing was hush-hush. Berkeley swore us to secrecy about the drugs situation. She was paranoid about the press finding out. Claimed she was trying to protect Jodie's memory but it was obvious she was more concerned with how it reflected on the academy. That said, I didn't want to drag her name through the mud – the media will take any excuse to imply the victim had it coming and the idea of Jodie being mixed up in drugs after just a few weeks here was upsetting to her parents, to say the least.'

'You're not wrong about the media,' said Kitt. 'But the drugs found in Jodie's locker, they alone were grounds for expulsion?'

'I take it Grace has filled you in on how the funding here works?'

'I used to study here myself, actually,' said Kitt. 'So I'm familiar with it anyway. They don't accept students with government loans so you have to have a decent pot of money or, in a somewhat Dickensian manner, rely on a wealthy benefactor.'

'Well, like I say, Jodie had a scholarship place. When it comes to what they found in her locker, someone with rich parents, who wasn't on a scholarship, probably would have got a slap on the wrist for something like that and then it would be buried to maintain the academy's impeccable reputation.'

'But someone like Jodie, who was here on scholarship funds, wasn't granted the same leniency?' Kitt said, bristling.

Patrick shook his head.

'In the recording, Jodie made some reference to "the way things are at Venerable Bede's",' said Grace. 'Is this what she was talking about? The double standards?'

'That, and the atmosphere here had become . . . oppressive is a strong word but let's just say Berkeley runs a tight ship and suffers no fools,' said Patrick.

'Sounds increasingly like Regina Berkeley is the first person I need to speak to about all this,' said Kitt.

'It's worth a go, though whether she'll tell you anything, I don't know. Jodie was livid about the accusations Berkeley made against her.'

'I can imagine,' said Kitt. 'You were engaged, is that right?'

'Yeah. Let me guess: you think we were too young to get married,' Patrick said with a knowing smile.

'It is quite unusual for people to get married so young these days,' Kitt conceded.

'I know. We got that a lot,' said Patrick. 'But we had been together for a good few years by the time I got around to proposing.'

'How long?' asked Grace, wondering, given how young they were, if he was about to tell some story in which he and Jodie had got married on the playground when they were seven and decided to make it official once they were old enough.

'I started dating Jodie during my GCSE years. We both grew up in Chester-le-Street and went to the same school. Her family inherited a house in the area but weren't in the same income threshold as the rest of the school's students. One day I defended her from some idiot bullies who were getting at her for being poor and within about a week we were going out.'

'Very gallant,' Grace said with a smile.

Patrick shrugged. 'I was just trying to do the right thing but it did work out quite well. I was in the year above. We stayed together during sixth form and when it came to choosing a place to study community justice, I decided to study in Durham to stay close to her. We kept the relation-ship together for the first year I was here before she got a scholarship place. In all the time I've known her, I've never seen her use drugs. She could drink as well as the rest of us – actually, better than me sometimes – but she used to joke that she was too hard up to indulge a drug habit.'

'So, where did the drugs come from if they weren't Jodie's?' asked Grace.

'That, I don't know. The day she disappeared, we met in the morning. She told me about the letter and said the drugs weren't hers, that they'd been planted there. She said she had an idea what had happened and was going to look into it. I offered to help but for some reason she wasn't having it. We . . . argued . . .' Again, tears rose in Patrick's eyes. Again, he blinked them back. 'We didn't part on the best terms that morning. I was angry at her for not letting me help. I didn't see why she wouldn't just let me do what I could to sort it out. But she was adamant. She could be so stubborn,' he said. 'Ironically, that was one of the qualities I loved most about her.'

Grace and Kitt offered Patrick a small smile apiece.

'In the end, we agreed she'd come round to mine that evening to let me know what she'd found. Next thing I know, I'm woken up by the police barging into my house at five a.m. I realize Jodie isn't there and then the police told me about what had happened. It was only then that I found out she went to the radio station with whatever she'd found when she couldn't wake me.'

'Why do you think she went to the radio station?' said Grace.

'I wish I knew. The police weren't giving much away right after Jodie disappeared so I was reliant on Bertrand for information, and he wasn't much use either.'

'Ber— Oh, Randy? Randy Hobbs?' Grace said.

'Yeah, that's what he calls himself on air. And he insists you call him that if you dial into the show but nobody who knows him can bring themselves to call him that off mic.'

'Hardly surprising,' said Kitt. 'What did he have to say for himself when you approached him? About Jodie calling in to him?'

'He didn't have any answers,' Patrick said, running a hand through his hair. 'All he could tell me is that Jodie had uncovered a secret about somebody senior at the academy and that she'd called just after three o'clock begging him to let her on the show as soon as possible. It had the makings of a major scoop so he didn't need too much persuading. As soon as he'd played the music he had queued for the next twenty minutes, he called her back so they could do the reveal live and, well, you know the rest.'

'Why did she choose Randy's show?' said Kitt. 'Surely revealing a big secret is going to have a bigger impact on prime time?'

'From what Bertrand told me, there wasn't any real planning behind it. She called into the show at the last minute to try and get on air. She was probably hoping she'd be able to come to me about it and when she couldn't reach me, felt she had to go public for some reason. If anything happened to her after that, even if not many people had heard the show, there would be a recording of whatever she'd uncovered. But, as you know, she didn't get that far.'

'Whatever she was uncovering couldn't have been of national importance though,' said Grace. 'Otherwise she could have just gone to one of the big media outlets that run news twenty-four seven. It must have been something at a local level – something that largely affected the community at Venerable Bede's.'

'And Randy didn't know what the secret was or who it involved?' said Kitt.

'He said he tried to get Jodie to tell him before she uncovered it on air,' Patrick said. 'But she wouldn't give anything away. The whole thing is just weird and totally out of character for her.'

'Well, it's too early to draw any conclusions just yet about what was really going on with her,' said Kitt. 'Like Grace says, given the way Jodie handled it I can't see this being of national importance. But Jodie's been missing for more than a year and nobody's seen her since that night. The last thing she was trying to do was reveal a secret about somebody in this community. I'm sorry to say that, for now, you need to prepare yourself for the worst. By the sound of things, the secret she uncovered might not have meant much to the world at large but it seems to have been big enough that somebody here could have thought it worth killing for.'

THREE

A silence fell over Patrick, Grace and Kitt and for a moment all of them avoided eye contact. Grace tried to make the avoidance look natural by gazing out over the city below. From this vantage point she could see how leafy Durham was. The trees dazzled in rich shades of red and gold. Between this and the ornate historic buildings the place seemed nothing short of idyllic. It was hard to believe that such tragedy had struck in the sacred resting place of not one but two saints.

Patrick was the first to break the silence.

'I understand what you're saying. For the last year, every day, I've half expected to see Jodie every time there's a knock at the door. Or to hear her voice whenever I pick up the phone – even if my caller ID says it's not her. I've been trying to keep my hopes up that she'd find a way to get in touch with me. But you said it yourself, it's been just over a year since she disappeared and I've heard nothing. If she was alive, and wanted to get in touch with me, by now I'm sure she would have found a way. Much as I hate to admit it, I know you're right. And I've got to start preparing for the fact that Jodie's really gone for good.'

Kitt took in a deep breath and rested her pen on her notebook.

Not really knowing quite what else to do to show how sorry she was about the whole thing, Grace reached her hand across the table and gave Patrick's hand a quick squeeze. She coupled this with a sympathetic smile. He was, understandably, unable to smile in return but his eyes shone with gratitude.

Clearing her throat, Kitt picked up her pen again. 'Just like the police, we'll need to keep our minds open when it comes to any circumstances surrounding Jodie's disappearance. I know you said Jodie didn't take drugs herself but you also said the bag found in her locker was sizeable.'

'That's the way it was described in the letter Jodie received. In the words of Dean Regina Berkeley,' said Patrick.

'I know it's not a pleasant thought but is there a chance Jodie was dealing drugs? If she didn't have much money, maybe she resorted to that to get by?'

Patrick frowned, thinking for a moment, but then shook his head. 'She just wouldn't be involved in something like that. Frankly, I don't think she'd have time. She was one of few female mechanics students and had to work like fury to prove herself just as good as any of the lads she worked with. We had plenty of fun nights out while she was here but during the day she was focused on her studies.'

'And she definitely was hitting the books all the times she said she was studying?'

'I . . . well, I didn't check her homework or anything but her tutors did some initial assessments in the first couple of weeks of term and she did really well in them so I assume so. And besides that, we'd been together nearly five years by that point. We were going to get married. I've got plenty of money and she knew I would always sub her. She'd come to me before she did anything shady, or worse.'

'I know you'd like to think that,' said Kitt. 'But if she was ashamed of something she might not have come to someone she loved about it. I know when something happens to someone we care about we only want to think the best of them but are you sure there's nothing Jodie might have been hiding? Was there any odd behaviour, anything at all?'

'The police asked the same question,' said Patrick. 'Especially after the drugs came to light. They thought, if she really had been attacked or taken, that she might have been up to something on a bigger scale that had had much worse consequences than being expelled. Like maybe she'd got on the bad side of a local drug lord or something. But the weirdest thing about her disappearance is probably that it came out of nowhere. Until the day she disappeared, she wasn't acting any differently than she had been all the time we were together at school and sixth form. She was just the same old Jo.' Patrick opened his mouth as if he was going to add something but Kitt interrupted him with yet another question.

'Can you think of anyone that might have wanted to hurt Jodie? Or anyone she wasn't on good terms with before she disappeared?'

'Nobody springs to mind. But then, she hadn't been at the academy very long and, to be honest, Jodie was a bit of an introvert. She was pretty particular about who she let into her inner circle. She was just starting to make some new friends here but it was all very early days.'

'Good to know,' said Kitt. 'There is one more thing I need from you and I'm sorry to ask you this, Patrick, but I have to. You said you were at home asleep on the night of the disappearance. Can anyone verify this?'

'No, it's just typical of my luck. Studying community justice, I know that suspicion is bound to fall on me in a case like this. And the night Jodie disappeared there was nobody to verify my whereabouts. I do share a house but my housemates were out at a gig at the student union that night. They didn't get home until five a.m., which is why they didn't hear Jodie either when she came knocking in the early hours. There are cameras here and there between our house and where Jodie was found. I wasn't caught on any of them but the police informed me there are routes I could have taken to avoid them so, by my own admission, my alibi isn't exactly what you'd call airtight.'

At these words, Kitt eyed Patrick in a manner Grace found a little bit surprising. She understood all too well that when it came to investigative work you had to be careful who you trusted, but Patrick's demeanour was that of a bereft fiancé. There was no mistaking it. Couldn't Kitt just look into Patrick's mournful brown eyes and know he wasn't the one responsible for Jodie's disappearance? Grace could. And Kitt was usually such a good judge of character that Grace was taken aback to find she didn't see it too.

'Well, I appreciate your forthrightness about that particular issue,' Kitt said, her eyes still a little narrowed. 'A true investigation has to follow every line of enquiry so you'll have to forgive any further questions I might have to ask later.'

'I understand your position and I've got nothing to hide. Just do what you need to do to find out what happened to Jodie and send any invoices or receipts to me here,' Patrick said handing Kitt a card.

'A business card by the age of twenty, that's . . . efficient,' said Kitt.

'Oh, you're not kidding. Mum insisted I had one before I left sixth form, even though I wasn't doing anything remotely business related – unless you count watching reruns of *Revenge* in my pyjamas a business.'

Kitt and Grace chuckled at that image.

'Your mum sounds even pushier than mine,' said Grace.

Patrick adjusted his glasses. 'She means well. The divorce settlement from my dad helped but she did make some of her own money. She ran a company that manufactured luxury furniture and it did really well so she was obsessed with me making business contacts even before I'd proved I could do anything useful.' Patrick's eyes lowered, just for a moment. 'After it became clear I wasn't going to let Jodie's disappearance go, she suggested I get some new ones printed up so people could easily get in touch with me about the appeal to find her.'

'Was she close to Jodie?' asked Kitt.

'Relatively. They saw a bit of each other when me and Jodie were at school and sixth form together, and once we got engaged they talked a lot more often. I wasn't really the expert on chair covers and china that Jodie needed at a time like that. But on the whole I liked to have Jodie to myself, sans parental supervision.'

Grace grimaced. 'Yes, parents can get in the way a bit, when they want to.'

'Think I've seen Dad a whole five times since the divorce so it was just my mum but that was bad enough; sometimes it seemed like she was actually trying to ruin any romantic moments I managed to orchestrate.'

Kitt laughed. 'Oh, I'm sure she was just keen to check in on you and make sure everything was OK.'

'She was,' Patrick said with a grudging smile. 'Unlike Dad, she's always been there for me. Especially after Jodie disappeared. I . . . I lost my way a bit. Failed quite a few modules at the academy. Thought about dropping out. I think Mum just threw money at the problem in case there was someone out there who could give us some closure. Not to mention Alec and Jean – Jodie's parents.'

'Naturally, I'd very much like to be the person to offer some closure,' said Kitt.

'Me too,' Grace chipped in.

'So, if you can think of anything else that might be important, please don't hesitate to get in touch with myself or Grace.'

'There is one other thing you need to know about the day Jodie disappeared,' said Patrick. 'It's going to sound a little out there but you should have all the same information I gave the police.'

'Go on,' Kitt said.

'When I met Jodie in the morning near the campus lake – when she told me about the drugs and the expulsion letter – there was a guy. I think he was watching us.'

Grace shuffled in her seat. Several of the cases Kitt had worked on in the past had taught her how often stalking and murder went hand in hand. The thought of someone watching her every move creeped her out. Had someone been keeping tabs on Jodie? And if so, why?

'What did this man look like?' asked Grace.

'It's hard to remember much from that general period in my life but he was wearing a long black coat and sunglasses.'

'Bit of a strange combo,' said Grace.

'Maybe in summer but it was autumn and it started out

as one of those bright chilly days, so I didn't think much of it at the time.'

'Can you remember anything else about him?' Kitt pushed.

'He had short brown hair, and quite a bulky build.'

'And you told the police about this mystery man? Did they come up with any leads?'

'I did tell them, but I don't think they really believed me. At the time, I was at the top of their suspect list with no alibi. I had voicemails on my phone from Jodie asking to meet. They were convinced I either met up with her or followed Jodie down to the river after she left my house and . . . did something terrible to her. Even though they never had any forensic evidence against me, I think they thought I'd just made this guy up to put them off the trail.'

'I see,' Kitt said with a nod. From her tone Grace suspected Kitt was also wondering if Patrick had invented the man in black. She had to admit it sounded flimsy but then, why would Patrick make that up? He just said there was no forensic evidence, no witnesses had stepped forward, and given the fact the body was never found, the police didn't have a case against him. He had no reason to just invent some imaginary, would-be attacker. At least, not one that Grace could think of.

'And you have no idea who this man could have been?' Kitt said. 'Jodie didn't give any signs that she recognized him?'

39

'There . . . was something vaguely familiar about him but with the sunglasses I couldn't see his full face. I didn't even point him out to Jodie because at the time I was focused on other things – largely trying to convince her to let me in on what was going on. I thought maybe I'd just seen the guy around at some point on campus, and that's why he seemed familiar.'

'Maybe you had,' said Grace. 'There are thousands of students here, not to mention the number of part-time employees.'

'That's what I told myself but in retrospect, I don't think so,' said Patrick. 'I've never seen him since. Just on that day. Just at that moment. His movements didn't mean much to me at the time but after Jodie went missing, I realized she left and, less than a minute later, so did he. The last I saw of him, he was headed off in the same direction as Jodie.'

FOUR

Grace and Kitt walked single file down Moatside Lane, retracing the last steps of Jodie Perkins. The lane was a narrow, back-street cut between the high street and the cathedral area that reminded Grace of York's many snickelways. Brick walls stood on either side of the path, overgrown in places with shrubbery showing early signs of bending to autumn's will.

'Why on earth would Jodie come down here so early in the morning?' said Kitt. 'It's creepy enough during the day.'

'I think you were right about Jodie running,' said Grace. 'It sounded like she was running on the clip and she was out of breath like she'd been running for a little while. If she was trying to get away from someone in particular she might have run down here to try and lose them, and failed.'

The pair emerged on Silver Street which, for a Monday afternoon, was surprisingly buzzing. Shoppers and couples meandered by, chatting and laughing their way along the cobbled streets as they went.

'At three thirty on a Wednesday morning this place would have been desolate,' said Grace, as she turned towards the river and took the cut down to the water just before Framwellgate Bridge. The same cut through that Jodie had taken before that fateful call to Castle Rock FM.

'It doesn't seem to me like she took the shortest route back to the campus,' said Kitt.

'Which adds weight to the theory that she was trying to lose someone who was following her,' said Grace. 'Assuming she was heading back to the campus after visiting Patrick's house.'

The pair set off against the flow of the River Wear, retracing Jodie's steps. They had been walking for a few minutes when Grace's phone rang. Her breath caught in her throat as she looked at the caller ID. It was her mother. She went to touch the accept call button but something held her back. The last words her mother had said before she left to get settled into her dorm room still echoed in her ears. Having deliberately thrown herself into a possible murder investigation to distract herself from the family situation, it seemed counterproductive to give her mother another opportunity to make her feel small and ungrateful. So, instead, she watched the call go to voicemail and then, lowering her head just a touch, shoved the phone back in her coat pocket.

'That your mum, by any chance?' Kitt said.

'No, it was George Clooney. He called last week to say he

couldn't live without me and I've had to screen his calls ever
since.'

'Bit old for you, isn't he?' Kitt said, fighting a smile.

'You tell me. There's a few years between you and Halloran.'

'Halloran's not old enough to be my father, thank you
very much. And don't think I can't see straight through you
trying to change the subject.'

Grace chuckled. Nothing got past Kitt. Ever. And there
was something comforting about that. The other students
on her library studies course were nice enough but she
missed the wisdom of her friend, who so often displayed
knowledge and insight far beyond her thirty-seven years.
She'd never let on to Kitt how much she'd missed her
because they weren't in the habit of getting all mushy about
the fact they were grateful for each other's companionship.
A continuous exchange of banter bordering on mild insult
was closer to the Yorkshire brand of affection, but Kitt had
the distinction of being the only person significantly older
than her who hadn't shouted her down or silenced her
when she tried to express an opinion. Yes, there were times
where Kitt had had cause to rein in some of Grace's more
mischievous behaviour, but it was always done in good
humour.

'Yes, all right, super-sleuth, it was Mum.'

'Still not talking to her?'

'I'm not talking to any of them. Mum. Dad. My brothers.'

Kitt stared hard at Grace. 'Look, I know you feel like they ganged up on you – '

'All four of them against one, hardly a fair fight. Even if I am sharper than both my chump brothers put together. Them two only count for one between them.'

Kitt laughed. 'They just care about you, Grace. It's difficult to see sometimes but often family do things we don't like much out of love.'

'I know. But it didn't have to be like this; they're the ones who gave me the ultimatum. If that's love, I don't need it right now. There are other ways to show you care about someone than railroading them into what you think their future should be.'

Grace winced at the memories resurfacing. She had done all she could to block out her mother's face when she had said she would give Grace the money to study at Venerable Bede's but if she went, it was the last thing she'd get off them and the last they wanted to see of her.

'I know, I know. And if you think library studies is where your heart lies . . .'

'I'm not totally sure if it is yet,' Grace admitted. 'How can anyone really know at twenty-two what they want to do with the rest of their life? Don't answer that, because I bet you did.'

'I may have had an idea that my future lay in whatever direction had the biggest available bookshelves,' Kitt said.

'I can imagine,' Grace said. 'With this course, though, I

just wanted to give something that was more "me" a try. Something that wasn't law or business or a branch of medicine just because that's what everyone had always told me I was going to do. I took that psychology degree at the Vale of York as a compromise but it didn't turn out to be my passion. And don't I have the right to decide my own life?' Grace all of a sudden realized that her voice had become louder than she meant it to and took a deep breath. 'I just, I need to find out who I really am without them. Up until now, they've done everything they could to prevent me from doing that. As though they're worried what I'm going to get up to, left to my own devices.'

'That's a thought that keeps me awake at night, too.'

Despite herself Grace laughed at this and, true to form, Kitt kindly changed the subject.

'We're not far now. Once I get a look at the spot where Jodie disappeared I should be able to put together some theories about what might have happened to her between the phone call to the radio station and the hour or so it took for the police to arrive on the scene.'

The pair had parted ways with Patrick about ninety minutes ago. After booking an appointment with Dean Regina Berkeley later that afternoon, Kitt had insisted they revisit the stretch of river where the police had tracked Jodie's phone to. A little way in the distance, the blocky outline of Durham Cathedral loomed from above. The eleventh century building was part-obscured by autumn trees and the sun struck the golden bell towers in such a way that Grace couldn't help but smile at the view – even in spite of her family situation and the macabre purpose of their early afternoon ramble.

'Is there really a chance of us finding something down here that the police didn't? Especially given how much time has passed since Jodie disappeared,' Grace asked, noticing that her shoes were already clarted up with mud. She'd largely facilitated Kitt's previous investigations through rigorous online research. Now she was out in the field she realized she'd much rather be hunting down local drug rings at the academy library than muddying the new pair of salmon-pink Moschinos she'd bought for the start of term.

'No, I shouldn't think we'll find any physical evidence after all this time but I need to get a look at the place if I'm to get inside the head of whoever presumably assaulted and abducted her that night, and while we're there it can't hurt to look around. I suppose you never know.'

'I suppose . . . but Patrick said there was heavy rain the night Jodie disappeared.'

'Yes, although I've got no reason to take Patrick Howard's word for anything just yet.'

'I thought you gave him a couple of suspicious looks. But he's the client. And he was giving you lots of help.'

'Oldest trick in the book,' Kitt sniffed. 'If you're the one helping the investigation, you can help steer it. I've learnt that one the hard way. More than once. Personal experience aside, just look at *The ABC Murders*.'

Grace resisted the urge to roll her eyes. She thought it had been too long since Kitt had referenced a mystery book. 'One of Agatha Christie's?'

'A very good one. But even if you haven't read that you must have seen an episode of *Columbo* in your time. It doesn't matter how old you are, the sheer number of repeats makes that show inescapable. The person most eager to help the investigator is always the killer. Granted, we don't know if Jodie is dead or alive yet. But from the sound of that recording something happened to her down here and I'd bet my first editions that the person behind it was someone close to her, like Patrick. Trust me, the truth behind all this will be no more surprising than the end of a *Point Horror* mystery.'

'But this is real life,' Grace tried, already knowing that Kitt wasn't going to appreciate her next comment. 'You can't investigate a real-life case based on fictional cases.'

'Hasn't hurt so far, no matter what Halloran might have to say about it,' Kitt said with a small smile. 'Sometimes the best way to solve a mystery is to work out the story behind it. That's all motive is, really. The story of why the culprit did what they did.'

'All right, so what do you think Patrick's story is?' said Grace. 'What's his motive for allegedly getting rid of Jodie?'

'Could be anything, from a well-hidden abusive streak to an argument that went too far – he did admit, after all, that they had a disagreement the day she disappeared. But the most obvious explanation, given that radio show recording, is that the big secret she was about to expose affected him, as well as the high profile person at the academy. Or that, for some reason, he wanted to protect that person more than he wanted to protect Jodie.'

'I can't really match that theory to the man we've just been talking to,' Grace said, shaking her head.

'Well, think about it. Jodie wasn't willing to let Patrick help her with this for some reason. She went to him in the early hours but only after she'd done a day of digging for herself. For some reason, she didn't want to tell him about her suspicions that morning. Maybe because it was some-thing that involved him. Perhaps she wasn't going to Patrick's house that evening for help. Perhaps she was going there to confront him with what she knew.'

Grace paused for a moment. She couldn't deny it was strange that Jodie hadn't been willing to let Patrick help her with whatever she was grappling with the last day she'd been seen alive. It's not like they'd only just started dating. They'd been together nearly five years and were due to be married so that didn't add up. Especially since he had seemed so gentle during their meeting and, consequently, she couldn't imagine there being anything that Jodie couldn't tell him. 'That bit is strange. But she did tell him about the drugs and that she was going to look into it. If she was concerned that whatever she uncovered had something to do with him then why would she even tell him that much? That's more than enough information for him to know the jig is up if she gets incriminating evidence against him – or someone he's trying to protect.'

'Making a person disappear, especially one that you claim to love, is an extreme measure. At that juncture she had only suspicions, no proof. He may have hoped that she wouldn't find anything concrete and that he would find a way of defusing the situation some other way. I'm not suggesting Patrick is evil, not yet. I'm just suggesting that making Jodie disappear somehow might have been a last resort to resolve some difficult situation we're yet to understand.'

'So you think the same as the police did: that Patrick followed Jodie down to the river after her visit to his place and . . . did something to her?'

'We don't know for sure that Jodie didn't talk to Patrick that night. He says he was asleep but maybe he wasn't and she confronted him with whatever evidence she had. She may have threatened to phone into the radio station and that's why he followed her. Or, maybe he didn't talk to her. Maybe he just followed her down there.'

'But the timing of the assault, it was just as Jodie was about to reveal this big secret. If Patrick was the one to assault her, he would have to have had a way of knowing that she was going to phone into the radio station. Otherwise he wouldn't have had to take such drastic action at that exact moment.'

'He may just have seen her on the phone to someone and panicked that she was reporting him – and whoever else is involved. But he seems to know Ran– er, Bertrand Hobbs off the air. Or is at least acquainted with him – he made that crack about his name. Maybe he got a tip-off. Bertrand Hobbs is near the top of my list of people to interview. I'll be very interested to hear what he's got to say for himself.'

'I agree interviewing Randy is a priority given he was the last one to talk to Jodie, but the way Patrick was talking about her, I just find it hard to believe he'd do something like this.'

'He might not have done it himself,' said Kitt. 'He might have known that if he had to look her in the eye he couldn't hurt her, or worse. Maybe that elusive man in black does exist but Patrick hired him.'

'You really think he'd go to those lengths and then set up a fake appeal for information about her? If I'd done something like that I'd keep my head down.'

'Yes, but if he's managed to get away with offing Jodie somehow, it might have made him feel as though he's cleverer than everyone else. The appeal website could be just another layer of deceit. He hired us quick enough on his mother's money. If he's got money enough to be hiring a PI they're not a poor family, that's for sure. Maybe he paid someone cash to follow Jodie and alert him if there was anything he needed to worry about?'

'Why not just invite Jodie back to his place and threaten her, or whatever, there?'

'Maybe he didn't want anyone seeing her going into his property before she disappeared? You saw how the police responded to the fact that Jodie's phone was tracked to his house that night. Probably the only thing that saved him from arrest was the fact that, thanks to the radio show, there's confirmation that she left his house alive. The river banks, on the other hand, are a pretty anonymous place for a person to disappear.'

'It just seems like a lot of effort, if you ask me.'

'I know,' said Kitt. 'But if that secret Jodie uncovered was big enough to destroy someone's career or reputation then it's less surprising that people would go to great lengths to keep it quiet.'

'Hopefully Randy will let something slip that lays the matter to rest,' Grace said, wondering what – if anything – the DJ really knew about Jodie's disappearance.

'He's on the list, but first we need to know more about these drugs that were reportedly found in Jodie's locker. If we sound like we know more than we really do about the whole situation then we might be able to trick Randy into revealing something he'd rather not. He knew Jodie was going to reveal something on the radio when seemingly nobody else did, which means he was in a unique position to alert someone to what Jodie was about to do or set something up with an accomplice.'

'That's true. There was about twenty minutes of music played between Jodie's original call to the station and him calling her back for the big reveal. As for Berkeley, do you really think she's going to tell you anything about the drugs?'

'We'll find out at four o'clock.'

Grace nodded. She had watched Kitt place a call to the dean's office almost the second that the pair had left the library. Kitt had made out her meeting with the dean was about some grand collaboration between the academy and the Vale of York University. Exactly how she was going to segue from there to drugs uncovered in a missing student's locker, Grace couldn't say. But knowing Kitt she would find a way.

'Oh, hang on. This is it,' Kitt said, looking around and then checking her surroundings against a hand-drawn map she'd asked Patrick to sketch for them. 'According to Patrick, this is the spot the police tracked Jodie to. It makes sense, look: the weir is a little further downstream from here. That's where her phone was found. Now, what story played out here the night Jodie disappeared?'

FIVE

The pair spent the next few minutes not speaking but searching. Kitt circled a couple of nearby trees, looking at the ground and beating back overgrown bushes. Grace, in the meantime, trudged through the longer grass at the edge of the river; kicking aside long blades that would soon shrivel as the November frosts took hold. After a few minutes, the pair looked at each other, shaking their heads. It had been too much to ask that any evidence would have survived and remained in place for over a year while exposed to the elements.

Grace's heart started to sink.

Maybe she had watched too much *Line of Duty* but, despite knowing it was a long shot, deep down she had got her hopes up that she might catch something unusual the police had missed the first time round. Or even uncover something that proved without any doubt that Patrick wasn't behind his fiancée's disappearance. If she had, she could have taunted

Kitt about being a better judge of character until the end of time. But no such luck. Even if it hadn't rained heavily on the night of Jodie's disappearance, like Kitt said, too much time had passed, and even though Patrick felt the police investigation had been lacking in some respects, they would undoubtedly have combed this stretch of the river.

'All right, worth a shot, but let's focus on formulating a theory about where Jodie went after that phone call with the station ended,' Kitt said.

Grace shivered, imagining this stretch of the river in the eerie light of the early hours. 'If she had been running from whoever made her disappear, she must have been petrified when they caught up with her.'

'I imagine so,' said Kitt. 'Which means she might have tried to scream, or call out or otherwise draw attention. Possibly putting up a struggle. So how did her attacker make her disappear so seamlessly?'

'This spot is quite sheltered by the trees,' said Grace. 'More sheltered than in other parts of the path. The attacker probably chose this stretch on purpose. Maybe they took her off guard, approaching from behind with some kind of weapon? A knife, maybe?'

'I agree that the element of surprise would be an advantage to an attacker, but we know from the audio that they didn't have that. Jodie saw and seemed to recognize her attacker which is unlikely if they approached from behind.'

'Oh . . .' Grace nodded. 'Yes. You're right. OK, but if they approached her head-on, which they must have done, why didn't she run or something?'

'If it was someone she knew, and it seemed to be, she may not have known how much danger she was in until it was too late.'

'What could have made her scream out like that other than a weapon of some sort coming towards her?'

'I don't know,' Kitt admitted. 'But whatever took place down here I doubt Jodie was conscious for long. Sheltered or not, this is a public place and even in the early hours of the morning, anyone could have come walking along and witnessed it all.'

'Couldn't the attacker have just held a knife to her back or something? To make her comply and walk wherever they wanted to take her?'

'It's a possibility but it feels a bit too neat for that. No witnesses have come forward but the attacker couldn't be one hundred per cent sure they wouldn't meet anyone along the way. All Jodie would have had to do was scream for help as a stranger passed and the attacker would have more on their plate than they probably wanted to deal with.'

'So . . . when you say she wasn't conscious for long . . . you mean you think she was killed down here?' A sudden chill came over Grace at that thought.

'There are three obvious possibilities. Firstly, the attacker killed her on the spot and threw her body in the river. But there is lack of forensic evidence for that. Besides anything else, dead bodies may sink in water at first but more often than not post mortem changes eventually cause them to float. Even when they're weighed down they usually wash up somewhere. Jodie's body has had a year to wash up and nothing's been reported. At least, not according to the searches I ran last night.'

'So we can rule that out?'

'Not quite. Not everybody floats. It depends on many variables but I would say it makes it less likely.'

'What are the other two possibilities?'

'That Jodie was killed down here and her body was then transported once it was safe to do so and otherwise disposed of. Or Jodie was knocked unconscious, possibly with a hard blow, and was taken somewhere else alive. Given that the attacker knew she was on the phone at the time and they would be expecting the police to show up sooner rather than later, the odds are they didn't kill her here.'

'Because if they rushed to kill her they might make a mistake that got them caught?'

'Exactly. You suggested the attacker chose this place because it was more sheltered but in fact they didn't get to choose when they attacked Jodie.'

'Because of the phone call,' Grace said.

'Yes, Jodie putting that call in would have forced their hand. They had to attack then or it would be too late. It was just lucky for them and unlucky for Jodie that this stretch of the river is more sheltered.'

'But the phone call would have limited their options about what they could do next.'

'Right. They could have killed her on the spot but making a body disappear without a trace isn't easy, especially when there's a time limit attached to the task. Many a serial killer has given it a good go but sooner or later evidence comes to light and a body – or parts of it – are discovered.'

'But Jodie really did disappear.'

'Which means either the person or people who attacked her did a very, very good job of disposing of the body, or she is still alive somewhere.'

'I really hope it's that last one,' said Grace, remembering the look in Patrick's eyes as he'd talked about his lost fiancée. Wouldn't it be amazing if she and Kitt found Jodie alive after all this time? Sure, there was a chance she had her reasons for not getting in touch with Patrick – other than being held under duress – but either way at least he would know she was safe and he could draw a line under that part of his life, move on.

Kitt opened her mouth to say something but seemed to think better of it. She squinted and fell silent for a moment before starting on another track. 'If the attacker did transport Jodie somewhere else, dead or alive, they'd need to be very strong or have an accomplice working with them to lift the body.'

'I don't know; I've seen pictures of Jodie on the appeal website, she was tiny.'

'You're one to talk,' said Kitt.

Grace smiled. 'Anyroad, it probably wouldn't take too much to lift her – assuming the attacker was male.'

'Not necessarily. It's harder to lift a person if they're unconscious, due to the poor distribution of weight. But if they'd left her here the police would have found her, so, where did they take her?'

Grace looked along the river back to the stone arches of Framwellgate Bridge. 'Maybe they had a vehicle waiting up on the road.'

'Maybe, and certainly that's one area of exploration. The problem is, CCTV footage a year after the incident is unlikely so we might be reliant on whatever eye witnesses can remember about that morning. Besides, regardless of what Patrick thought of the police investigation, I'm sure they would have at least checked that.' Kitt craned her neck, looking up and down the slight curve of the river. 'The only other thing I can think is that they could have found somewhere to temporarily stash Jodie along here.'

'Why would they bother doing that? They'd have to come out of hiding at some point, even if they did find somewhere.'

'They would know the police would be on their way and would spend the next couple of days at least scouring that stretch of the river. They had two choices: make a run for it or hide somewhere nearby until the police had moved their investigation on.'

'Well, there's nowhere round here, except for the bushes. And it was a wet night so I doubt that would have seemed like a master plan. There'd be no way of sheltering under the bridges without the risk of being seen either.'

Kitt's eyes narrowed. 'You're right.' She pulled her phone out and started tapping away at the screen. 'Hmm.'

'What?'

'What's this building here?' Kitt turned her phone so Grace could take a look at the map she'd brought up. She'd zoomed in and was pointing at a small rectangular building on the other side of the river between Prebends Bridge and Kingsgate Bridge. 'All the other buildings are labelled but not that one. I don't remember any significant buildings along that stretch from my time studying here but of course that's going back ten years now.'

'Er, I'm not sure but there is an old outhouse that sits on that side of the river. It could be that. But that's a good twenty minute walk at least. They couldn't have carried Jodie all that way, surely?'

'Oh yes, you're right, I remember now. There is an out-house down there. They might well have hidden there, you know? Even if it's a bit of a walk. You'd be surprised what people will do in moments of desperation. If it was a wet night, it would beat standing outside in the cold northern rain.'

'Anything does,' Grace said with a nod. 'Take it from a lass who grew up in Leeds.'

'Well, until I can enquire about CCTV footage along the main roads that night, it's our most promising prospect,' Kitt said. 'So there's only one thing for it.' Without another word she set off along the river path at a pace Grace could only just keep up with.

No less than twenty minutes later, Kitt and Grace approached an old ramshackle outhouse made of weathered brick that had become part of the scenery for Grace even in the short time she'd been living in Durham. She couldn't count how many times she'd already walked between campus and town. Although not the quickest route, the riverside walk was without a doubt more picturesque and was a good opportunity for a bit of brisk exercise – something to offset all the pizza she'd been comfort eating during her first few weeks at Venerable Bede's. Her stomach clenched at the idea that she had walked past this building on so many occasions and now it seemed there was a chance it could have some link with Jodie's disappearance.

Kitt gave the wooden door, that looked to be rotten in places, a hard yank. When it didn't at once give, she tried a couple more times. 'It's locked,' she said with a sigh.

Grace looked around the side to see if there was another way in but Kitt had already tried the only door and the windows were too high up to see through.

Grace took a couple of steps backward. 'You . . . you don't think Jodie's body could still be in there, do you?' She had seen her fair share of horror films in her time and this was exactly the kind of structure where something creepy was likely to happen.

'Highly unlikely. The odds are someone has accessed this building between now and last October. Besides, if there was a body in there anyone who walked past would probably have been able to smell it, and without a doubt we'd be able to smell it right now. Dead bodies tend to give themselves away like that. But that doesn't mean the attacker didn't use it and leave behind some more subtle clues that only a trained eye could single out. If the attacker – or more likely attackers – wanted to hide out this would be the perfect place to do it, and given how open a space this is, it's hard to know where else they could have gone without being noticed – unless, like you suggested earlier, they did make their getaway in a car.'

'The thing is, it's a bit of a walk from where Jodie's phone was last tracked to.'

'So is the road. In fact I'd say getting the body up on the road where there are more likely to be witnesses would have been riskier. The fact that this is a bit more isolated and a little way from where Jodie was last seen probably made it even more perfect for the attackers. Remember, her phone was found in the river. The attackers knew they would be tracked and went to certain lengths to make sure that didn't happen. This place is far enough away from where Jodie disappeared that the police probably didn't think to check it.'

Despite Kitt's reassurances that there wasn't a dead body behind the outhouse door, Grace stared warily at the rusted lock. She knew it was daft, but she still had to try with all her might not to imagine Jodie wide-eyed, alone and decomposing on the other side. She had a dark, nagging feeling that she just couldn't shift. Perhaps it was because it took cunning to make a person disappear – assuming they didn't disappear of their own accord. There was something about this case that suggested cold calculation and if Jodie had met her end that night, Grace wondered if the killers had found a way to stash the body here without anyone noticing, right under everybody's noses.

SIX

After what seemed like an eternity of watching Ms Polly Smyth, Dean Regina Berkeley's secretary, alternate between sending an email, filing her nails and checking text messages on her phone, Kitt and Grace were at last waved through a heavy oak door into their meeting.

'Ms Hartley?' Berkeley said as Kitt and Grace walked into her office. Grace had seen Berkeley's photograph in the prospectus but had never crossed paths with her in person. When she had glanced at her picture, Grace had been struck by Berkeley's over-powdered aesthetic and it was no less striking in the flesh. She was clarted up with heavy foundation that not only emphasized every wrinkle on her long, thin face but also seemed a bit too dark for her skin tone. A line ran along her neck where the make-up stopped. Clearly the contouring craze had passed her by.

Berkeley's fondness for slapping on a lot of foundation was however the only flaw in an otherwise prim appearance. Her grey hair was tied back in a tight bun with a neat, if unflat-tering, Austenesque centre parting and her clothes looked well-tailored so it seemed she was paid well for her services here at Venerable Bede's. The lines on her tartan cardigan, on which she wore a silver brooch shaped like a peacock, were particularly sharp. Despite the fact that the dean must have weighed all of seven stone, this gave her a somewhat severe, intimidating appearance. Kitt had better watch her step with this one, she didn't look like anybody's fool.

Berkeley was sitting behind a large oak desk and when it became clear that she had no intention of rising to greet them, Kitt stepped forward to address her.

'Yes, I'm Kitt Hartley, and you may be aware of Grace Edwards who is enrolled here with you currently on the library studies course – just as I once was.'

'Yes,' Berkeley said, indicating two chairs in front of her desk which Kitt and Grace promptly took. 'I've already done my homework on you, Ms Hartley.'

'H-homework?' Kitt replied.

'I took the liberty of pulling your file. I thought it might make for some nostalgic reading. Can't have you travel all the way from York to Durham without giving you a chance to relive the good old days at Venerable Bede's, can we?'

'Oh, well, I . . .' Kitt began, flustered.

Berkeley flicked open a manila folder sitting on her desk with a single fingertip. 'Hartley, Katherine Anne. Exemplary first-year grades – top of your cohort, in fact.'

Kitt's slightly panicked look fell away and she raised her chin with pride. 'I did work very hard to achieve that position.'

Unable to resist, given her phone was in her hand and Berkeley was engrossed in Kitt's file, Grace quickly tapped the word 'Geek!' into a text message and sent it to Kitt. Kitt's phone buzzed. On looking at the screen she gave Grace a suspicious glance out of the corner of her eye followed swiftly by a glare when she read the message.

'Let's see, what else do we have? You were captain of the debate team, I see, and won the academy a trophy or two.'

'Seventeen, actually,' Kitt corrected. 'During my reign as captain, that is. Twenty-two if you count the months I spent learning the ropes. There are probably one or two of them still lying around in a display cabinet somewhere on campus.'

Twenty-two trophies for debating? Conveniently this factoid had never come up during the many back and forths Grace had had with Kitt over the time they'd known each other. Now Grace understood why winning an argument with Kitt was almost impossible.

'A bit of a lull in your grades in the second year,' Berkeley continued, not paying any attention whatsoever to Kitt's interjections. Licking her finger, she flicked to a page marked by a blue tab. 'And you seem to have been disciplined for . . . running across the football field in your underwear.'

'Wh-wh-what?' Grace sputtered out before exploding into laughter. Kitt was so prim and proper, the image of her

65

streaking across a football pitch was just too much for her. Kitt could be quite private so extracting information to use as part of a prank or material for future wind-ups was always difficult. A penetrating warmth spread through every inch of Grace as she realized she was going to be able to dine off this nugget of intelligence for the rest of time.

'This is not a laughing matter,' Berkeley snapped and rapped her knuckles on the desk to sober Grace up. Grace at once straightened her face. The last thing she needed was to make an enemy out of the dean after just five weeks at the academy. It pained her to admit it but all teasing related to Kitt's public displays of indecency would have to be postponed to a future date. 'And if you're studying with us at this institution I'll thank you for not getting any ideas. We will not tolerate this kind of lewdness. I'm amazed they let you graduate after that.'

'There was nothing lewd about that incident,' Kitt said quickly, a blush rising in her cheeks. 'It was a deliberate and important protest about body shaming.'

'I've not heard of too many protests taking place at two in the morning,' said Berkeley.

'Yes, well, it was a different time.'

'It was 2009.'

Kitt's mouth hung part open but no sound came out. It might have been the first time in recorded history that Kitt Hartley was lost for words. Certainly, Grace had never witnessed such an occurrence. She considered capturing the moment on her phone camera but getting into Venerable Bede's had been no easy task. She'd already enraged the dean once in this meeting and from the looks passing between Kitt and Berkeley she got the impression neither of them would see the funny side.

'But you're right in a certain respect, I suppose. The academy was under different leadership then. More lax leadership.'

That was rich, Grace thought. Coming from a woman who had let a student disappear on her watch. She glanced over at Kitt who had regained her composure and was no doubt thinking along similar lines.

'My predecessor was far too lenient. They didn't keep the small things in check which is so important when you're responsible for training the next generation of workforce leaders.'

'Is that so?' Kitt said. 'The new leadership is certainly adept at managing difficult situations, I'll give you that.'

'Are you driving at something, Ms Hartley? If so, I'd appreciate you getting to the point. I'm a rather busy woman, in case you hadn't noticed.'

'I was merely complimenting you on the way you handled the extremely difficult circumstances surrounding the disappearance of Jodie Perkins. That's the kind of situation any leader of an educational institution would dread. Losing one of your own like that.'

Berkeley flipped the folder closed. She didn't speak but it

was clear from the distinct tightening of her face that she would have given almost anything just then for Kitt to change the subject.

'We did our best to control the situation and handle it as sensitively as possible.'

'Seems to me you did a very efficient job of controlling the situation. Her disappearance didn't even make it into the alumni newsletter. I read it religiously every year and didn't hear a thing about it.' Kitt continued to rub it in.

The dean reached across to a jug of water sitting on the desk and poured herself a glass. Though there were enough glasses for everyone, she didn't offer Grace or Kitt a drink but focused instead on taking a big gulp of water before speaking.

'It isn't exactly something you want to broadcast when the future of your institution relies on young people from affluent families feeling safe enough to come here and study.'

'But there must be more to it than that,' Kitt pushed. 'I mean, it surely wasn't just about making sure you had enough students to fight another year. I'm sure the loss felt very personal to you, as the one who is ultimately responsible for the safety of students.'

'What happened to Jodie Perkins is without doubt the deepest regret of not just my academic career but my life as a whole. Nothing like it has ever happened on my watch before or since and it is my mission to make sure nothing like it ever happens again. There's no other word for it but tragic. Senseless and tragic.'

'We're agreed on that score. And since you seem to feel as strongly as we do about the tragic nature of Jodie's disappearance you'll be pleased to know there may yet be a way of helping her,' said Kitt.

Berkeley frowned. 'Help her? In what way exactly? Some kind of memorial, or a scholarship initiative in her name so that she's not forgotten? Is that the collaboration you came to speak to me about? It's a great sadness that we can't bring her back but, if your institution is interested in some kind of partnership, we could look into something to help her live on in people's memories.'

Kitt paused before responding. Grace assumed Kitt was biding her time, trying to think up a plausible collaboration between the academy and the Vale of York University but instead she had noticed something that had totally passed Grace by.

'Excuse me for asking,' Kitt said with a sharp note in her voice, 'but do you know something we don't about Jodie?'

'What? No. What do you mean?' Berkeley said, tilting her head.

'Well, it's just, I'm not sure a memorial or scholarship in her name is particularly appropriate, given that for all we know she might be still alive.'

At Kitt's words, Berkeley's face froze.

SEVEN

A hard silence filled the room. The dean cleared her throat and took another sip of water before responding. 'Oh, well, yes. Of course. I wasn't thinking. I'm sorry. It's just, she's been gone for so long and nobody's had any word from her. Privately, sad though it is to think about it, I've sort of accepted that there's a good chance she's no longer with us.'

'I see,' Kitt said. 'Unfortunately, you may be right to assume that but that's where my help might come in. The thing is, although I am a librarian at the Vale of York University, I've also had some experience as a private investigator. As such, I'm interested in trying to uncover what really happened to Jodie that night. To give her family and friends some closure.'

Berkeley shook her head, firmly. 'No, I'm sorry. I understand if you have a personal attachment to the case as this terrible thing happened to a girl who studied at the same institution as you but I don't think we want to go digging all that up again.'

'I'm afraid it's a bit late for that. I've already been hired by someone with connections to the academy,' said Kitt.

'Who?' Berkeley said, sitting up in her seat.

'That's confidential information, so I can't disclose it. But their intentions are good and we have no desire to just dig things up. I'm going to solve this case so the matter can be settled once and for all.'

'Be that as it may, you are not welcome to conduct an investigation of that sort on our campus. Our community has been through enough and we want to put this terrible incident behind us,' Berkeley said with a dismissive wave.

'But —' Kitt tried, though she was soon cut off.

'Nothing can be gained by dredging that sorry affair up all over again. It's been difficult enough to make the students feel safe here after what happened to Jodie.'

'What if they're not safe here?' said Grace. As a member of the student population she couldn't say she felt particularly safe given that nobody was ever held accountable for Jodie's disappearance. 'What if the person who did this to Jodie strikes again?'

'If I say they're safe, they're safe. And I will thank you for not saying things that are akin to scaremongering.'

'I see,' said Kitt. 'Are you forbidding me to conduct my investigation?'

'On academy grounds, yes. What you do outside the academy grounds is none of my concern.'

Grace suppressed a sigh. How was Kitt going to conduct

71

an investigation on Jodie's disappearance if she was banned from the campus? There were ways around it, of course, but it would make everything a lot more long-winded. Kitt was only here for a few days and with every day that passed the trail only grew colder.

'Well, I'm very sorry to hear that,' Kitt said at last, standing from her chair. 'I had hoped it wouldn't come to this but I suppose you've left me no choice. Oh dear, oh dear, oh dear.'

'What are you talking about?' Berkeley didn't quite snap but she came close.

'Hm? Oh nothing, it's just that I'll have to pass the new leads I have on to the police if you won't let me conduct my business discreetly.'

'The police? Wait, wait, wait, what new leads?'

'It wouldn't be proper procedure to discuss them while the investigation is ongoing – don't you worry about it. You've made your position clear and I can't blame you. I have contacts in the force. They know my intel is sound and they'll revisit their findings from before and hopefully get a bit closer to the truth.'

'Do you really need to go to the police?' said Berkeley. Was that a pleading note in her voice? Not quite, but almost. 'We dealt with all that once last year. If the press get even a sniff of it I'll have a media circus on my hands all over again.'

'I was trying to deal with it quietly but you don't want me around so I'll have to let the police take over from here,

I'm afraid, I can't just sit on new information when it could mean uncovering what really happened to a missing young girl.'

'Now wait a minute.' Berkeley at last rose from her chair. 'I didn't know you had new information on this case. That wasn't clear. If you really have uncovered something that wasn't known before, then that changes things, obviously.'

'Oh, does it?' Kitt said, her eyes wide and innocent enough for Grace to recognize that this had been Kitt's plan all along.

'Yes, of course,' Berkeley said. 'If it was just a matter of dredging up old material again, well, I wasn't going to stand for that. It wouldn't be sensitive to the students who are studying here. Not to mention the staff who worked with Jodie in the short time she was with us. But if you really might be able to draw this matter to a close, quietly, then I suppose that's a good thing.'

'It will require the disclosure of some details,' Kitt said, sitting down again and pulling a pen and notebook out of her pocket.

'Like what?' The thin smile on Berkeley's face disappeared as she also resumed her seat.

'Firstly, confirmation that Jodie received a letter from you on the day of her disappearance stating that she was expelled from Venerable Bede's.'

'Oh, well, yes,' Berkeley said, looking down at her desk for a moment before meeting Kitt's eye once more. 'This is confidential information.' Her stare then fixed on Grace. 'I

73

assume you know a little something about discretion, Ms Edwards, since you are, what, assisting Ms Hartley? I can count on the fact that this information won't be floating around campus tomorrow morning or appear in the student press because you've opened your mouth?'

'I've assisted Kitt – er, Ms Hartley on several previous investigations,' Grace said. 'And I'm well aware of the need for tact.'

Grace thought she heard Kitt snort at that statement, but if she did she promptly turned it into a cough so as not to arouse Berkeley's suspicions. All right, so maybe tact wasn't Grace's number one quality but if it meant getting justice for Jodie she would double down on it, starting now.

'Very well. We kept the letter quiet because we didn't think it would do any good to drag Jodie's name through the mud after she went missing. As far as the outside world was concerned, Jodie was a model student.'

'But behind closed doors, you thought differently of her?' Kitt said, jotting down a few notes that Grace was sitting just too far away to read.

'I did after one of our caretakers found a large quantity of drugs in her locker during a random search. The rules of attendance here are very strict for scholarship students. Jodie knew that and yet she still violated the terms of our agreement. Not that she seemed to have much discipline. The day she disappeared, she barged into my office without an appointment, ranting about the letter I sent her.'

'What did she say, exactly?' asked Grace.

'I'm ashamed to say I didn't let her get very far. She was promptly escorted out by security. I thought she was just having a recalcitrant reaction to the letter. If I had known there was some greater web, that she might have disappeared the way she did, I'd have taken the time to listen.'

Grace stared hard at Berkeley's face. It looked somehow even thinner than it had when they first walked in. Patrick seemed to think that Berkeley was only concerned about the reputation of the academy but from where Grace was sitting her remorse over her part in Jodie's disappearance seemed genuine. But did her involvement stop at the letter she sent to Jodie? Or was there more?

'Who discovered the drugs in Jodie's locker?' asked Kitt.

'Elvis McCabe. He was one of our caretakers.'

'Was?'

Berkeley sighed. 'He left about six months after Jodie disappeared. I tried to reason with him that Jodie's disappearance wasn't his fault. That he had just been doing his job when he brought the drugs to my attention. I was the one who issued an expulsion letter, for Heaven's sake, not him.'

'So, he decided to leave his post because he felt guilty?' said Kitt.

'Yes.' Berkeley nodded. 'He was an excellent employee but I couldn't persuade him to stay.'

'I see,' said Kitt. 'There's just one more thing I have to ask, and I'm sorry for any offence caused, but one of the first things I always have to do is establish where everybody involved was at the time of the crime.'

Berkeley puffed up her chest at this. 'As yet, there's no evidence there was a crime – except for the drugs Jodie was either taking or dealing. But I had to tell the police at the time so I know exactly where I was the night Jodie disappeared – at a dinner for a charity that supports autistic learners in education. I was there until midnight and then booked a car ride home. I have an alarm system on my house that registers entry and exit. The records confirm I got back at one a.m. and did not leave the house after that. My secretary has the details of the dinner I attended, so if that's all?'

Berkeley rose from her seat to indicate that this wasn't, in fact, a question.

'That will be all for now,' Kitt said, packing away her notebook and pen.

Grace offered Berkeley a polite smile and followed Kitt out of the room.

The pair paused briefly to leave Kitt's card with Berkeley's secretary and asked her to forward the details of the event Berkeley had attended the night Jodie disappeared.

After that, they exited the main reception building and found a spare bench near the lake. The striking lines of the nearby library building reflected in the water in an almost dreamy fashion, caused by the slow dimming of the late-afternoon sunlight.

'What did you think of that performance?' Grace asked once the pair were seated.

'Performance is the right word. She knows something she's not letting on about,' Kitt said. 'She implied Jodie was dead.'

'I agree she was acting weird but we're going to need more evidence than that if we want a confession out of her about what really went on. After the amount of time Jodie's been missing, it's not unreasonable to think the worst. You were trying to prepare Patrick for that eventuality yourself just a couple of hours ago.'

'I know. But something's off. She didn't want me here and no matter what she says I don't believe it's just to protect the academy's reputation.'

'Maybe she's covering for someone. Elvis McCabe, for example. He might have left the academy out of guilt, like Berkeley said, but there might be more to it. Something Berkeley was keen to cover up.'

'Like what?'

'Patrick said the drugs didn't belong to Jodie and she was mortified anyone would think they did. If Jodie was going to reveal a secret about a powerful person, they might have bribed McCabe to plant the drugs and get Jodie expelled. Maybe Berkeley found out about that and McCabe jumped before he was pushed.'

'That's . . . a possibility,' said Kitt. 'Berkeley was trying to keep a lid on the scandal as it was. If it came out that an employee had a hand in Jodie's disappearance and possible death the odds are all those rich parents who hand over tuition fees every year would send their child, and their money, somewhere else.'

'There's also the fact that the outhouse we were looking at is not very far from the campus grounds,' said Grace. 'I wonder if it belongs to the academy? Or if Berkeley has some other connection with it?'

'Worth trying to find out. Hunting down the owner of that building is number two on my to-do list, after getting in touch with Bertrand Hobbs. I'll also need to interview people who live and work along the main roads Jodie's attackers must have taken if they did drive her out of here around the four o'clock in the morning mark.'

'Are there really likely to be any witnesses at that time of day?'

'It's a long shot but you never know. Never underestimate the observation skills of shift workers and insomniacs. They see the world, and all its happenings, at times the rest of us don't.'

'So that's how you've been catching all those cheating spouses?'

'It has helped,' Kitt admitted. 'Can you see if you can uncover what happened to McCabe after he left the academy? If he did receive some big bribe for framing Jodie he might have used it to buy something a custodial worker might not normally be able to afford. A flashy car, a house extension. See what you can dig up?'

'Happy to make a start on that this evening, but right now I've got to get off to my lecture on cataloguing.'

'No problem. That'll give me a breather and, more importantly, an opportunity to find a good cup of tea round here. Who's teaching cataloguing these days, out of interest?'

'Dr Harriet Lowenthal. Do you know her? She seems . . .' Grace trailed off. Kitt's face had darkened in a way she had never seen it darken before. Not even last April Fool's Day when Grace had thought it a grand idea to adjust Kitt's office chair and duct tape an air horn under the seat. The look on Kitt's face when she readjusted her chair and the horn rang out across the entire third floor was priceless but it took her two hours to see the funny side of the incident.

'What's wrong?' Grace asked, trying to forget the air horn incident in case she accidentally started laughing and Kitt took offence.

'I *hate* Harriet Lowenthal.'

'What? Why?'

'She's my arch-nemesis.'

EIGHT

If asked, Grace couldn't have told anyone quite how long it took her to stop laughing at the revelation that Kitt Hartley had an arch-nemesis. But it was long enough that she only just made it to her lecture on time. Between this and the news that Kitt had been involved in a streaking incident, Grace was beginning to think this might be the best day of her entire life. She had marked the day on her online calendar so that next year she could present Kitt with a cake topped with a candle and christen it 'Arch Streaking Day'. She could already picture the look on Kitt's face as she handed it to her. The moment would be golden.

'All right, that's all we've got time for but we'll pick up the issues Lauren raised next week,' Harriet Lowenthal said over the lectern mic while shuffling her papers into a pile.

Oh dear. Grace had been so preoccupied with her plot to wind up Kitt, and all that had transpired that day with the investigation into Jodie's disappearance, that she'd zoned out of the lecture for at least the last forty minutes, and the lecture was only an hour long. Perhaps it was incidents like this that made Kitt crinkle her nose up so often when in Grace's company.

The rest of the students began to move but Grace, as instructed by Kitt, pulled on her coat and scarf, before reaching under her long cardigan and flicking the switch on a radio unit clipped to her belt. The mic at the lectern buzzed for an instant. Just long enough for Lowenthal to frown at the device until another student approached to ask a question, distracting her. A faint ringing sounded out in Grace's earpiece.

This was it. She was online.

Ensuring her voice was little more than a murmur, Grace said: 'Dark Halo to Carrot Top. Come in, Carrot Top.'

'*Grace!*' Even with the distortion through the earpiece there was no missing the disdain in Kitt's voice. '*That's not my code name and you know it. I'm Red Flame. This is not a game, you know?*'

Grace put a hand over her mouth to stifle a giggle so the rest of the students didn't think she was crackers for laughing to herself. 'Anything can be a game if you let it,' she muttered down the mic.

'*In my experience, people who live by that rule don't get to play many hands.*'

'I'm sorry, I forgot your code name.'

'*Forgot, my foot. Stop messing about and focus on the task in hand, will you?*'

'Are you sure about this? As far as we know Lowenthal has no link whatsoever to Jodie. She was a mechanics student and Lowenthal is in the social studies department. I can't imagine them crossing paths.'

'Trust me, if something unsavoury is going on around campus, Lowenthal will know all about it.'

Sighing, Grace made sure the wires from the radio set weren't visible beneath her scarf. Kitt wouldn't be drawn on exactly what Lowenthal had done to deserve the title of arch-nemesis but she had to assume it was something pretty serious for her to be so convinced of Lowenthal's involvement. Slowly, she walked down the steps next to the raked seating to the front of the lecture hall where Lowenthal was answering a question about cataloguing fiction subgenres. Grace watched on as Lowenthal explained the merits of using the Library of Congress Classification system.

Harriet Lowenthal looked to be a similar age to Kitt. She had a head of tight chestnut curls that shook with her enthusiastic gesticulations and Grace had noticed since the very first class that she favoured thick, dark lipsticks. Today was no exception. Her lips were a deep purple and seemed to move twice as fast as those belonging to the average person.

'Yes, Grace?' Lowenthal said.

'Hi. I'm sorry to bother you but there's something I need to ask about and you seem the most approachable tutor on my roster.'

'Ha! That's not saying a lot for the other tutors on your roster,' Lowenthal said with a smile that didn't quite make it to her eyes.

Grace returned the smile in as genuine a fashion as she could. She needed to get Lowenthal onside here if she was going to somehow casually ask if she knew anything about Jodie's disappearance and simultaneously have any hope of passing her cataloguing module. 'What can I say? I just get a good feeling in your lectures. They've really opened my eyes.'

'Flattery won't get you a grade-raise but that's nice to hear,' Lowenthal said, packing some pens and a notebook into her handbag. 'What is it you wanted to ask about? I'm only on campus for a few more minutes so I'll need to make it quick. If it's something sensitive or time-consuming we could always book an appointment tomorrow.'

'Oh no, this won't take long at all. The thing is, I ran into another student at a freshers' event – Patrick Howard – and he told me what happened to his fiancée, Jodie.'

'Oh yes, that was tragic,' Lowenthal said. Though she was saying the right thing about Jodie's disappearance, her tone of voice didn't betray any sadness or remorse at all. In fact, her response was pretty much the definition of lip service. Lowenthal snatched up the rest of her papers and began heading out of the lecture hall slowly enough that it was clear she meant for Grace to follow her.

'Tragic, yes, you won't hear any argument from me on

that score,' Grace said, as they headed out into the corridor, which smelled vaguely of warm custard due to its proximity to the department canteen. The sickly sweet smell never failed to turn Grace's stomach. Probably because she'd never forgotten seeing the canteen custard for the first time. She was no custard connoisseur but she was pretty sure it wasn't supposed to be that shade of brown.

'And is there some reason you wanted to talk to a faculty member about this?' Lowenthal said, re-establishing Grace's attentions.

'Patrick mentioned, in passing, that he's hired a private investigator to get to the bottom of her disappearance once and for all. It's been a year and the police haven't found anything so he decided to take matters into his own hands. Apparently, the PI has already come up with lots of new leads the police didn't uncover.'

'And I'm sure if Patrick Howard keeps throwing money at them, they'll keep finding leads.'

'*Oooh, what would* she *know about it?*' Kitt hissed into Grace's ear. Grace bit her lip to keep from smiling. Thankfully, Lowenthal would likely put any amusement on show down to her cynical quip.

'You might be right about that but hearing what happened to Jodie last year really spooked a lot of us first years. I think secretly we're all hoping she'll turn up somehow – *we're really working hard to fulfil our weekly quota of gullible first-year behaviour* – and I wondered if you had any contact with Jodie or knew of any faculty members who were close to her so that the PI could talk to them and get some background information.'

Lowenthal paused and looked Grace up and down. 'I appreciate you're only trying to help but that episode is one the whole academy would rather forget. If Jodie was going to be found, or wanted to be found, I'm sorry to say she would have been by now.'

'But –'

'Look, a word of advice that you'll thank me for. Don't rock the boat. Just put your head down, get along with your studies, and you'll do fine here. I have to go. I have another appointment.'

Don't rock the boat? Was Lowenthal trying to say that this was a dangerous path to travel down? If so, why, and what did she know that she wouldn't outright say? Unfortunately, Grace was never going to get the chance to ask her these questions directly as she had already walked away and turned down a connecting corridor that led out of the social studies building.

'The weasel is out of the den. I repeat –'

'Yes, thank you, Grace, I heard the first time. I'm in position. Subject is heading left past the library in rather a hurry.'

'Moving out that way now,' Grace said, taking a different exit to the one Lowenthal had used and walking out into the crisp October evening. Dusk had fallen now, which wasn't likely to make the task of surveillance any easier.

85

'Damn it.'

'What? Did you lose her?'

'No, give me some credit. I've only been on her tail two seconds. The subject is on her phone. I bet she's calling somebody about Jodie and what you've just fed her about the new leads. I knew she was in on this.'

'I'm not sure that her making a phone call really means –'

'You don't know what she's like. Oooh, what I wouldn't give to be able to hear what she's saying right now. She's cutting between the social care and sports technology buildings.'

'She's probably heading to the faculty car park. She did say she was leaving campus so looks like she was being honest about that, at least.'

'Yes, you're right, I remember. There's a cut through the halls complex to the car park. Whether she's changed her mind about where she's going based on what you said to her is another matter. If she gets in a car and drives off straight away this is going to be a very short surveillance op.'

'Well, I see you, so keep moving. If she changes direction just let me know. It won't take long for me to whip round the other end of the building if she changes course,' Grace said. She quickened her step, barely glimpsing the long shadows reflecting across the lake, hardly noticing the formidable silhouette of the library in the fading light or the ornate outlines of the academy's many prestigious buildings. Her one focus was to keep her sights on Kitt who had her sights set on Lowenthal. Her heart was beating fast at the thought of catching Lowenthal up to something she shouldn't be, and she decided right then that she was a fan of exhilaration.

Soon, however, Kitt paused just where the halls opened out into the campus shopping complex and the faculty car park. The whole area was cast in the orange glow of street lamps, probably to deter any car thieves who might be looking to knock off one of the many expensive cars parked up. Grace wasn't sure what could have caused Kitt to hang back like that but she was less than thirty seconds' walk from her so she'd soon find out.

'She turned this corner about a minute ago,' Kitt explained when Grace caught her up. 'It might be better to stick together from here on in and just make out like we're going to get a few things from the campus shop. If she clocks us I can just say I'm visiting you because I used to go here. That I'm here to reminisce.'

'All right,' Grace said with a nod. 'Seems like a believable story.'

When they turned the corner, however, both of them cried out in shock. Harriet Lowenthal stood not three feet around the edge of the building. Her eyes narrowed. Her purple lips tight and her arms crossed over her chest.

A moment later her expression slackened ever so slightly as she said: 'Kitt Hartley, is that you?'

NINE

There was a moment's stunned silence before Lowenthal sneered: 'At least I see you've finally replaced that raggedy blue hat you used to wear.'

Grace couldn't believe the switch in Lowenthal's attitude between here and the lecture hall. If she was hiding that kind of snark behind a respectable appearance, what else might she be hiding? And what on earth had passed between her and Kitt all those years ago?

'It wasn't raggedy, it was well-loved, that's all,' Kitt replied, though she tailed off at the end of her sentence in such a way that she didn't sound one hundred per cent sure.

'Never mind that,' Lowenthal said with a scowl. 'Perhaps you'd like to explain why the pair of you are following me?'

'Don't flatter yourself,' said Kitt. 'We're not following you, we're on our way to the shops. Running into you is just one of life's unfortunate coincidences.'

'Don't give me that. You couldn't be more obvious if you

tried. I may not have recognized you at first but I did notice you the second I stepped out of the department building. Grace tells me there's a PI on campus and the next thing I know a mysterious figure in a hat trails after me, speeding up when I do, slowing down when I do, hovering around a corner when I turn it. How stupid do you think I am?'

Kitt opened her mouth to answer Lowenthal's question but Grace, knowing Kitt's temper and fearing for her future at Venerable Bede's, interjected before she had the chance.

'Kitt, I think we should tell Ms Lowenthal what's really going on here. If you do she might be able to help us.'

Kitt glared at Lowenthal for a moment and then sighed. 'Fine. I am conducting some surveillance on various faculty members to gather background information on the disappearance of Jodie Perkins. I've taken to doing a bit of PI work lately and Patrick Howard has hired me.'

Lowenthal smirked and looked Kitt up and down in what could only be described as a patronizing manner. 'Well aren't you the little adventurer? Who knew you had it in you?'

Making what Grace thought was an admirable effort to ignore Lowenthal's condescending tone, Kitt replied: 'My track record of solving cases like this is strong, Harriet. So if you know anything about Jodie's disappearance you'd do well to tell me now before I uncover it for myself. Is there anything you can think of that will help us find out what happened to Jodie?'

Lowenthal looked slowly from Kitt to Grace. 'What did Ms Hartley tell you about me?'

'I didn't tell her anything,' said Kitt before Grace had a chance.

'You must have told her something. Otherwise, why did she agree to follow me knowing the risk to her academic career?'

Grace swallowed hard at that comment. When she agreed to tail Lowenthal, she hadn't thought about the consequences of their little surveillance game going wrong. Enrolling at Venerable Bede's had likely cost her her relationship with her parents. She didn't relish the thought of having to go back and explain that she had been expelled for being part of an amateur private investigation. That said, there was something really off about Lowenthal's attitude; she had a dark side to her that definitely wasn't apparent when she was standing at the front of a lecture hall, and if it ever did become a choice between keeping her place at the academy or finding out what really happened to Jodie Perkins, she knew which one she would choose.

Then again, wouldn't it be nice if she could do both?

'I didn't tell Grace anything specific. Though you are hardly my favourite person in the world, I believe Grace should have the chance to make her own mind up about you.'

'How very virtuous,' Lowenthal said, though she eyed Kitt in such a way it was clear she didn't totally believe her.

'Don't think I didn't notice that you dodged my question

about Jodie. Why don't you do the right thing for once? A missing girl's life could be at stake, you know.'

Lowenthal rolled her eyes. 'I don't know anything about Jodie's disappearance. I never even met the girl.'

'Who were you on the phone to just now, then?' Kitt said, looking at Lowenthal askance.

'Not that it's any of *your* business but I was talking to my boyfriend. Got yourself one of those yet? Or are you still pining over what's-his-face? Leo?'

'Theo,' Kitt corrected, a slight blush rising in her cheeks. 'That's all in the past but thanks a bunch for dragging it back up. A class act, as ever.'

'Look, sheer prejudice aside, I don't know where you got the idea that I would know anything about Jodie going missing but the last thing I need is you buzzing about me while I'm trying to get on and do my job. So here's what you really need to know: the night Jodie disappeared I was out with several faculty members at The Library.'

'The campus library?' asked Grace.

'No, the pub in town. We were trying to take the edge off the beginning of term with a few glasses of wine. There were quite a few people there but Karen Flacky and Julian Riddsdale were two of them. They're both in my department and once the pub shut we continued the party round at Julian's house until the early hours. If you're desperate to waste yet more of your time you can double check it with them.'

'Checking anything you have to say is above board won't be a waste of time,' Kitt countered.

'Suit yourself.'

'And I assume, since you haven't mentioned it, that there's no one else you can think of that I should talk to in connection with this case?' said Kitt.

'Not on the academy faculty, no,' Lowenthal said with a sly smile.

'What about people who aren't part of the academy faculty?' said Kitt.

'There may have been a rumour just after the investigation was closed that the police didn't have the guts to go after a suspect in the case who so happens to be a prominent student here at Venerable Bede's.'

'Who's that?' asked Kitt. 'Come on, out with it.'

'If I tell you, do you promise I won't need to see you or speak to you again for the duration of your stay here?'

'Assuming you're telling the truth, yes,' said Kitt.

'Fine. Selina Grant.'

Kitt frowned. 'Who's that?'

'You've heard of Grant Computing, haven't you?' Lowenthal said with a sigh.

'Everyone has,' Kitt said with a shrug.

'Selina is Humphrey Grant's daughter. Far as I know, the police never questioned her. Probably because they know millionaires can afford good lawyers.'

'I think I've heard of her,' said Grace. 'She's studying

sports technology. Second year . . . which means she was in the same year group as Jodie.'

Lowenthal nodded. 'That's her. From what I understand from staffroom gossip she and Jodie were pretty much inseparable until about a week before Jodie disappeared.'

'So, they were friends and had some kind of altercation?' said Kitt.

'You're supposed to be a PI. Why don't you find out yourself?' Lowenthal said. 'I've done you a favour by not shopping you to the dean for harassment. Don't expect another one. If I find you sniffing around me again I'm going straight to Berkeley about it.'

'You can't blame me for wanting to check in on you, given our history, can you?' said Kitt.

Lowenthal shook her head. 'Same old Kitt Hartley. Too serious for her own good and won't let a damn thing go. I gave my apology for what happened years ago. If you'd had the decency to just accept it maybe you'd be making better use of your time more than ten years after the fact.'

Kitt raised an eyebrow and didn't so much as flinch. In Grace's experience, Kitt was a pretty forgiving person. Certainly, she'd had a lot of things to forgive Grace for over the time they'd worked together, including her impromptu impersonations of Kitt and an assortment of deliberately embarrassing secret Santa gifts. Last year Grace had really pushed the envelope by purchasing Kitt a hardback copy of a book entitled *How to Bonk at Work*. Come to think of it, there wasn't much forgiveness involved in that instance because to Grace's surprise and slight disappointment Kitt sat reading it earnestly at her desk for the rest of the afternoon. Apparently in a bid to make the point that, as far as she was concerned, a book was a book. At any rate, Grace's pranks didn't always go according to plan and Kitt had never given any impression that their friendship was in jeopardy. Thus, if Lowenthal had apologized for whatever she did and Kitt had still refused to forgive her then it must have been something truly heinous.

As it quickly became apparent that Kitt wasn't going to rise to her digs, Lowenthal didn't bother trying to continue the conversation any further. Instead she simply grimaced and walked in the direction of the faculty car park. In a matter of minutes she approached a silver Audi and slipped into the driver's seat. She sat there for a moment before the engine revved up. Kitt and Grace stared after her as she drove off.

'Do you believe her? That she doesn't know anything about Jodie's disappearance?' Grace asked, now that she could be one hundred per cent certain her lecturer was out of earshot and couldn't kick her off the course for doubting her.

'Yes, I think so. Though it grieves me to say it, she didn't give any of the physical cues that might suggest she was lying. From past experience I know she's well practised at lying but even so, there really were no signs. That said, I was right on one point. She may not be directly involved but she did know something about it.'

'So, are you going to tell me what happened between you two now?'

'Nope.'

'Oh come on. Don't I need to know for my own protection? I mean, if she's my lecturer and I'm going into my relationship with her unprepared, who knows what could happen?'

'Nice try. Ask me another time, when I haven't just had to face her for the first time in a decade, will you?'

'Oh all right. But I'm holding you to that. I suppose we'd better start looking into Selina Grant and find out if there's any suggestion the police should have taken things further with her.'

'Yes, I suppose we had,' said Kitt. 'We'll need some other avenues to pursue while waiting to get hold of Bertrand Hobbs. When I checked his Facebook page there was an update saying he was on a class visit to various London media centres this week. He's not back until late on Friday.'

'No hope of an interview until the weekend then,' said Grace. 'Anything on his page that suggested trouble?'

'Other than his insistence on spelling media "meeja" seemingly without any irony, no.'

'Ugh,' Grace said, scrunching her nose up. 'That's bad enough, isn't it?'

'You're not wrong. We can't risk interviewing him over the phone in case he really is party to Jodie's disappearance and we tip him off. Best to talk to him face to face when he gets back.'

'And in the meantime we'll look into Selina?'

'Yes, it's a job for tomorrow though. I need to visit the shops and residences along the road near the river, see if anyone saw anything strange the night, or rather early morning, Jodie disappeared.'

'I would come with you, but I've got quite a few assignments due tomorrow,' said Grace.

'No bother, I've already left a few voicemails about the outhouse; hopefully someone will come back to me about the owner, and Mal is coming over tonight so he can come with me to question any potential witnesses.'

'How romantic for him after a day of . . . questioning potential witnesses,' Grace teased.

'He won't mind so much if he's with me,' Kitt said.

Grace thought about passing a comment on the unmissable smile on Kitt's face at the mention of her inspector boyfriend but thought better of it. Kitt's best friend Evie could get away with that kind of banter because they'd known each other for a lot longer, but she would without doubt get a scolding and a hard stare if she tried the same thing.

'I wonder how a millionaire's daughter is connected to Jodie?' Grace said in lieu of the many other jibes she would have liked to dish out.

'I've got a better question for you,' said Kitt. 'I asked Patrick directly if there was anyone Jodie wasn't on good terms with before the worst happened. If Selina was close to Jodie and had some falling-out with her just before she disappeared and was never heard from again, why didn't Patrick mention her?'

TEN

The next morning, just after nine o'clock, Grace, Patrick, Kitt and DI Halloran stood by the old outhouse near the River Wear. They were joined by the man who owned the property, local builder Kenneth Sweeney, and Patrick's mother Cynthia who, given she was paying for the investigation, had travelled down from Chester-le-Street to meet Kitt and check everything was above board. Cynthia was a lot more glamorous than Grace had expected. Her bobbed blonde hair was cut perfectly in line with her chin and she wore a full-length leopard-print winter coat made of faux fur that looked more like the kind of garment someone would wear to turn heads at a red carpet event than to a small meeting on the banks of the Wear one idle Tuesday morning.

They all looked on solemnly as Kenneth unlocked the outhouse door. It swung open with a creak and one by one they approached the building.

'Stay by the entrance, if you don't mind,' Kitt said to

Grace, Cynthia, Patrick and Kenneth. 'We don't want to accidentally damage or contaminate any evidence.'

Grace sighed. Even when she brought Kitt in on the investigation she was forced to stand on the sidelines. Since finding Jodie was the most important thing, Grace, for once, did as instructed. As a trained professional, it seemed Halloran was getting a free pass to go deeper into the building with Kitt to see what they could unearth.

'Well, like I told you,' Kenneth said in his broad Geordie accent, 'I've bin in this building a couple of times since last October, like, and I've not noticed anything untoward.'

'Except that when you visited in November last year the lock was broken,' said Kitt, and silently Grace agreed with her that this would definitely be categorized as 'untoward'.

Kenneth scratched his head. His fingernails were yellowed by either age or nicotine – maybe both. 'Aye, but I don't know how long it'd been broken for. Autumn was reet rainy last year. I remember because I couldn't get many outdoor painting jobs done. Odds are a rough sleeper broke the lock and was using the place as a shelter. Wouldn't be the first time, like.'

'Even so,' said Kitt. 'I might not have troubled you if the property had remained locked and secure. It was just a hunch, after all. But I can't think it's a coincidence that you found the lock broken so close to Jodie's disappearance.'

Kenneth shrugged. 'It didn't seem like owt to worry about at the time. If I thought there was a link I'd have phoned the police about it. I saw her picture in the paper, she was a canny lass. But I'd be surprised if this place had owt to do with her disappearance.'

'Well, we'll know soon enough,' said Kitt, taking a few steps further inside. She was closely followed by Halloran.

Grace looked around at the boxes of tools and various lengths of wood stored near the walls. She then glanced over at Patrick and Cynthia to see they, too, were examining the place as best they could from their remote vantage point. Kitt and Halloran continued to scour the room, their expressions equally intense.

'I'm no detective but, at a glance, it doesn't look like there's anything here,' said Cynthia, disappointment in her tone. She glanced at Patrick out of the corner of her eye, probably wondering how her son would handle another dead end on a case he was so desperate to solve. Grace stared at Patrick's face in profile for herself. Even from this angle she could see that wounded look had returned to his eyes. What torture for him to live all these months and be left to wonder.

'It's too soon to say, we don't know that yet,' Kitt said, putting on a pair of plastic gloves she'd pulled from her pocket before walking towards the back of the room and moving some boxes of nails aside. 'I interviewed every shop owner and resident from Pimlico to North Road who'd open their door to us last night and –'

DI Halloran cleared his throat.

'Sorry, we. We interviewed everyone along the main drag nearest the river. But for the most part we were just rehashing work the police did a year ago. They remembered hearing about Jodie's disappearance on the news the day after but they didn't remember anything strange from the early hours. Most of them were in bed but the few that weren't didn't see or hear anything. Which makes it more likely that if Jodie was attacked that night they didn't make it up to the road.'

'Or maybe they did take that road but nobody saw them,' said Patrick. 'It was very early in the morning.'

'It's possible,' said Halloran. 'But often someone sees something on a main road, even at that early time of day. It would have been about four a.m. Some people are getting up for shift work at that time. Some people are coming back from last night's party. Either way, Kitt won't leave any stone unturned, and that's ultimately the way a lot of these kinds of investigations are resolved. By entertaining every possibility.'

Grace thought she saw a certain look in Halloran's eyes that she had noticed once or twice before. He was evaluating Patrick as he spoke to him. Did Kitt only bring him along to get his professional opinion on whether he thought Patrick was in on it? Something tightened in her chest at the thought.

Kitt and Halloran started systematically moving the many boxes and trays around, checking in and under each one before setting it aside. No luck. Next, the pair started on a pile of paint-splashed linens resting on the window sill. Each one was unfolded and inspected and then refolded.

'Those are just some sheets we use for interior decorating jobs,' said Kenneth, 'nothing suspect about them.'

'What about these?' Kitt said, pointing to a pile of rags on the floor. 'Are these yours?'

'Er, whey aye, suppose they must be. We do use rags from time to time.'

'But you don't immediately recognize them.'

'Well no, but it's hard to tell one rag from another, like, you know? I do a lot of jobs and if they're sitting in the back there it could be a couple of years since I last put my hands on them.'

One by one, Kitt picked up the rags, inspecting them first with her eyes and then sniffing them. She paused on the fifth rag, and narrowed her eyes.

'What is it?' said Halloran.

'I'm not one hundred per cent . . . What do you think this is?' she said, handing it to Halloran.

Halloran held the rag near his nose and inhaled. 'Smells like some kind of ether to me. Sweet-smelling enough to be chloroform.'

'That's what I thought.'

'Chloroform? You mean like the anaesthetic?' said Cynthia, before biting her bottom lip and looking over at Patrick. Every muscle in his face seemed to be clenched tight.

'I use some strong substances,' said Kenneth, 'but nothing like that, and at any rate, all my liquids are kept in a different storage space.'

Kitt studied Kenneth's face with a little more keenness than she had before but then returned her attention to the rags again. 'There's just this one that seems to have the smell about it.'

Halloran produced an evidence bag from the pocket of his dark grey coat and started placing the rags inside.

'Hang about,' Kitt said. She pulled a small box from her satchel and opened it. Inside, as far as Grace could see, there were various small tools including a pair of tweezers. Leaning forward, she picked something off the rag with the tweezers; something that Grace had no hope of seeing without getting a bit closer.

'What is it?' asked Patrick, a note of urgency in his voice.

'Fibres,' Halloran said.

Kitt placed it in another bag Halloran held out for her and then took the bag over to where Grace, Patrick, Cynthia and Kenneth were standing. They all leaned in to get a better look at the bright red fibres that looked to be mohair.

'Oh God,' Patrick said. Grace looked back at him to see all the colour had drained from his face. 'Jodie had a cardigan that was that colour.'

'Yes, you're right. I remember it,' said Cynthia. 'There's no doubt it's the same colour. I always admired it whenever she wore it. Most of the times I saw her she was in jeans and an oil-stained T-shirt so I remember thinking it was nice she had something a bit more feminine in her wardrobe.'

'There's not much point getting dressed up when you're

spending most of your days under a car, is there, Mum?' said Patrick with a snap to his voice Grace wouldn't have expected from him.

'No, I know, love. I just wished she'd got the chance to dress up a bit more, that's all. Before all this happened.' Cynthia put an arm around Patrick.

He offered her a weak smile. 'I know. She never even got to pick out a wedding dress for our big day.'

'Oh, don't, pet,' Cynthia said, pulling a tissue out of her pocket and dabbing her eyes. 'You'll set me off.'

'Sorry,' Patrick said, before returning his attention to the bag Halloran was holding. 'She was wearing that cardigan the day she disappeared, or at least, the last time I saw her that morning.'

'So Jodie was here,' said Grace. 'Before she disappeared, wherever she went, she was here first.'

Halloran turned on Kenneth. 'I'm going to need to report this finding to the local nick and submit it as evidence. They'll probably have some questions for you when I do.'

'A few fibres don't prove anything,' said Kenneth. 'She could've broke in here of her own accord, for all we know.'

'True,' said Kitt. 'But unlikely given her disappearance and the fact that the last time we heard from her she was screaming on local radio.'

'Well, I've got nothing to hide,' said Kenneth. 'The police can ask owt they want.'

Halloran nodded and then began to usher everyone, Kitt

included, out of the doorway. He proceeded to search the area for any further clues. After ten minutes, he was satisfied they had found all they could without the use of more specialized equipment.

'We'll need to cordon this building off,' said Halloran. 'If Jodie was . . .' He paused and looked at Patrick before correcting himself. 'If anything happened to her, this is likely where it happened.'

'Oh, this is horrible, just horrible. I can't stand to think about her in here, trapped and scared,' said Cynthia, looking back into the outhouse. Grace looked again at the building and tried, without success, to stop a shudder in its tracks. Nobody wants to die before their time but the outhouse was cold and dank and very much the last place you'd want to take your final breath.

'Well, we don't know anything for sure yet,' Halloran said. 'But even if Jodie did leave here alive, this place is a new lead in her case. We need to protect it.'

'How long for, like?' Kenneth said.

'I don't know yet,' Halloran replied, with an edge to his voice that made Kenneth visibly shrink. 'You said you don't use this building very often anyway, so it shouldn't be any trouble, should it?'

'I don't, but you never know when you're going to need access to your stuff, do you?'

'I've had a quick look round but I don't want to step on any toes at the local nick and besides which they'll need specialized equipment to be sure they've caught everything. I'm sure they will do all necessary work as swiftly as they can. In the meantime, nobody is to go in or out until they get here to conduct a thorough search.' And with that, Halloran pulled some yellow tape out of his pocket and began securing it on a nearby tree.

'Does he, er, always carry crime scene tape around with him?' Grace asked.

'Oh yes,' Kitt said with a hint of pride in her voice. 'Mal's always prepared for anything.'

Grace would have smiled at Kitt's strange admiration for her boyfriend's access to crime scene essentials if it wasn't for the look on Patrick's face. Those brown sorrowful eyes looked even sadder now than they had done in the photograph on the appeal website.

'She isn't alive, is she?' Patrick said quietly.

'Look,' Grace said in a gentle voice. 'I'll be the first to admit this doesn't look good, but like Halloran says, we don't know anything for sure yet. In fact, there are other leads we can explore while the police are working on this bit.'

'You've found other leads already?' said Cynthia, her tone admiring. 'That is quick work. I wish we'd had you around when all this first happened. If we had, we might have been able to draw a line under it all much sooner.'

'Yes, we . . . try,' Grace said, unsure if conducting less than discreet surveillance on a faculty member Kitt had a long-running vendetta against really counted as work. 'I looked into the man who found the drugs in Jodie's locker, Elvis McCabe. Does his name sound familiar?'

Cynthia and Patrick both shook their heads.

'He resigned shortly after Jodie's disappearance. Berkeley said he felt guilty but we wanted to be sure it wasn't because he'd taken a bribe and was fleeing the scene.'

'And did you find anything suspicious?' Patrick asked.

'I'm afraid not,' said Grace. 'If Elvis McCabe took some big bribe off anyone he hasn't spent it. He still lives in the same housing estate on the edge of Durham he lived in when he worked at the academy. His Facebook profile shows him in a photo with four kids. I called the company that manages that estate this morning, pretending to be a potential tenant, and they said that the biggest flats they had were three bedroomed, so their living quarters aren't exactly spacious, given the size of their family.'

'What about a car?' said Cynthia. 'Or gadgets, things like that?'

'I'm going to do a bit more surveillance work when I get the chance but on the surface there are no red flags.'

'Oh, so you haven't really found any new leads then?' Patrick said.

'Actually, we were given one name, though the source was dubious,' said Kitt.

'What was the name?' asked Cynthia.

'One of the lecturers we talked to said we should interview Selina Grant about Jodie's disappearance,' said Grace.

'Selina Grant?' Patrick frowned. 'Why do they want you to talk to her?'

'Apparently she and Jodie had a falling-out just before her disappearance.'

'Oh . . .' Patrick paused for a long moment, seemingly thinking hard. 'Yes. I do remember Jodie saying she'd decided to cut ties with her.'

'That never struck you as odd at the time?' said Kitt. Grace wished Kitt's tone could have been a little kinder. Even if she wasn't letting go of the idea that Patrick had something to do with Jodie's disappearance anytime soon, she could be a little bit more sensitive given the discovery of those fibres, just on the off-chance he was innocent, and especially since Kitt knew what it was like to be wrongfully accused. Besides anything else, was Cynthia likely to keep funding the investigation if she caught on to the fact that her son was Kitt's chief suspect?

Patrick, seemingly too fazed by all they had uncovered at the outhouse to notice Kitt's insinuation, replied, 'Not really, they hadn't known each other very long. It's not like it was a very dramatic parting of ways. Not as far as I knew, anyway.'

'Why did she make the decision to stop communicating with Selina?' said Kitt.

Patrick shrugged. 'She didn't even say. I didn't think anything of it at the time because she was a bit of an introvert. She was picky about who she was friends with so not every relationship stuck. All I knew was they'd been close for the first few weeks of term and then for some reason Jodie just decided to distance herself. At least, that's all I knew then. I have heard a few rumours since that might give some sense as to why she decided not to bother with her any more, though it's very silly.'

'Silliness doesn't scare me,' said Grace.

'No, that's because it's your bread and butter,' Kitt said, before turning back to Patrick. 'What rumours have you heard?'

'Well, I don't know how much there is in it, but apparently there's been some secret society at Venerable Bede's for generations.'

'Oh! Yes, I heard rumblings about that kind of thing when I was studying here,' said Kitt. 'If the rumours are to be believed, they call themselves the Scarlet Stocking Society.'

'What kind of name is that?' said Cynthia, her face scrunching up in distaste.

'These things always have silly names,' said Kitt. 'It's one of their hallmarks and is the primary reason why people outside the circle can never really take them that seriously.'

'What does this secret society do, exactly?' said Grace.

'Not entirely public knowledge, given they're a secret society,' said Kitt. 'But the rumours were that they got together to attempt daring, death-defying feats and, like any secret society, manipulate institutions and other people in their favour whenever the opportunity arose.'

Grace stared at Kitt. 'You were one of them, weren't you?'

'Don't be absurd,' said Kitt.

'A-ha. That's exactly what somebody who belonged to a secret society would say,' said Grace, determined to find some way of lightening the mood after the sadness that had settled over them. 'All this time you've been playing the part of a prim librarian who accidentally finds her way onto murder investigations, when really you've had the taste for danger all along.'

Kitt crossed her arms. 'Prim?'

'Maybe not prim. But you've got to admit you're a bit . . .'

'A bit what?'

'Can I suggest that you don't finish that sentence?' said Halloran, who had, apparently, finished his cordoning duties. 'Unless you are a member of the Scarlet Stocking Society and are currently trying to engage in a death-defying feat.'

The frown on Kitt's face slackened and she chuckled at Halloran's dig.

'Ooh, give over,' she said. 'My hard stare is disquieting but it's hardly lethal.'

'Only on subjects tested so far,' Halloran continued to joke.

Kitt shook her head at him but within a few seconds she was back to thinking about Selina Grant. 'From what I remember about the rumours, every few years the society has to choose a new head. It's always somebody rich and powerful. A millionaire's daughter like Selina Grant would be the perfect choice.'

'The recording,' said Grace. 'At the end of the radio recording, Jodie was trying to say something that just came out as a sssssssss sound. Maybe she was trying to say Selina but was cut off before she could?'

'Or Scarlet Stocking Society,' said Kitt.

'Or both. What if Selina wanted to induct Jodie into the society?' said Grace.

Patrick shook his head. 'There's no way Jodie would be up for that. She was far too focused on doing well on her course. She had a scholarship here and knew she had to work hard to stay in the academy's good graces. Besides anything else, she kept herself to herself.'

'Exactly,' said Grace. 'Which is why she cut off ties with Selina. How secret is this society? Given you've both heard rumours about it while you studied here?'

'When I was here it was just a silly rumour nobody really believed,' said Kitt. 'It was a campus Big Foot of sorts. Nobody gave it any credit.'

'People believe it now,' said Patrick. 'But nobody knows exactly who is involved or what they really get up to. Sometimes there are rumours about certain people being involved, like there were about Selina, but of course they always deny it and nobody knows who's really calling the shots.'

'Honestly,' said Cynthia. 'It sounds like they've got a bit too much free time on their hands to be coming up with nonsense like this.'

'Can't disagree with you there,' said Kitt. 'Berkeley was

acting very strangely in our interview yesterday and we thought she might have been trying to cover for someone. What if it's Selina? Berkeley's fixated on keeping the college income up. No doubt she wouldn't want to lose a student as high profile as Selina. If she suspects Selina is involved she might be willing to lie for her.'

'I called DI Thompson who coordinated the investigation at Durham nick this morning,' said Halloran. 'I asked him what he thought about Berkeley and if they'd uncovered anything. They checked both her financial records and phone records at the time and there was nothing out of place so if she was acting strangely it makes more sense that she was covering for someone else rather than up to no good herself. Especially since she has an alibi.'

'So what if Jodie knew too much about the society and someone involved was worried that she was going to reveal it?' said Kitt.

'Yes!' said Grace. 'When she called in to the radio show she said it was about an important figure at Venerable Bede's. Being a millionaire's daughter here must have made Selina a minor celebrity.'

'There was a lot of buzz when she enrolled,' Patrick conceded. 'And Berkeley did take full advantage of the media opportunities that came with it. Selina has her own bodyguard assigned by her father. That guy follows her everywhere. Nobody can talk to her unless she wants them to so everyone knows her on sight. The thing is, I really can't see Selina being involved in this. I only had limited contact with her but she seemed incredibly down to earth – for the daughter of a millionaire.'

'Limited contact is, unfortunately, probably not enough to make a judgement one way or another,' said Halloran. 'If she was involved in Jodie's disappearance she'd make sure any connection was well hidden, especially given her high profile. People like that often have connections and influence that the rest of us simply never will. They operate in a whole other world.'

'This theory does seem to hold some water,' said Grace. 'It wouldn't look too good if the society was exposed when Selina had only been running it for a few weeks. Who knows what the consequences would be?'

'And who better placed to make a person who knows your darkest secret disappear, than a millionaire?' said Kitt.

ELEVEN

'Grrr, nothing!' said Grace, putting her head in her hands. 'You?'

''Fraid not,' said Kitt, dropping her phone down on the desk.

Despite Patrick's scepticism about the idea that Selina could be involved in Jodie's death, the second Grace's morning lecture was done she and Kitt had headed straight to the library to conduct as much online research as possible on their suspected millionaire murderess.

That was two hours ago, however, and the search had not proven fruitful.

'I tried hacking – I mean accessing – the academy database but they don't keep anything in the student files except core contact details. All the other stuff – like details of students streaking across the football pitch at two a.m., for example – must be kept in those paper files in Berkeley's office.'

Kitt issued Grace with a hard stare but didn't reference

her cheeky comment about the streaking directly. 'The academy has always been a bit behind the times. Although, knowing how concerned Berkeley is about reputation, she probably just wants to maintain the option to shred any evidence that might reflect badly on her, or Venerable Bede's.'

'Well, I've tried every combination of search terms I can think of to find a link between Selina and the Scarlet Stocking Society but there's nothing there. Which, I suppose, is what you'd expect for a secret society, but I thought someone somewhere would have leaked something.'

'I've not found anything linking her to the society either,' said Kitt.

'It's not just that though,' said Grace. 'For a millionaire's daughter she's led a pristine, if adventurous, life.'

'How do you mean?'

'I mean, there are videos of her on her YouTube channel skydiving from ten thousand feet, bungee jumping in South America and white-water rafting in Colorado, but there's no headlines about a drug addiction or a drink problem or any petty criminal acts that you might expect from someone who might be more inclined than most to go off the rails in their teenage years.'

'Maybe her father is rich enough to keep anything like that quiet,' Kitt suggested.

'Perhaps, but I doubt it in today's clickbait climate. He'd have to pay a journalist off pretty big to squash that kind of headline. Is someone who hasn't had any minor infractions likely to kidnap or kill? Can someone really go from nought to murder in sixty seconds?'

'It happens,' Kitt said. 'People who feel threatened will do a lot to protect the status quo and in this case, Selina's reputation was at stake. If she's got a pristine record then arguably she had a lot to lose.'

Grace tapped a couple of keys on her laptop. 'She still hasn't responded to that email I sent to her academy email address.'

'Who knows if she even checks it?' said Kitt. 'Even if she did, after what you wrote in said email she'd probably think it a scam.'

'My email was totally plausible, thank you very much. Given her lifestyle, she might well have won an award for Adrenalin Junkie of the Year.'

'There was probably a more believable tack, though I admire your attempt at getting the subject to come to us,' said Kitt.

Grace shook her head. 'No smirches on her name and no easy way of getting a quiet word with her. I even looked her house up online and it's a gated mansion. Something tells me whatever staff she has to run the place won't be letting us in for a cosy chat. So now what do we do?'

'I don't know,' Kitt admitted. 'I'll have to have a think about it but if, as Lowenthal suggested, even the police were edgy about going after her, then we'll have to tread carefully. I'm meeting Mal for dinner tonight so I'll ask him and hopefully he'll have word about the police response to the new evidence we found at the outhouse. Maybe I'll even get invited onto the case to consult.'

'Doubtful that'll happen again unless the DI at Durham fancies you as much as Halloran,' Grace said.

'That's not the only reason I was asked to consult on his cases,' Kitt said, though she didn't sound too sure. A moment later her phone started buzzing. 'That's probably him now.'

She picked up her phone and glanced at the screen. 'Oh, it's a Skype call from Evie.'

Kitt tapped to accept the call and Grace shuffled round so she could say hello.

'Greetings, chums,' Evie said with a little wave.

'Now then, Marilyn,' Grace said. Over the last six months or so this had become Grace's pet name for Evie. With her full pouty lips and golden blonde curls she looked a lot like Monroe and Evie's love for all things vintage only made it more appropriate. At first Evie had resisted the nickname – likely because she was sensitive about her facial scars which were still visible a year after her brush with death. Over time, however, she'd just accepted that as far as Grace was concerned she was still film star material.

'Everything all right? Where are you?' said Kitt.

'Yeah, just having a cuppa at Tea by the Tower,' Evie replied.

'And you've Skyped in just to make me jealous, have you? I don't know what they do to their Lady Grey but, as far as I'm concerned, it's the best in the city of York.'

'Funnily enough, I didn't call to discuss the tea,' Evie said with a little giggle.

'Then do put me out of my misery, you know I'm working a case and time is of the essence.'

'Well, Ruby's here with me' – ''Ello, love,' Ruby chipped in off-screen – 'and I was just telling her about this missing student you're trying to find. She wants to have a quick word with you about it.'

Kitt closed her eyes for a moment as if preparing herself for an ordeal. Grace wagered that if Ruby hadn't been listening in to the call she would have had a thing or two to say to Evie about discussing the case with her. As it was, unless she wanted to be cruel, she'd have no choice but to acquiesce. 'All right, put her on.'

Evie's face disappeared as she passed the phone over to her companion but unfortunately it didn't seem Ruby was particularly au fait with Skype. She was holding the phone so close to her face, all Grace and Kitt could see was her chin.

'Oh my giddy aunt, Ruby! Move the phone back a bit so we can see your face, will you?' said Kitt.

'Eh? What's that?' said Ruby. But a second later, Evie must have taken matters into her own hands as the phone moved back and Ruby's wrinkled face came into view.

'I 'ope you don't mind me getting in touch but when I 'eard about the case you're working on I thought of a couple of things you may not have thought of.'

'Without any background information or evidence, that's impressive,' Kitt said, her voice as dry as it always was when she was conversing with the Vale of York University library's unofficial psychic. Grace nudged Kitt's arm to signal she was being a touch harsh when the old woman only wanted to help. 'But do continue,' Kitt added with half a smile.

'Well, for starters, I understand that this lass 'as disappeared. Now these things do happen but not without some kind of disturbance in the ether. Given she was studying in the Durham area there's a chance she might 'ave been spirited away by St Cuthbert. 'is presence is very strong in Northumberland.'

'Spirited away,' Kitt repeated.

'Or!' Ruby said, getting herself even more excited. ''ave you passed any odd-looking hills while you've been in Durham?'

'Hills? No. Nothing out of the ordinary, why?' said Kitt.

'Well, I 'ate to think it but there's always a chance the poor lass was eaten by the Lambton Worm.'

'Lambton Worm? What's that?' asked Grace, not sure if she wanted the answer, given she was supposed to live in Durham for the next three years and worms, though useful in the garden, weren't exactly her favourite creatures.

'It's a giant, poisonous worm that curls itself around hills near the Wear. Killed by John Lambton not long after the Crusades.'

'Oh God, that sounds grim,' Grace said.

Kitt tutted, shaking her head at Grace and Ruby simultaneously. 'If the worm was killed after the Crusades, how on earth could it be responsible for the disappearance we're looking into now?'

'Well, it must've 'ad a mother. Or maybe it 'ad babies. And who knows how long those things live?' said Ruby, before frowning. 'But you're right, there's probably a more likely explanation.'

'That we agree on,' said Kitt, her nose crinkling. A sure sign that her patience was wearing thin.

'Now that I think about it, I wonder if she's been lured away by Jimmy.'

'Jimmy?' said Kitt.

'Aye – Jimmy Allen.'

'Who's he?'

'He was the piper to the Duchess of Northumberland for a couple of years. He died in 1810, like, but people are still seeing 'is ghost round and about. If 'is ghostly piping led her off somewhere then finding her might prove quite difficult, but I could do some scrying for you to see if the powers that be want to reveal anything that might be of use.'

'OK, first things first, what have I told you about referring to famous local ghosts by their first names like they're your best mates?'

'Well, it's not my fault that those who 'ave passed on feel at peace in my company. That Roman soldier had been marching for a thousand years before he stopped to rest at my 'ouse. No wonder he was ready for a cup of tea when 'e got there.'

Kitt pursed her lips, ignoring Ruby's madcap explanation. 'And second, are all of these "helpful suggestions" by chance coming out of the book of Durham Folklore?'

Ruby sat silent and still for a moment. 'I might have glanced at it for reference.'

To Grace's surprise, Kitt managed not to roll her eyes. 'All right, Ruby, well, we'll take what you've said into consideration. Can you put Evie back on?'

There was a bit of shuffling as the phone was handed back to Evie. Evie's face was red, probably from the strain of trying to hold in a lot of laughter.

'Thank you for that. It was such a productive use of our time, especially as we just hit another dead end.'

'I thought it best to convey this important information to you as soon as possible,' Evie said with a grin.

'You are in for it when I get back to York,' Kitt hissed.

'For all you know, you'll be coming back to thank us for the important leads we've provided,' Evie said, clearly confident enough to really push her luck, a confidence that was no doubt dependent on the fact that Kitt was seventy miles away.

'I wouldn't hold your breath on that score,' said Kitt. 'I'll be back Thursday morning to have a word with you.'

'All right, you take care, Kitt,' Evie said with a chuckle before ending the call.

121

'Oh dear me,' said Kitt, putting her head in her hands. 'Sometimes, between you, Ruby and Evie, I wonder how I cling to what little sanity I have left.'

'Whoever said sanity was so great?' Grace said, giving Kitt a playful nudge with her elbow.

'I suppose I shouldn't worry. If I'm not driven mad by you lot I'll probably be driven mad by not being able to get at the chief suspect on this case. Maybe Mal will do us a favour and use his badge to bypass Selina's security detail and encourage her to be a little bit more forthcoming, although I really would like to solve this case with minimal input from him. I've got to stand on my own two feet – can't always be pulling in favours with the police if I want to run my own agency.'

As Kitt said this, a plan started to hatch in Grace's mind. It wasn't the kind of plan you could share with a prim librarian turned PI who played by the rules, or her police detective boyfriend. But it might be the key to getting close to Selina Grant. If she mentioned it to Kitt she'd never hear the end of how risky it was, but if having a sit-down with Selina Grant was the most likely way of moving the case forward then surely it was worth a little bit of peril? Something told Grace that Kitt wouldn't agree, so for this outing she'd have to find another accomplice.

TWELVE

'You're going to get me expelled,' Patrick hissed as the pair scuttled down the corridor in the main reception building. Their footsteps echoed on the hard lino and at this time of day it was the only sound in the usually bustling hallway. 'Do you know how frustrating that's going to be given how close I am to completing my course? It hasn't exactly been an easy ride getting to this point after all that's happened, you know?'

'I wouldn't ask you to do something that I thought would get you into trouble. But even if you do get caught just act like you had no part in it. Like you wanted to make an appointment with Dean Berkeley about something else and just happened to be here while I was snooping around. I'll take the fall and back up your story. It's my plan and part of that plan is affording you plausible deniability,' said Grace, flashing him her most impish smile. 'Relax.'

'You know I'm not going to let you take the blame like that,' said Patrick.

'Then, for the sake of your bright future, I guess I'm going to have to work doubly hard not to get caught.'

The pair continued down the corridor towards Berkeley's office. Like most interiors around the academy it was over-sanitized and painted from ceiling to floor in a depressing shade of grey. The windows ran the length of all the corridors on the exterior wall but as it was dark outside there wasn't even the view of some shrubbery to take the edge off the otherwise dismal decor.

Half an hour ago, Grace and Patrick had sat on a bench outside pretending to be engrossed in some reading for their respective courses. They had both watched the dean leave the building. Fifteen minutes after that, her secretary, Ms Smyth, left for the day and the office cleaners arrived ten minutes later. This was the final green light they had needed to go ahead with Grace's plan.

There was no doubt that Berkeley's secretary would have locked her office door when she left. But the cleaners would have keys. A little bit of misdirection and a dash of luck and Grace's cunning scheme should come off without a hitch.

'I'm not exactly in the habit of making light conversation with the custodial staff,' said Patrick. 'Won't she wonder why a student is coming up to her out of the blue? What am I supposed to say to her?'

'You're smart, I'm sure you'll think of something,' Grace said, giving him a playful punch in the arm.

'I think you overestimate my small-talk skills. It's not my strong suit.'

'Just . . . dazzle her with your charms,' Grace said.

'Very funny.'

Grace laughed, even though she wasn't exactly joking. If circumstances were different and Patrick stopped her to talk in the corridor, she would definitely want to listen to what he had to say. Of course she couldn't let Patrick know that. She was trying to solve the case of his fiancée's disappearance so it would be highly inappropriate for her to act on or even admit an attraction. Still, she couldn't help the places her mind had wandered to since they'd met in the library the day before . . . could she? After all, it wasn't like thinking about how Patrick's hands would feel on her was hurting anyone, right?

'Look,' Patrick said, snapping her out of her thoughts.

The cleaner, wearing a less-than-fetching lime green tabard, approached the secretary's office and was toying with some keys. A moment later she started to unlock the door.

'Now's your chance,' said Grace. 'Walk her as far as possible in the opposite direction without rousing suspicion. I'll be as quick as I can.'

Taking a deep breath, Patrick strode towards the office while Grace crept further down the corridor where she could stand out of sight.

'Excuse me,' Patrick said, before the cleaner could enter Ms Smyth's office.

'Yes, sonny, what is it?'

'Sorry to bother you, but . . . er, could you help me? I think I've got something in my eye. Can you just take a look under the light over here and tell me if there's something there?'

Something in his eye? Was that the best he could do? Patrick really wasn't selling himself short when he said small talk wasn't his strong suit.

'Aye, all right,' the cleaner said with a nod and followed him to the section of the corridor Patrick had indicated.

The second the cleaner moved away from the door, Grace zipped inside the office. After a quick look around, she clocked the filing cabinet marked A–Z and headed straight to G. She spent an agonizing twenty seconds hastily flipping past names like Geller and Granger before she came to Grant.

Glancing at the door to make sure she wasn't going to be interrupted, she pulled out the file, opened it to the page that listed Selina Grant's academic timetable and snapped a quick photo on her phone. She was just about to close the file when she noticed a blue tab sticking out of one of the pages. It was the same kind that had been stuck to the page about the early morning streaking in Kitt's file. Perhaps Selina Grant wasn't as pristine as Google would have everyone believe? That said, it didn't seem too difficult to get into trouble here at Venerable Bede's and it was likely that, even with her status as the daughter of a millionaire,

Selina's wild streak probably wasn't a good match for the kind of rules people like Regina Berkeley liked to enforce.

Any evidence that might draw Selina's otherwise impeccable record into question would surely be of vital importance. Grace flicked to the page and gave it a quick scan, just to check it wasn't some minor infraction like walking across the grass after Berkeley had just had it mowed. As she read the document, however, her eyes widened. It was a statement written by Selina describing a physical fight she had had with another student. The other student was Jodie Perkins and the fight had taken place a week before she disappeared. In the statement, Selina admitted to starting the fight because Jodie had been taunting her about Patrick. Apparently Selina wanted Patrick for herself and Jodie had made it clear that was never going to happen. It seemed Selina Grant didn't like being told she couldn't have the things she wanted. Was wanting Patrick for herself enough to motivate Selina into making Jodie disappear? Certainly, this was the most solid motive she and Kitt had uncovered so far.

As quickly as she could, Grace snapped a photo of that page too, closed the file, refiled the folder and pushed the drawer shut. It made a loud thundering as it closed. Oops. That wasn't very smart. She stood stock-still for a moment, listening for any sounds outside that might indicate someone was on their way to investigate. If it really came to it she could probably hide until the coast was clear. After ten seconds or so, however, it became clear she'd got away with it.

All she could hear was the cleaner laughing at something Patrick had said. It sounded like he had taken her literally when she told him to use his charms.

She raced to the door and eased it open. The cleaner had her back to Grace so as long as she didn't make any noise she could slip out unnoticed. Without any further hesitation, she flew out of the door and off down the corridor towards the main entrance. She heard Patrick make his excuses and started walking at a more casual pace so he could catch her up. He was just a few paces behind her, and Grace was just about to congratulate herself on pulling off the perfect stealth operation, when she happened to glance through the window and notice a figure walking down the adjoining corridor. There was no mistaking the figure, it was Berkeley's secretary, Ms Smyth. She was going to round the corner any moment. They couldn't be seen near the office after hours. Grace was ninety-five per cent sure she'd put everything back the way she found it but if the secretary noticed anything out of place and she was seen near the scene of the crime they would know she'd broken into the office and there was no question that would mean definite expulsion.

'Oh God, quick, in here!' Grace hissed.

Patrick frowned but followed her. 'Why are we hiding in the cleaning closet?'

'Shh. Berkeley's secretary is coming back. I don't want her to be able to link me to a break-in if she notices anything different.'

'Oooh, Ms Smyth,' the pair heard the cleaner say on the other side. 'I was just starting on your office. Did you forget something?'

'My phone,' said Ms Smyth. 'I thought I'd put it in my handbag but I must have been distracted on my way out. I won't be a minute, sorry to get in your way.'

'No problem. I haven't really started on your office yet. I'll go get the hoover out and give you a few minutes to collect your things.'

'Oh-oh,' said Grace.

'What?'

Grace picked up the end of a hoover – there was just enough light coming through from the window above the door for Patrick to see it.

His eyes widened. The pair fell silent. The sound of the cleaner's footsteps on the hard lino grew closer and closer. Biting her lip, Grace tried to think quickly. What was a valid excuse for hiding in the cupboard? A game of hide and seek? No, that wouldn't work. They weren't twelve. Stock-taking cleaning products? But she didn't know anything about the person in charge of facilities at the academy. Not even a name. There's no way she could make that story fly. And besides, the cleaner had already seen Patrick so she might wonder why he hadn't mentioned during their chat that he'd been sent over by a faculty member to stock-take cleaning products.

Then, a thought came to her.

'Er, why are you looking at me like that?' Patrick murmured.

'Patrick, kiss me.'

'What?'

'We're young people. We do stupid things like kissing in closets. It's less suspicious than just hiding here.'

'You really think she's going to buy that?'

'It always works on TV,' Grace said with a shrug.

The cleaner's footsteps were close now. Maybe only a couple of feet away. Nodding at each other, Patrick and Grace leaned in. Gently, Grace pressed her lips against his. They were soft and somehow tasted like citrus. Perhaps it was that delicious taste that prompted her to lightly suck on Patrick's bottom lip. Who was she kidding? She had wanted to do that even before she knew what he tasted like. A small gasp escaped him as she did so. She scrunched her eyes shut, concerned that she had overstepped but the next thing she felt were Patrick's arms wrapping tight around her. She was surprised by how firm they felt. How steady. She circled her arms around his waist, pulling him closer, and the kiss intensified. His hands gripped the back of her shirt as he pressed his body harder against hers until there was no space between them at all. A moment later their tongues met and Grace heard herself make a small, satisfied moan that only made Patrick kiss her deeper. It had been too long since she was last kissed and, by her own admission, Grace had never quite been kissed like this.

'What's going on in here then?' a familiar voice said.

Grace and Patrick parted with a start, both of them breathing heavily. Neither had heard the closet door open. Grace wondered if she was blushing, her face certainly felt very hot.

'Sorry,' Patrick sputtered. 'My, er, girlfriend here surprised me and things got a bit out of control. Sorry. I'm very, very sorry.'

'Yes, sorry,' said Grace. 'We didn't know anyone would be going into this cupboard anytime soon. You probably could do without seeing stuff like this when you're trying to do your job. We didn't mean to get in the way.'

The cleaner stared at them for a moment and then shrugged. 'I used to clean hotels. After that there's not much that can shock you. But you better get out of here before Ms Smyth comes back. She tells Berkeley everything and between the pair of them they might not be so understanding.'

'Right. Thanks,' Grace said, adjusting her shirt which had ruffled during her kiss with Patrick. She stepped out of the closet. Patrick followed and the pair walked as quickly as they could without drawing too much attention to themselves, neither quite able to make direct eye contact after the kiss they had shared but also unable to stop themselves from smiling when they thought the other wasn't looking.

THIRTEEN

'See, there she is now,' Grace said, as Selina Grant walked out of the Sports Science faculty building and started towards the main reception block. Grace recognized her from the many YouTube videos Selina had uploaded onto her personalized channel. As those videos invariably depicted Selina doing some death-defying feat, however, she had adopted a totally different look for campus life. Gone were the racer back T-shirts and Lycra shorts. Instead, she wore a short pleated skirt that barely covered all it needed to and a denim jacket that you could tell from the cut hadn't been bought off the rack at New Look. Her long blonde hair wasn't tied up as it always was in the videos but fell loose about her shoulders, poker straight to the point that it looked like a salon job. Did millionaire's daughters have their own in-house hairdressers? Looking at Selina's perfectly tamed locks, Grace would have to say it was a sure bet.

'I didn't say your plan wouldn't work,' Kitt said, following after Selina Grant who, just as Patrick said she would, had a square-jawed, square-shouldered bodyguard in tow. 'I said your method of obtaining the information to make the plan possible was both unethical and dangerous.'

Grace walked along with Kitt, maintaining visual contact with Selina and her bodyguard while making sure to keep her distance. 'Don't exaggerate. I didn't do anything mind-blowingly illegal.'

'You broke into the dean's office,' Kitt said through her teeth.

'Now, technically, I didn't break in anywhere, the door was unlocked,' Grace countered.

This seemed to give Kitt pause. 'Well, you broke data protection law then, by accessing Selina's file.'

'And who is ever going to know about it?' said Grace. 'I'm not going to sell her academic timetable to the tabloids; I'm going to delete the photos as soon as we've managed to make contact with her. Nobody is going to get hurt over it. If there'd been another way I would have taken it, but you're only here until the end of today. It's bad enough that Randy Hobbs is out of touch until the weekend without another suspect also eluding us. We need to talk to Selina before you leave. Time's running out for us to make some headway here.'

'I'm not going to give up the case just because I'm headed back to York,' said Kitt.

'No, but if we uncover something concrete before you go

then I can start doing some of my world-class online research.'

'Dubious cyber-stalking, you mean?'

'Potato, potarto. If we don't uncover something then it's going to be at least the weekend before we can move things on. It's already been a year. We don't need the people who abducted Jodie to get any more of a head start on us than they already have.'

'I'm aware of all this,' said Kitt. 'I still think there was a more ethical way of going about it.'

'You know, being a PI is probably going to require some tough decisions between greater and lesser evils sometimes. In case you missed it, the lesser evil is me accessing Selina's file; the greater evil is Selina possibly being responsible for Jodie's disappearance and/or death.'

'Yes, thank you, Grace, I got that.'

'Anyroad, I only took photos of her timetable.'

'That's bad enough. It's still personal information. And as for enlisting Patrick to help you, did you really have to jeopardize the investigation for the sake of a little crush?'

Grace looked aghast. Not at the insinuation, per se, but at the fact Kitt had figured it out so quick. That's what you get for making friends with a detective. Still, Grace had already made a pact with herself not to admit her attraction out loud so denial was the only logical course of action. 'I do not have a crush on Patrick. I'm helping him find his missing fiancée. Developing a crush on the guy would be wildly inappropriate.'

'Wildly inappropriate behaviour is your speciality, isn't it?'

Grace smiled in spite of herself. 'The only reason I enlisted Patrick is that I knew he'd understand the ends justified the means. He wants to find Jodie more than any of us.'

'I'm not so sure,' said Kitt. 'And by the by, you didn't just take photos of the timetable, let's not forget the misdemeanour statement.'

'Ah yes, but that doesn't count. I didn't go in there intending to take a photo of that. It was just a happy coincidence,' said Grace, checking that Selina and her bodyguard were still in view ahead of them.

'Not so happy for Patrick's status as a suspect,' Kitt said, raising her eyebrows.

'What? But he didn't have a physical fight with Jodie a week before she disappeared – surely your money's on the millionaire's daughter after everything we've learned?'

'A little louder, I don't think Selina's bodyguard quite heard you.'

'Sorry,' Grace said, lowering her voice. She hadn't realized she'd got so loud.

'Your theory holds true only so far. If he happened to like Selina back he could have taken the opportunity to get rid of Jodie for good so they could be together. I can't think that Patrick would mind dating a millionaire.'

'Surely he wouldn't need to make Jodie disappear, he could have just ended things with her. They weren't married yet.'

'No, but maybe Patrick was too cowardly to break up with her, so Selina arranged for Jodie to be expelled by planting drugs in her locker. In that case, if Jodie sussed what they'd done, then that would be motive enough to make her disappear.'

'I'm sorry, you're wrong. I just don't believe that he'd do that,' said Grace.

Kitt narrowed her eyes. 'What happened between you and Patrick last night?'

'Nothing . . . well, nothing that wasn't in the spirit of good old-fashioned undercover work,' said Grace. 'I just know he's not guilty.'

'I hope you're right,' said Kitt. 'But I still think you should prepare yourself for the possibility that he's not giving us the whole story.'

Not wishing to discuss this any further, Grace decided it was time to change the subject. Kitt was a good friend and she didn't want to have a falling-out with her over this. They'd have to just agree to disagree about who the chief suspect was right now. 'Look, they're heading into the cafeteria, that's useful. We can sit nearby and then when the time is right, make our move.'

Keeping plenty of distance between themselves and the subject, Grace and Kitt entered the main cafeteria, which was panelled with dark wood and set up with long tables that stretched almost the width of the hall. The pair headed straight for the serving stations and picked up a few items that would help them look more natural but that they could also shove in their pockets if they needed to move quickly. They then found seats on the table a couple of rows down from Selina. They watched her chatting with her friends while her bodyguard stood near the end of the table. Before seeing Selina's bodyguard in the flesh, Grace had thought it would be just a matter of pinpointing Selina's whereabouts based on her timetable and then politely approaching them, explaining the situation and their desire to strike Selina off the suspect list.

One look at Selina's bodyguard in person had meant an abrupt end to that idea and a plan B had to be quickly formulated. The bloke was at least eighteen stone of pure muscle. He seemed almost as broad as he was tall and was the kind of chap you looked at and wondered if even Dwayne 'The Rock' Johnson could beat him in a fair fight.

For all Grace knew he was a perfectly reasonable fellow but, given how his narrowed eyes seemed to be assessing each and every individual in the room with almost Terminator precision and objectivity, she didn't fancy trying her luck.

'Did you manage to check into Berkeley's alibi?' Grace muttered to Kitt. The last thing she needed was somebody on a nearby table overhearing their conversation and sending the Venerable Bede's rumour mill into overdrive.

'Yes, she was telling the truth.'

'Well, what about Lowenthal?'

'I followed that up too,' Kitt said with a sigh. 'Both of them check out.'

'And given that you're here with me rather than following a DI around, I take it you didn't get an invitation to join the investigation down at Durham police station?'

'Yes, thank you, Grace. You don't have to look quite so smug about that. I may not have been asked to consult but the police have reopened the investigation and are making a fresh appeal for information. I'm supposed to share anything we find that might prove useful to them. It's all pretty one-way although DI Thompson, who Halloran spoke to, said if they did get a major break they'd let us know, and to be fair he did disclose one unusual thing about their tests on the rags in the outhouse.'

'What's that?'

'The rag we singled out had large quantities of limestone dust on it.'

'Limestone? What's that used for?'

'Name anything in your house and it's probably got limestone in it somewhere – glass, tiles, the list goes on. But this was in raw form, powdered – almost like a dust, according to the police tests.'

'Is it so surprising that they found it in a builder's outhouse then? Surely if he's working around houses he must come into contact with limestone sometimes.'

'We're not sure,' said Kitt. 'There's a chance it could have rubbed off Kenneth's clothes or equipment but the police questioned him about every substance they found and the only one he couldn't account for was the limestone powder on the rag. He said he uses that outhouse to store wood and tools but all raw materials are usually kept on site wherever they're working.'

'Are we taking Kenneth's word? I mean, evidence relating to a missing girl has been found in a building he owns.'

'He's been questioned and Halloran says the police will scrutinize his bank and phone records to make sure he hasn't got a connection with the victim. Apparently he did come up with an alibi when he checked his paperwork and bank transactions from last year. He was doing a long-term job over in Penrith and stayed the night near there in a B&B. It's one of those B&B's where they lock the doors at midnight and Kenneth was in their bar when they did . . .'

'So he couldn't have come back to Durham and had a hand in Jodie's disappearance.'

'I suspect the police will be checking traffic cameras and talking to the staff at the B&B to verify he really was in that area, mind, and didn't just lend his bank card to someone for the sake of an alibi.'

'But it's not looking likely that he's a suspect.'

'He's certainly further down the list than Selina Grant is.'

Grace sighed. 'It's a pity limestone powder is such a common substance. That means even if it was left behind by Jodie's attackers, it's not particularly likely to help us narrow down our suspects.'

'No, but it might be a piece of evidence that helps us prove who the culprit is later on.'

There was a pause as Kitt glanced in Selina's direction. She was forking quiche and salad into her mouth and laughing at something one of her friends had said.

'So, tell me more about what happened with Patrick last night.'

'Happened? Nothing. I already told you.'

'You told me about stealing into Ms Smyth's office, you didn't say anything about how Patrick was acting. Given that Selina had a fight with his fiancée over him just before she disappeared, we've got to keep a keen eye on him. How was his behaviour?'

How was Grace supposed to answer that question? She could hardly reply that she could vouch for his kissing skills. Kitt was cross enough that she'd used him to help the investigation along, so telling her they'd locked lips wasn't an option just now.

'He didn't do anything out of the ordinary,' said Grace. 'He was actually against my plan – worried about getting chucked off his course – so if anything he was trying to be a good influence on me.'

Kitt raised an eyebrow at Grace, indicating – or so Grace thought – that such a quest was a waste of time.

'Hang about, looks like Selina's on the move,' said Kitt. 'She's heading to the ladies.'

'And her bodyguard is following her,' said Grace, her voice flat with disappointment.

'He's probably just going to wait outside, and he can't stop you going in there so this is probably as good a chance as any to approach her.'

'OK,' Grace said, taking a deep breath. 'I won't be long but if anything happens to the coms, you should probably come and find me.'

'All right. Be careful. And for once in your life don't do anything rash.'

Grace nodded but made a silent agreement with herself that given this might be the only opportunity she had to cosy up to Selina Grant, she'd do whatever she needed to do to get her attention.

FOURTEEN

Grace passed through the doorway to the women's toilet, slipped her hand under her scarf and switched the two-way radio on. As Kitt had predicted, Selina's bodyguard was waiting a few feet away from the door. Perfect. Women were somewhat notorious for taking their time in the bathroom. She probably had a good ten minutes before the bodyguard suspected anything untoward. Of course, she didn't have a strong track record of hanging out with the daughters of internationally recognized millionaires so if she was going to find a way of cosying up to this woman, it seemed sensible to adopt a slightly different personality for the job. An undercover persona that the suspected head of a death-defying secret society might warm to.

Inside, a few girls were washing their hands and reapplying make-up in front of a row of mirrors. Grace made a show of rearranging her hair and pulled some make-up out of her bag. She was applying her third layer of coconut lipgloss when Selina stepped out of one of the stalls. Grace gave her a moment to wash her hands before striking up a conversation.

'Oh my God, you're like, that girl from the kick-ass YouTube channel, aren't you?' Grace said, looking across at Selina.

Selina offered Grace a smile that was nowhere near polite. 'Yeah. That's my official title.'

'Oh, I'm so sorry, you probably get people approaching you all the time about it. I didn't mean to bother you, it's just, I really love what those videos stand for, you know? The freedom, the courage, the boldness. They're totally inspiring.'

'Really?' Selina said. She still had a suspicious note in her voice but she'd asked a question, which was at least a sign of engagement.

'Are you kidding? At the risk of coming across as creepy, you should know that I am like, shamefully addicted to your channel. I mean I'll tell you upfront that I've re-watched some of your videos like ten times. That skydive you did in Dubai was one of the most amazing things I have EVER seen in my life. How did it feel? Must have been a total buzz.'

'*Tone it down, Grace,*' Kitt hissed into her earpiece. '*She's a British millionaire's daughter, not a sorority girl from SoCal.*'

But despite Kitt's critique of her impression of a vacuous cool kid, Selina's previously reserved body language relaxed just enough for Grace to believe she was making headway.

'It was a hard, fast ride,' Selina said. 'Definitely in my top ten skydives of all time.'

'Now you see, I haven't even been skydiving once and you've got a top ten already. No wonder you didn't scream. You were all laughs and cheers. There is no way I'd be able to handle a skydive and look that cool about it.'

Selina chuckled. Apparently, plying people with platitudes was a sure-fire way of getting them to warm to you.

'So you've never done it yourself then? Been skydiving, I mean?'

Time for a bit of method acting.

'I've like, always wanted to do something that wild but my parents would literally kill me if I did. The fall from the aeroplane wouldn't kill me but they would, know what I mean?'

'*Oh Grace, really, you sound like a character from* Queen Bees and Wannabes,' Kitt said into Grace's earpiece.

'They've kept me buttoned down my whole life,' Grace said, trying to keep her focus despite Kitt's somewhat unwelcome notes on her performance. 'I never get to do anything remotely interesting. What I really want is to be out chasing thrills like you. That's why I enjoy your channel so much. Embarrassing though it is to admit it, I live vicariously through the videos you post on there. If my parents have their way, I'm never going to get the chance to do that kind of thing.'

'Well, what your parents don't know won't hurt them,' Selina said, a slow, sly smile creeping across her face.

'My parents know everything, I don't know how they

know but they always, always find out,' said Grace. There was no acting required at that point. She must have some kind of tell because whenever she'd been up to something her parents wouldn't approve of they had a knack of figuring it out. Maybe she got her generally suspicious nature and love of private investigation from them.

'There are ways of fooling even parents like them. Ever thought of trying a few things out behind their back?' asked Selina.

'I – wouldn't even know where to start with that.'

'Well, you can start small and build up to skydiving from ten thousand feet.'

'Small sounds good,' said Grace, suddenly concerned that if this undercover thing went too far she might find herself in an aeroplane hangar with a parachute strapped to her back. She wanted to solve the case, for sure. She wanted to find Jodie and find justice for her. But there was no way she was going to take the method acting that far. Skydiving was a hard red line.

'You don't have to sound so nervous,' Selina said with a laugh. 'You're not in a plane now.'

'Fine thrill-seeker I am,' Grace said with a chuckle. 'Knees knocking together with my feet on the ground.'

'You'd get the hang of it. Skydiving is a lot like sex. The first time is nerve-wracking and a little bit painful. But after that you start to figure out how to make it work for you.'

'Nice tip,' Grace said with a nod, whilst wishing Selina

had picked a different analogy. She didn't need any reminders of her exceedingly disappointing first time.

'Well, I wouldn't usually do this but you seem like you could use a little nudge in the right direction. I'm having a house party tomorrow night with some like-minded people who are, shall we say, big on the thrill-seeking scene. If you're such a fan, why don't you come along and meet some of them? Get inspired?'

'I'm not sure that's such a good idea, Grace,' Kitt's voice warned through the earpiece. *'She might have seen through your approach, and luring you to her house might be part of a trap. Probably best to get out of it. Say you've got a family dinner or something.'*

'Really?' Grace said, ignoring Kitt's warning – this might be their only chance of infiltrating Selina's house: she couldn't pass it up. 'You wouldn't mind having a total newbie there? I wouldn't want to cramp your style.'

'No, it's cool. I know a lost girl looking for a little guidance when I see one. I was one myself once. Here, give me your phone.'

Grace obliged and Selina added her number to the contacts. 'Text me later today and I'll reply with the time and the address.'

'I can't believe this is happening,' said Grace. 'A party with my YouTube idol. Nobody's going to believe it. Then again, I lead such a quiet life I think the most unbelievable thing to anyone who knows me is that I'm out at a party on a Thursday night. Let alone with a vlogging sensation.'

'Didn't you hear? Thursday is the new Friday.' Selina beamed. 'But, do me a favour, will you? Don't tell anyone else about the party until it's over? It's only for people I've invited and I don't want outsiders trying to crash. I keep a fairly close eye on the entry system but like to let my hair down too so it's easier if I can count on the fact that just the people I invited will show up. You can brag about whatever craziness you get up to after the fact. Deal?'

'I totally understand,' said Grace. 'I won't say a word. I'm like, SO grateful for the invite. You know, I ran into a guy at Freshers' Fortnight. I happened to mention how much I loved your channel and this guy said he vaguely knew you. He only had good things to say. Now I know first-hand he was right.'

'Oh, and who was this mystery man?'

'Patrick Howard.'

The smile fell from Selina's face. 'Patrick, wow. Vaguely is the word. I haven't seen him in . . . a long time.'

'He did say it had been a while. Someone else in the group was trying to talk trash about you but Patrick totally defended you and came down on them hard about judging people just because they've got money. Like anyone at Venerable Bede's has the right to judge you on that score – you've pretty much gotta be loaded to come here unless you're one of the chosen few scholarship students.'

'Exactly. It's pretty cool to hear that Patrick's still got good things to say about me though. After all this time, I mean. Hey, why don't you bring him along?' said Selina. 'It'd be a nice little reunion.'

'Sure, we stayed in touch after meeting at that freshers' event,' said Grace, suddenly seeing an opportunity to test the waters where Selina's attraction to Patrick was concerned. 'Truth be told I have a little crush on him so an excuse to invite him to a party would be awesome. But only if you're sure you don't mind me bringing a guest? I know what you said about not wanting people crashing the party.'

Selina's smile had only widened at the news that Grace was attracted to Patrick. She didn't flinch or look disconcerted. Maybe she had got over him and anything that had passed between them? Or maybe she was just a very good actor. 'No, it's OK if I know a person is coming in advance and I've invited them, so don't worry about that. Look, I've gotta go. My dad has me under bodyguard protection – you may have noticed the guy standing outside the door who looks like he hadn't had a laugh since 1983.'

'That guy's your bodyguard?'

'Yeah, so, you know, I totally understand the overprotective parent vibe.'

'Wow, nothing says concern for your safety like a guy who could fell trees with a single punch following you around twenty-four seven.'

'Thankfully he's only tasked to shadow me while I'm outside the house. Though, that's more than enough.'

'I can imagine. Let's just promise to never let our parents

meet. I have a feeling that my dad and your dad could give each other a lot of ideas. Ideas neither of us ever want them to have.'

'Ha, that's a deal. I'll see you at the party, OK?'

'OK. See you tomorrow night for thrills and spills, sister.'

Selina looked mildly embarrassed on Grace's behalf but then smiled and waved her goodbyes.

'*Thrills and spills? Sister?*' Kitt said. '*What on earth were you thinking?*'

'Your intermittent critique of my undercover work was very helpful, thanks,' Grace returned. 'Anyroad, I got the invite, didn't I?'

'Yes, you did,' said Kitt. '*A little too easily for my liking.*'

FIFTEEN

Grace took a deep breath right before she pressed the buzzer near the gates at Selina's mansion situated three miles or so outside the city centre in Durham's sprawling suburbia. She exhaled slowly, trying to focus on the task in hand and not how handsome Patrick looked in his blue blazer. Or how she found the fact that he smelled vaguely of almond oil more appealing than she should.

There was a beeping sound and then Selina's voice said: 'Who is it?' The beat from whatever music was playing pulsed in the background.

'Grace. We met yesterday, and I have Patrick with me.'

There was a buzzing sound and the gates started to open inward. As soon as they'd opened far enough the pair stepped through into the driveway. It was lined with olive trees and led straight up to the main doorway which was set in a decorative arch.

'*Can you hear me, Grace?*' Kitt said over the radio. She had returned to York as planned late the night before but had yoyo-ed back to Durham again the moment her shift at the library was done. Though Halloran was working and was thus unable to join them, she had managed to borrow his car and was sitting in his black Fiat a little bit further up the road. They had toyed with the idea of trying to get Kitt into the party. She still believed that getting an invitation to this little shindig had been easier than it had any right to be and was concerned Selina might be luring them into some kind of trap. With all this in mind, Kitt would've preferred it if she could tag along in person to look out for Grace. Kitt was an alum of the academy, after all, and probably could have bargained her way in. Ultimately, however, it was agreed that, after Selina made it crystal clear that no invitation meant no entrance, trying to get her into the party might risk losing the opportunity to search for clues in Selina's home. That was a risk they knew they couldn't take. Especially when, in a relaxed atmosphere, Selina might slip up of her own accord and inadvertently implicate herself through casual conversation. Consequently, Kitt was there for back-up purposes only.

'Loud and clear,' Grace confirmed.

'In and out, all right? Remember, you're not there for the hors d'oeuvres.'

'I remember,' Grace said. Though if there was food on the go she wasn't going to pass it up. She suspected that the catering at this party was likely to be a lot better than the stuff she could afford on a student budget. So long, sausages and beans in a tin, hello, smoked salmon.

As they walked up the driveway, Grace recalled some of the things she had learnt about Selina's home in an online feature about Selina starting her academic career at Venerable Bede's. Apparently it had seven bedrooms and had cost her father £3.5 million. Grace made a mental note not to spill any wine on the carpet. Who knew what the cost of cleaning a carpet in a £3.5 million mansion was? She wasn't keen to find out.

Selina opened the door and stood in the frame. She had a cocktail in her hand and had curled her long blonde hair into soft waves for the occasion.

'Well, if it isn't my biggest fan,' Selina said with a grin, taking Grace's hand and pulling her over the threshold. 'And Patrick, it's been a long time,' she said, leaning in to give him a peck on each cheek.

'Just over a year,' Patrick said in a manner Grace thought a bit too telling. Grace shot him a look. Was he trying to tip her off as to their real business that evening or what?

'Time flies,' Selina said, opening the door further so he could follow them inside.

Grace resisted the urge to look in the direction beyond the mansion walls to where Halloran's Fiat was parked. She was hoping they wouldn't need any back-up but it was good to know Kitt was only a minute away if things went south. How she would get over the high walls or past the locked gates was another matter.

'Oh my God, this is the COOLEST house,' Grace said. She could see Patrick looking very confused over the sudden change in her demeanour. She probably should have filled him in on her undercover persona before they arrived. 'I'm sorry, I don't think I'm going to be able to play it cool here,' she added. The part of an impressed super-fan wasn't difficult to play as Grace scanned Selina's open-plan living room and kitchen. The floor was made of polished marble. The sofa was white leather. There was a bar set up in the corner of the living room. Not just a table with some drinks on but a real bar with a uniformed bartender shaking cocktails. At the other side of the room was a pool table, and lavish chandeliers hung from the high ceiling. Most of the furniture had been pushed back to the sides of the room to make space for a dance area.

'Why are you talking like that?' Patrick muttered into Grace's ear.

'It's a sort of undercover thing,' Grace whispered back. 'It's all part of the plan, just play along.'

'Come on,' Selina said with a chuckle. 'Why don't you two go and dance and I'll bring you each a drink over.'

'That sounds, like, perfect,' Grace said, taking Patrick's hand and leading him to the edge of the dance floor where several other couples and some small friendship groups were dancing to a Lana Del Ray record.

Patrick put his hands around Grace's waist and slowly she looped her arms around his neck before starting to sway in time to the beat. She stared up at him. This was the first time since they shared that kissed that she'd looked him in the eye. Neither of them had spoken about it and that was probably for the best but being so close to him, her face close enough to his that she could feel his breath on her cheek, was driving her crazy.

'Grace,' Patrick said, 'there's something —'

'Hang about. I've just been looking for more details about Selina's mansion online. Apparently there are CCTV cameras outside the property.'

Grace held a finger up to Patrick so he could see she was listening to Kitt.

'If there are cameras inside the house you've got no chance of getting into her bedroom. Look in the corners of the living room, up at the ceiling, can you see any cameras?'

Grace leaned in close to Patrick's ear and it took all of her strength to talk into it rather than nibble on it. 'Turn me around, will you? Kitt needs me to check the room for cameras.'

Without a word, Patrick obliged and started to turn. Grace pressed her head to the side of his and kept her eyes on the ceiling as they turned.

'I can't see anything,' said Grace. 'They must just be outside.'

'Here you go,' said Selina. 'Two Deadly Poisons.'

Grace split herself off from Patrick at once and looked at the glasses Selina held. The drink was somewhere between purple and black in colour.

'*Deadly Poison? Be careful, Grace. There's no telling what's in that. Remember, she might be on to us and is possibly trying to get you drunk so you'll reveal your true agenda here.*'

'I don't think so,' Grace muttered back to Kitt.

'Sorry, what was that?' said Selina.

'Er . . . I just said I don't think I've ever heard of Deadly Poison,' said Grace, trying not to let her dubiousness show as she eyed the glass. 'Sounds, like, totally off the hook. What's in it?'

'That would be telling, now, wouldn't it?' Selina said, winking at Grace.

Oh dear, it didn't look as though there was any getting out of drinking this, whatever it was. Grace took a big gulp and spluttered a little bit.

Patrick and Selina chuckled at her reaction.

'Well, there's definitely vodka in here,' Grace said, prompting more laughter from her companions. Patrick took a sip from his glass without flinching. Grace opened her mouth to pass some glib comment about the fact that if he was used to drinks of that strength he probably needed to lay off the sauce, but then it occurred to her that he might be used to drinking as a way of handling the grief after Jodie's disappearance so for once she decided to engage her brain before opening her mouth. Instead, she looked around the other guests at the party. 'I, like, can't believe how many people are here,' she said. 'You have so many friends.'

'I wouldn't call them all friends,' Selina said, staring

around the room. 'Most of them are just people I've met doing the stunts for my YouTube channel.'

'Are they all as daredevil as you?' Grace asked, taking another mouthful of drink. After just the second mouthful, she began to realize a flaw in the plan they'd agreed with Kitt. She was supposed to down her drink and then go upstairs to 'use the facilities' while Patrick, the apparent object of Selina's affection, an affection she was hiding well so far, kept her occupied. After a glass of whatever was in this cocktail, however, Grace doubted she would be able to walk up the stairs, let alone conduct a surreptitious search of Selina's bedroom.

'Actually, some of them make me look like a rank amateur. See Vinny over there?' Selina pointed to a man chatting to a big group of lads with a pint in his hand. Vinny seemed to be covered from neck to toe in ink. His face appeared to be the only part of his body where he didn't have a tattoo. Granted, Grace couldn't see exactly what was going on under his T-shirt, but the artful designs sprawled all around his neckline and up and down his arms so it wasn't clear if or when the ink stopped.

'He actually wrestled a croc last summer,' said Selina.

'Mindless brute. The things rich kids will do for thrills.'

Distracted by Kitt's interjection and already a little giddy due to the strength of her drink, Grace asked: 'Oh! Is the crocodile all right?'

Patrick and Selina exchanged amused glances and then looked at Grace.

'You're a real card, aren't you? That's not the question people usually ask when they hear about that story.'

'Oh . . .' Grace stuttered. 'I – I guess looking at Vinny I think even a croc might think twice before going into a fight with him.'

Selina chuckled. 'I know what you mean but the croc started it – well, technically Vinny started it by swimming in Darwin harbour which, as he well knows, is notorious for crocodiles.'

'So why did he go in?' said Patrick.

Selina shrugged. 'Felt good at the time, I guess.'

'Speaking of which,' Grace said, holding up her empty glass, 'this drink has hit me pretty fast, can I use your bathroom?'

'It's up the stairs, second on the left,' Selina said with a smile.

'Thank you,' Grace said, trying to hold in a hiccup. She gave Patrick a subtle nod to remind him now was the time to turn on the charm.

Turning away, she tried not to dwell too long on that idea. Though Selina was currently the most likely suspect in the case of his missing fiancée, a small voice laced with jealousy asked whether Patrick minded so much that a millionaire's daughter had taken a shine to him. The moment the thought surfaced, Grace scolded herself for focusing on such petty issues when the truth about a missing young woman was at stake. Besides anything else, she knew in her heart Patrick wouldn't want anything to do with Selina when there was a strong chance she had something to do with what happened to Jodie, even if Selina did have designs on him.

Shaking off any more analysis about what might happen between Patrick and their party host while she was upstairs, Grace made her way up to the landing. There was a corridor to the left and to the right. The bathroom was on the left and, assuming she didn't have an en suite, it was likely Selina had chosen a bedroom close to that room for ease. Veering left, Grace nudged open the first door. She peered in to see bookshelves and a desk.

'Red Flame, come in. I've found the study. Maybe any papers about the society will be in there rather than her bedroom? I don't have time to check both without being missed. What should I do?'

Try and find her bedroom. Anything about the society is likely to be kept in a hiding place you wouldn't expect rather than in a proper filing system in the study. If you have no luck in the bedroom tonight –'

Kitt was interrupted by Grace giggling. 'Having luck in the bedroom tonight isn't my top priority right now, Kitt, get your mind out of the gutter, will you? I'm working a case here.'

'Oh really,' Kitt said with a small sigh. *'I get enough of that stuff from Evie without you starting. As I was saying, maybe you can find a way to access her study at a later date with some academic excuse.'*

'Copy that,' Grace said, collecting herself. Knowing from Selina's directions that the middle door was the bathroom, she continued walking on to the third door. She knocked in case anyone was in there. It didn't seem like the kind of party where couples were getting hot and heavy but remembering what the academy cleaner had said about working in hotels, she'd rather be safe than sorry.

When she didn't get any answer from her knock, she pushed the door open and closed it behind her. Flicking the lights on, her mouth fell open at just how spacious and luxurious Selina's bedroom was. What looked to be a super-king-sized bed stood at the centre of the room, covered with what Grace wagered were sheets of the highest available thread count. The bed was littered with ten or fifteen throw pillows of various sizes. Grace had never quite understood the throw pillow thing but maybe rich people led a more leisurely life and thus needed more cushions to lounge on. Opening the walk-in wardrobe, Grace was greeted with rows of dresses, shoes, handbags and other outfits that were likely designer brands. Selina's closet was big enough to live in all by itself.

'Have you found the bedroom?'

'Just taking a look around now,' Grace said, remembering she was on a time limit and starting to rifle through the hanging garments with one hand while opening drawers with the other.

'Anything incriminating?'

'Not yet,' Grace said, rooting through a range of socks, bras and knickers and suddenly realizing what a horrible invasion of privacy this was.

'*Go straight to the bottom drawers.*'

'Do you really think that's . . . fair?' Grace said, hesitating.

'*Fair?*'

'It's just, a woman's bottom drawer is a very private place. You never know what you might find.'

'*Why, what do you keep in your bottom drawer?*'

'That's definitely top secret information,' Grace said, a slight blush rising in her cheeks. She was glad Kitt was talking to her over the radio and not face to face; Kitt would never let her live a moment of coyness down.

'*Look, we're not interested in her collection of sex toys. We just want to know there isn't anything in there that implies she had a part in Jodie's disappearance. Anything else can stay just between us girls.*'

'All right,' Grace said pulling out the bottom drawer and secretly hoping nobody had any cause to snoop around her bedroom the way she was in Selina's. 'Belts . . . a lot of them. Nothing saucy about that.'

'*Depends on how imaginative you are.*'

Grace giggled. 'Halloran's not here, you know? He can't hear you.'

'*It's a pity.*' Kitt said it in a tone that left Grace in no doubt about what kind of smile was on her lips.

Grace pulled out the bottom drawer on another chest at the opposite side of the closet. This one was full of papers. Old school reports. Old birthday cards and the like. Grace rifled through it all, trying to find any reference to the

Scarlet Stocking Society, when her hand hit against something hard and square at the bottom of the drawer. It was a picture frame laid face down. Grace picked it up and turned it over.

'Oh my God.'

'What? Have you found something?'

'Maybe. It's a picture of Selina . . . and Jodie. Must have been taken when they first met.'

'What's happening in the picture?'

Grace took a photo on her phone and sent it to Kitt via WhatsApp. 'Take a look for yourself. Check your notifications.'

There was a brief pause while Kitt checked her phone.

'Nothing particularly odd about it,' said Kitt. *'Except that most people don't keep hard copy photographs any more.'*

'And the quality is such that it looks like this was taken on someone's phone and printed off.'

'Maybe after Jodie disappeared she printed the photograph as a reminder of her.'

'Maybe—' Grace's phone beeped. 'Dammit,' she said, looking at the screen.

'What is it?'

'Patrick's just sent me a text message. He and Selina are heading upstairs to her bedroom, right now.'

SIXTEEN

Grace barely had time to switch off the light and pull the closet doors closed before hearing Selina's bedroom door creak open. There was a shuffling sound as she and Patrick walked in.

Slowly, so as not to make even the smallest noise, Grace lay down on the soft, beige carpet and peered through the small gap under the door. She could just make out Patrick's pristine pair of Nike Air Force 1s and Selina's bare feet with the toenails painted midnight blue. They were positioned in such a way that it was clear they were sitting on the bed together.

You see, Grace, this is your karma for kissing a bloke when you're supposed to be solving the case of his missing fiancée – now you have to sit and listen to a millionaire's daughter hit on your not-so-secret crush. And when you go to hell for your sins, you'll no doubt relive this moment on a loop.

'So what did you want to talk to me about?' Patrick said, loud enough, she thought, that he might have guessed where she was hiding and he wanted her to be able to hear the conversation.

'Sorry to drag you away from the party, and to bring up sad topics, but actually I wanted to talk to you about Jodie and say, you know, how sorry I was about what happened to her.'

Grace heard a little crack in Selina's voice that suggested she might be on the brink of tears. Was that genuine sympathy or was it guilt?

'Thanks,' said Patrick, 'it is a terrible thing.'

'It is, and I'm sorry I didn't get in touch with you after it happened.'

'I don't blame you. You weren't the only one who didn't know what to say.'

'I wanted to reach out. But it was complicated. When Jodie disappeared we weren't on good terms.'

'Yeah, I know,' Patrick said. 'She mentioned at the time you'd had a falling-out. If it makes you feel any better, me and Jodie had a bit of a spat on the morning she disappeared, too, so I know how it feels to not be able to get closure.'

'I'm sorry. It's the worst feeling. Did Jodie . . . Did she say what our falling-out was about?'

'No.'

'Well, that was good of her. If she'd told anyone at the time, I would have been screwed.'

'Screwed in what way?'

'Every way but the good way.'

There was a pause where Grace imagined Patrick was frowning just as hard as she was, trying to figure out what was going on here.

'Did you have something to do with the drugs Berkeley said she found in her locker? Is that what it was about?'

'No, I— Well, if I tell you, you have to promise you won't say a thing to anyone until I say it's OK to talk about it.'

'As long as it's not illegal I'll agree to that.'

'Illegal? Wow, you do have a low opinion of me.'

'It's not that,' said Patrick. 'Venerable Bede's is pretty strict for us non-millionaires and I don't want to get myself into something I can't get out of.'

'Fair enough.'

Another lengthy pause.

'The truth is, Jodie and I fought because I liked her. A lot.'

'I don't understand why that would —'

'Romantically, Patrick. I liked her like you liked her.'

'Oh.'

Silence fell between them for a moment before Patrick asked the question that was on the tip of Grace's tongue.

'Why did that result in a fight between the two of you? I didn't have anything to do with it, did I?'

'The word "fight" is a bit of an exaggeration but it happened in the cafeteria and all people really saw – and by people I mean the supervisory lunchtime staff members who will take any excuse to report you – was me and Jodie shouting and pushing each other around. It was my fault. She wasn't upset that I had feelings for her, she was upset because I told her I couldn't be friends with her any more.'

'Because she was going to marry me and it was too hard to be around her?' said Patrick.

'Not quite. I realized I was bi in sixth form and tried to come out to my parents. I say "tried" because they absolutely lost it, especially Dad. He went on and on about the family's reputation – as though being bisexual was some terrible smirch on the family name – and said if I went public with my news he would cut me off from any financial support. Not only that, he got so mad when I first told him, it got . . . physical.'

'He hit you?' Patrick said, with a sharp note in his voice that betrayed a spark of anger.

'I had two black eyes by the time he'd finished,' Selina said, and it was clear by the wavering in her voice that she was crying. 'He said nobody would want me looking like that so it would keep me out of trouble. I had to stay in the house for three weeks until I looked normal again.'

Grace couldn't believe what she was hearing. Selina behaved in this carefree, casual manner. On the surface she had everything that most people dreamt of having and yet behind all that was an abusive and controlling father. Was this the only time her dad had seen fit to 'put her in her place', Grace wondered. She couldn't imagine life at the hands of an abusive parent. Yes, she and her own parents weren't seeing eye to eye just now, but there was no way they'd ever get physical with her. That kind of pain was unimaginable. The bruises might heal but the betrayal would never go away.

'Jesus Christ. I'm so sorry you had to go through that,' said Patrick. 'I just don't have anyone in my circle who would react that way.'

'My dad was born in prehistoric times, apparently,' Selina said with a sniff. 'So when I realized my feelings for Jodie were growing into more than friendship I had to cut ties. It was silly really. I'd only known her a couple of weeks but the moment I met her, well, you probably know better than anyone how I felt.'

'Yeah, I tried to play it cool with her in the beginning, the way teenage boys do, but everyone else could see I was smitten with her from the get-go.'

'I can see why,' said Selina. 'I want to be clear: I wouldn't have made a move on her but having to hide who I am all the time is bad enough without hanging out with someone who stirs all those feelings up in you every day.'

'I get that,' said Patrick. 'But how did this exchange get physical?'

'Jodie was upset with me for wanting to break off the friendship and was trying to walk off before I had completely finished telling her my reasons why. I liked her a whole lot and didn't want her to just have half a story so I tried to stop her walking away. She tried to dodge and push past me a couple of times but I really wanted her to hear me out so I tried to hold her back. There was a bit of jostling, nothing violent, just a bit of back and forth, but unfortunately, the lunchtime supervisors saw it and shopped us to Berkeley, and you know what an old stickler she is. She insisted we both write a statement about what happened for our academy record. I sent Jodie a text message of the story I was going to use so our statements would match and when the matter wasn't taken any further it was clear she had gone along with it even though she never replied to the message, or talked to me again.'

'What was the story?' asked Patrick.

'I said that we were fighting over our affections for you so that there'd be no official record of what we really fought about but so the blame for the incident would still rest with me. I knew Berkeley would try to pin it on Jodie because she was a scholarship student and I couldn't stand the idea of her losing everything over my family politics. So I took responsibility for starting it – which I did really.'

'Still, I'm sure she appreciated you taking most of the heat.'

'I don't know, as I say, I never got to talk to her again. She didn't do anything wrong. It wasn't her fault my family is messed up.'

'Well, I appreciate you not trying to steal her away from me,' said Patrick.

'Like I ever could,' said Selina. 'I had no chance. She was totally in love with you.'

'I know,' Patrick said, in a tone that was laced with pain.

'I'm sorry to ask you to do this, but I need you to keep my sexuality a secret for now.'

'As far as I'm concerned it's nobody else's business.'

'Thanks. I never planned to live this way for ever. I made a promise to myself in sixth form that I'd find a way to become financially independent. That's why I'm building my YouTube channel. I hope to be able to stand on my own two feet at some point but I'm not there yet. I know a lot of people think my place here was a given because of my dad's status and money, but I worked hard to get into Venerable Bede's and can't afford the tuition without my dad's help. By the time I leave here I hope I'm going to be able to monetize my YouTube channel and then I'll be able to lead life on my own terms.'

'Sounds like a plan,' said Patrick. 'I am curious about one thing, though.'

'I would expect nothing less of a community justice student,' Selina said with a teasing note in her voice.

'Sorry, it's just, if you wanted to keep all this a secret and you weren't going to act on your feelings for Jodie, why tell her the truth at all? You could have just phased her out or something? She hadn't known you long. You took a big risk in telling her.'

'I couldn't just never talk to her again. I've been cut out

of friendship groups myself, without any explanation, and it's heartbreaking.'

'I find that hard to believe about the daughter of a millionaire,' Patrick said.

'You'd be surprised how many people can hate you or resent you for having money,' Selina said. 'At any rate, I wanted to be honest with Jodie and let her know she hadn't done anything wrong, it was just a bad situation.'

'But she didn't take the explanation well?'

'She wasn't bothered about the "revelation" of my true sexuality but she was mad that I wouldn't be friends with her any more. I think she thought I shouldn't wait to be who I really am deep down. But the money complicates things and I was afraid someone would guess I was into her and out me to the world before I had a chance to get myself into a stronger financial position.'

'Sounds like Jodie,' said Patrick, with a light chuckle. 'She was pretty fearless but didn't always understand that not everyone in the world was as bolshie as she was.'

'She was unapologetically herself, totally up front about her poor background and everything. It's understandable she wouldn't have much time for the first-world problems of a bona fide rich kid.'

'I'm sure Jodie didn't think what you were going through was a first-world problem. She was probably more angry at the situation you'd been put in than she was at you.'

'I hope you're right.'

Grace pondered Selina's story. It didn't quite match what was written in the misdemeanour report but she'd already explained to Patrick that she'd made the story up to keep her true sexuality under wraps. Fighting over boys was the kind of drama faculty probably expected from first-year students so she had decided to claim she was fighting over Patrick, and Jodie, probably just wanting to draw a line under the situation and likely fearing for her place at the academy if she made a fuss, just went along with it.

'We're still trying to find her, you know?' said Patrick.

'You are?' Selina said. 'But it's been a year.'

'She was never found. Until she is I can't give up hope or close the door on her. Hey, you could do me a favour, actually.'

'OK, what is it?'

'You could talk to the PI I've hired to try and find Jodie.'

'What good would that do?'

'She's compiling a lot of background information on Jodie. Anything you can tell her about the time you spent in her company might be helpful. Will you do it?'

'I don't know. I've got a dark secret of my own I'm trying to keep quiet here, I – '

'Please. I really, really need to get some closure on this if I'm ever going to move on with my life.'

'All right, I'll talk to her, but just the once for background information. My dad keeps a keen eye on me via the body-guard and I can't do anything to upset the applecart until I've got money in the bank.'

'Thanks, I appreciate it.'

'Well, we'd better get back to the party. Grace looked a bit wobbly going up those stairs – it's probably not a good idea to leave her unattended too long.'

Grace physically jumped at the sound of her own name and her heart started beating faster. Thankfully, Patrick and Selina couldn't hear. She listened to them shuffle out of the room, counted to sixty slowly and then made her exit. Hurrying down the stairs, she tried to think of an excuse that would explain why she was not already there waiting for them.

SEVENTEEN

The faint scent of almond oil was the first thing Grace was aware of the next morning. That and the fact that she felt warm, cosy even. In her family home this wouldn't have been anything out of the ordinary but the heating system in the halls at Venerable Bede's was temperamental, to put it politely – a feature not advertised in the academy brochure – and for the last week she had woken up shivering. This morning something was different. She felt safe. Cocooned. Slowly, she opened her eyes. Patrick was lying next to her; his arms wrapped around her. Their noses were almost touching. Still half-asleep, Grace smiled dreamily for a moment.

Now this was the kind of dream she always wanted to have. Waking up with the person she had a crush on. Feeling the warmth of them. Being able to just lie back and enjoy being with them. Instead, she usually had dreams about misfiling things at work, or being late for school even though she was twenty-two and there were no real consequences to being late for school any more. But this was a nice dream. She'd happily stay in this one.

Slowly, Patrick's brown eyes opened. He looked deep into Grace's eyes and then . . . he frowned.

This wasn't a dream.

Patrick was really here.

'Oh my God,' Grace said as she jumped awake properly.

Patrick's eyes widened as he seemed to have the same realization Grace had had just seconds ago. 'Oh . . . Oh!'

He untangled his arms from around Grace and she at once got out of bed.

'What the . . . what? Did we . . .?' Patrick said, fighting his way out of her Powerpuff Girls duvet and also standing. In the cold light of day, with Patrick across from her, the kitsch-cool bedding she'd carefully selected on eBay felt lame and childish. She could only hope he was so freaked out about waking up next to her he wouldn't notice.

'Did we . . . you know?' he said.

'No! I – I don't think so, we have our clothes on,' said Grace.

'Yes.' Patrick nodded frantically. 'Clothes on is good.'

'I agree, clothes on is good.'

'I mean, not that I don't . . . I mean, it's just, you know, you're investigating Jodie's disappearance . . . it's . . . it would be weird.'

'No, no, no, I know, I agree, it's sick is what it is. It's a sick, sick thought,' Grace said, and made a face like she was sucking on raw lemon.

'I mean . . . I might not go that far but, it's not cool.'

'Not cool at all. It's, you know, lukewarm.'

'What?'

'I don't know, I just woke up. I barely make sense after midday, let alone before,' Grace said, wondering why the ground never swallowed you up when you wanted it to. She ran her fingers through the worst of her bed hair, trying to even it out. Patrick, of course, looked deliciously dishevelled. He'd clearly taken his glasses off just before falling asleep and somehow his face looked more vulnerable without them.

As if reading Grace's mind, he picked them up off her bedside table and put them on, smiling. 'We must have just fallen asleep. That's all.'

'Yes, perfectly innocent explanation. It got late and we must have . . . I must have invited you in to talk about the case or something.'

'Sounds very plausible, and above board,' Patrick said.

'Yeah, it must have been that. Except, I really can't remember doing that. Do you . . . remember anything about last night?' Grace asked with a nervous little chuckle.

'Er . . .' Patrick frowned and ran a hand through his hair. 'No . . .'

'Ooh! Ooh! I remember Kitt looking deeply unimpressed with me!' said Grace with a note of triumph in her voice. But then her smile drooped. 'Though, to be honest, that could be a memory recovered from any day in the last few months or – in fact – three years.'

Patrick frowned again. 'It's weird, last night is a real blank. Last thing I remember is coming back downstairs from Selina's bedroom after our chat and then . . . nothing. Nothing at all. Just waking up here this morning.'

'Me too, well, almost. I think I remember Kitt driving us back to campus,' said Grace and then she giggled. 'If I can't remember anything else then I must have really been tipsy, and if I was that out of it then there's a strong chance that my recollection of Kitt giving me her unimpressed glare was indeed a memory from last night.'

'I must have told her I'd walk you back to your dorm room on the way back to my place – looks like I didn't make it that far.'

'Yeah,' said Grace. Although that made no sense at all. Kitt didn't trust Patrick and if Grace was off her face there's no way she'd let Patrick just walk her back to the dorm without checking everything was above board. 'I mean, the easiest way to settle it is to call Kitt in a bit and see if she can shed any light. She wasn't drinking so no matter what she'll have a better sense of what happened than us. It's a bit weird that everything's so hazy though. This is the first time I've had a blank like this. What about you?'

Patrick paused before speaking and a strange look crossed his face. 'I think maybe this has happened to me once before.'

Grace put a hand to her head; she could feel a dull pounding that she suspected was only going to get worse as the day wore on. 'Well, whatever Selina put in those cock-tails, I'm not going to be drinking them again in a hurry. Should have known better than to accept a drink off someone who thinks base-jumping is a relaxing Sunday afternoon activity.'

'Doesn't seem like I'm any wiser,' Patrick said. 'Look, I'd probably better go. I've got lectures this afternoon and I'm nowhere near finished the reading for them. Will you call me if you need me? For anything to do with the case, I mean.'

'Of course, no worries. After everything we found out last night I think Kitt will be taking the lead for a while – she'll need to question Selina further. Suss out her alibi and such.'

'Wait . . . Kitt's going to go back to Selina?'

'Yeah, I mean, you asked her to speak to Kitt and she agreed, so . . . is there a reason why she shouldn't?'

'Nothing specific, and I did ask her to do that as a favour in case you still wanted to talk to her. It's just . . . after every-thing she said, the story she told me about her father, you still think she had a hand in Jodie's disappearance?'

'Yes, er, well, I mean we certainly don't have enough information to discount her yet.'

'Even after what she told me, about what her fight with Jodie was really about? I mean, if she felt that way about Jodie she wouldn't hurt her. And you know, I've been thinking, how would she even commit an abduction or a murder with a bodyguard following her around everywhere?'

'She managed to give him the slip long enough to have a

scuffle with Jodie,' said Grace. 'If she's done it once I'd imagine she could do it again.'

'I suppose,' said Patrick. 'It's just, she doesn't seem a likely suspect to me.'

'That's probably because you're assuming she's telling the truth. What she told you last night is useful background information, and don't get me wrong, if she is telling the truth then what happened with her father is nothing short of tragic, but until we can prove where she was at the time of Jodie's disappearance, we can't remove her from the suspect list.'

'Oh, I see,' Patrick said, pursing his lips.

'What?'

'Well, you can't prove where I was at the time of Jodie's disappearance. So if that's the criterion you're working with am I on the suspect list too? I mean, I think I have the right to know.'

Not wanting to answer that directly, Grace tried to deflect with a question of her own. 'I don't understand. What's going on with you? Why are you being so defensive about this?'

'I'm not, I just want to know: if Selina's fair game in terms of suspects, am I too?'

'Well, you said yourself that your alibi wasn't airtight. Those were your exact words. And Kitt said she might have further questions.'

'So, is that a yes? You still think after everything I've told you that I would hurt Jodie in any way? That I would make her disappear or kill her?'

'I don't, or at least I didn't until about two minutes ago when you started acting really defensive.'

'Right.'

'I don't. Really I don't.'

'But Kitt still does? The person I hired?' Patrick picked his blazer up, which had been hanging on a chair, and threw it on. When he looked at Grace again he glared at her with those brown, sorrowful eyes and she felt a familiar stab through her heart. She hated to think she'd caused him pain, but what was her alternative? Lie to his face?

'Patrick, you told us when you hired us that you wanted to get to the truth. Selina's story will probably check out but we have to properly eliminate her from the line of suspects.'

'I said that when I thought you'd do a good job. You haven't said a thing about the man in black I told you about – when are you going to go after him? Don't you understand?' Patrick said, grabbing Grace by the arms. 'He's the one I need you to track down. He walked after her and then I never saw her again.' Tears started to form in his eyes but Grace could see he was working hard on holding them back.

'There wasn't much to go on with the man in black, and even if there was, the odds are he wasn't acting alone. If anything, the man you describe sounds exactly like the kind of person a millionairess might hire to do her dirty work.'

'You didn't look into Selina's eyes when she was telling her story, I did. There's no way she hurt Jodie.'

'I'm not saying she hurt her, but for all we know she might have used her ample resources to help her disappear.'

'So, your alternative theory is that if Selina didn't kill her, and I didn't kill her, then my girlfriend of five years left with no word and in the year she's been missing hasn't contacted me? Why would she do that?'

'I don't know.'

'You think she was running away from me?' Patrick's eyes filled with tears again.

'I have no reason to think that.'

'Yeah right,' Patrick said, shaking his head. 'I think hiring you and Kitt was a mistake. Next time you talk to her, tell her she's off the case. My mother won't be sending any more cheques her way.'

'What? Patrick, wait,' Grace tried, but it was no use. Before she had time to stop him he was out of the door, slamming it behind him.

Sighing, Grace went over to her desk, picked up her mobile and dialled Kitt. The phone rang and rang before eventually lapsing into Kitt's voicemail message. Grace caught sight of a picture of Jodie sitting on her desk next to some of the notes she'd made on Elvis McCabe. The words of Jodie's mother, Jean, used at the press conference they gave, came back to her again. *We will not let you become just another lost girl who's never found. We will never give up.* The tone beeping on Kitt's voicemail snapped Grace back to the present.

'Er, Kitt. Hi, it's Grace. I was just ringing to . . .' She looked again at the picture of Jodie and took a deep breath. 'To say I'm going to try and get myself invited around to Selina's house this afternoon. If you can organize to question her like she promised Patrick once you've finished work, I might be able to find a way of listening in on the interview without breaking my cover. Drop me a text when you get this so I know the game is on.'

Grace ended the call and leant her hands on the back of her computer chair, keeping her eyes on the picture of Jodie. She couldn't just abandon her: with or without Patrick's blessing, she had to give it one last shot.

EIGHTEEN

At seven p.m. on the dot that evening, the buzzer for Selina's front entrance sounded, interrupting the almost non-stop laughter Grace and Selina had been engaged in since four o'clock. Selina could be quite dry-witted when she wanted to be, a quality in a person that never failed to amuse Grace, and at times she had to remind herself that she was engaging in undercover work rather than building a real friendship. The only brief moment of seriousness happened when Grace first arrived and admitted to feeling out of sorts after the night before. Selina had been sympathetic enough, explaining that she had sent Grace home as soon as she had realized she'd drunk more than she should.

'Oh, who's that?' Grace asked, making her eyes as wide and innocent as she could without overdoing it.

Selina padded over to the door and pressed a button that presumably opened the front gates. 'It's just this favour I promised to do for Patrick. He's got a PI looking into the disappearance of his fiancée and because I knew her I said I'd give her a bit of background information on Jodie.'

'Oh, I'm sorry. I didn't realize you knew her too. I heard about it, obviously. Horrible. Do you want me to leave, then? I don't want to get in the way,' said Grace, praying Selina wouldn't call her bluff.

'Nah, it's not going to take long. You could just go up and chill in my bedroom while she's here.'

There was a swift, sure knock at the door just then and when Selina opened it Kitt introduced herself before stepping over the threshold.

'This is my friend, Grace,' said Selina. 'She's just going to go upstairs while we chat through whatever questions you have.'

'Nice to meet you,' Grace said, trying to keep a straight face as she addressed Kitt in such a formal, distant manner.

'And you,' said Kitt. 'I shouldn't think we'll be long.'

Nodding, Grace turned to walk up the stairs.

'My room is the third on the left,' Selina called after Grace, even though she was already halfway up the stairs.

'Oh, thanks,' said Grace, cringing over the fact that if Selina was even just a little bit more suspicious she could have just blown her cover. She turned to flash Selina a dopey smile. 'I probably would have figured it out eventually but directions make it much easier.'

Selina chuckled, then indicated that Kitt should follow her into the living room. As soon as they were out of sight,

Grace began to slowly creep back down the stairs. From the passage she'd be able to hear whatever was said quite clearly without Selina knowing that she wasn't up in her bedroom, as instructed.

'Cool hat,' Selina said, just before the creaking of the arm-chair indicated that the pair were now seated.

'Oh, er, thank you. I really appreciate you agreeing to talk to me,' Kitt said.

'Well, I've managed to convince Dad's bodyguard that – since I was having a night in – he deserved Friday night off. I probably won't be able to do any follow-up interviews though – at least not in person. He's supposed to keep his eyes on other people to make sure they're not a threat but I swear he spends eighty per cent of his time watching me and I don't need him listening in to conversations like these where we're likely to cover topics I don't want my dad knowing about.'

'Being watched constantly doesn't give you much room to explore yourself,' said Kitt.

'And that, of course, is my father's plan in a nutshell,' said Selina, coupling her statement with a small, awkward laugh.

'Well, I've no desire to get you into any trouble,' said Kitt. 'I'll try and get everything done this evening so we don't have to take up any more of your time.'

'I'll help any way I can when it comes to background on Jodie's life in the time that I knew her. I did hang out with her pretty extensively for a couple of weeks but, well, I take it Patrick told you about the fight I had with her just before she disappeared?' Selina said.

'He said you'd given him permission to, and I appreciate the information. It helps me to know what frame of mind Jodie was in just before that call to the radio station.'

'I don't really think our fight had any impact on her frame of mind, to be honest.'

'But she must have been upset about it?' Kitt pushed. 'According to Patrick, Jodie wasn't one for letting people into her inner circle easily, so it was probably a bit of a blow when she was just starting out at a new institution that someone she was friends with didn't want to see her any more.'

'She was upset when I told her. And a bit angry about it. But I'm not sure the impact was lasting. If it was a big deal to her, I never knew about it because unfortunately the fight we had was the last time I ever spoke to her. I heard a rumour that some drugs were found in her locker before she disappeared but they obviously didn't belong to Jodie, if the police had come to me at the time I'd have told them as much. She wasn't into anything like that – I should know, I tried to tempt her on several occasions.'

'But the drugs that were found in her locker, they weren't yours?'

'No,' Selina said with an indignant laugh. 'I enjoy a rush as much as the next person, a little more, actually, but I don't have a stash of that kind of stuff. It's all social and very intermittent. Besides the fact that Berkeley would lose it if she found something like that in your possession, addiction is not cool.'

'Noted,' said Kitt. 'I was quite surprised by the fact that you and Jodie had fought in such a public place. You mentioned your bodyguard earlier and I assume he's with you all the time, so did he just let you and Jodie push each other around without intervening?'

'No . . . neither my bodyguard nor my dad know anything about the fight. I told my bodyguard I was going to be at home for the rest of the day, arranged to meet Jodie at the cafeteria and then left my phone at home. My dad tracks it via GPS so the only way I can trick him is to leave the house without it and for obvious reasons I didn't want him knowing about my meeting with Jodie, or for my bodyguard to overhear the conversation I had to have with her.'

'I see,' said Kitt. 'I'm sorry you had to go to those lengths just to have a talk with your friend, and that it ended so badly.'

'Yep, I'm sorry about those things too,' said Selina.

'So, going back to Jodie's behaviour. It's fair enough that you don't know anything about the drugs that were found but can you tell me a little bit about Jodie's behaviour before you had your falling-out? Was there any secretive behaviour or anything like that?'

Selina shook her head. 'There was nothing out of the ordinary. We met on the first day of term at a freshers' event. After that we hung out around campus. We'd meet for lunch or go to club nights.' A smile flashed over Selina's face. 'She was different to other people I hung out with.'

'You mean, she came from a different background to the people you were used to associating with?' said Kitt.

'It wasn't just that. When you've got as much money as our family does, people mostly just want you around to pay for the drinks. Or to find some other way of weasling money out of you. But Jodie was different. She didn't have much but she wasn't interested in what other people had. She was caring and beautiful and . . . God,' Selina said. Though Grace couldn't see her face she could guess by the waver in her voice that she was upset. 'Why did she have to disappear like that?'

'That's what I'm trying to understand,' said Kitt. 'I'm sorry to have to ask, Selina, but before I can move to the next step of the investigation I have to ascertain where everyone was at the time Jodie disappeared.'

'You mean you're asking for my alibi?'

'That's right.'

'I don't have one.'

'You mean you don't remember or . . .?'

'No, I mean I was home alone that night studying and then I went to sleep. From what I understand, Jodie disappeared in the early hours of the morning and because I wasn't out that night I was already in bed.'

'I see, and nobody can confirm that?'

'Nobody should need to. I didn't have any cause to kill Jodie.'

'Except that she knew your deepest secret, something that you were trying to keep quiet and that would cost you your inheritance if it came out.'

'And you think . . . what? That Jodie was going to out me and so I got rid of her? Bit of a wild accusation to throw around, isn't it? Considering how expensive my father's lawyers are.'

Grace bit her lip. Selina was essentially threatening Kitt with a lawsuit. Knowing Kitt's temper Grace willed her to tread carefully. Of course they wanted to get to the bottom of Jodie's disappearance but they definitely couldn't afford to go up against the lawyers of a millionaire in order to do it.

'I am not accusing you of anything,' Kitt said, her tone surprisingly even. 'That much I want to make clear. All I'm trying to do is find out the truth about what happened to Jodie and I have to explore every possibility.'

'Well if I were you I'd be careful about what possibilities you explore until you have some evidence.'

'I'm only stating the obvious,' said Kitt. 'Jodie did have information on you that would be damaging to your income if it got out. And on top of that, several people I've spoken to have suggested that you have some rather unusual extra-curricular activities that may also have played a part in all this.'

'I'm booked to trek the Catskills during my mid-term reading week so you're going to have to be more specific if you expect me to have any idea what you're talking about,' said Selina.

Grace's shoulders tightened. Selina was growing more hostile by the second. She'd had an edge to her when Grace had first approached her in the ladies, but that was to be expected when you approach someone as a random stranger. Particularly a person with money who's used to people trying to squeeze it out of them. But otherwise, Selina had been perfectly friendly towards her. Her hostility towards Kitt right now probably meant one of two things: either she was innocent and resented the accusation that she would hurt someone she loved, or she was guilty and Kitt had hit a raw nerve with her questions.

'There is a rumour,' said Kitt, 'that you are part of a secret society here at Venerable Bede's. Off the record, and in the interests of making sure I have all the information I need to find Jodie, is there any truth to that?'

'Well if there was, I wouldn't be a very upstanding member of the secret society if I told you, would I?' Selina said with a mocking note in her voice.

'This isn't a game,' Kitt said. 'Justice for Jodie is at stake here.'

'Why would a secret society have anything to do with getting justice for Jodie?'

'Maybe she was mixed up in it and something went wrong? Or someone we haven't thought to question was a member and had something to do with her disappearance?'

'If there is such a secret society, I can guarantee you Jodie didn't have any part in it. If she did, I would know about it.'

'Because you're in charge of it?'

'Because I was her friend,' Selina said, with a slight waver in her voice. 'I wish more than anything we'd parted on better terms than we did. She didn't exactly say the words but I could tell Jodie thought I should break free and stand up to my parents so I could embrace who I really was. I suppose, in a way, that's how I got into all this thrill-seeking stuff. I've been trying to prove that I've got guts ever since. But you understand, don't you? That I couldn't stay friends with Jodie, feeling the way I did. That there was a lot at stake if the truth came out about who I really was? That I had to keep the secret?'

'Yes,' said Kitt. 'I understand all too well.'

NINETEEN

Approximately thirty minutes after Kitt left Selina's house, Grace walked to the end of the road on which Selina's mansion stood and turned left. Not far along, Kitt was waiting, as promised, in Halloran's Fiat, well out of sight of the CCTV cameras outside Selina's house.

Earlier that day, on one of the quick breaks Kitt had taken during her library shift, the pair had engaged in a text message exchange in which they arranged a little scheme for extracting Grace from Selina's house without raising suspicion. About half an hour after Kitt left Selina's she was to call Grace's mobile, pretending to be Grace's parents and claiming she was late for a family dinner she had forgotten about. This little trick worked a treat and enabled her to make her excuses to Selina and leave without blowing her cover.

'Anything to report from after I left?' said Kitt, dialling a number on her phone. 'I need to know before I ring Patrick.'

'Patrick? Oh, no, you can't ring him,' Grace said, reaching for Kitt's phone.

Kitt's head jumped back in surprise and she stared at Grace. 'What on earth is going on?'

Well, she'd managed to keep the truth from Kitt long enough to at least interrogate the main suspect on their list. Grace supposed, under the circumstances, she couldn't have asked for any more than that. It was time to come clean.

'Long story short? Patrick sort of . . . fired us.'

'Fired us? Why?'

'I – I don't know exactly. He was acting really weird this morning when I –'

'This morning?'

'Yes. Oh, but no. No, it's not like that. Nothing happened, we just fell asleep talking about the case – I think. If I'm totally honest, last night is a blur. Not so much a blur, actually, but a blank, and I haven't been feeling quite right. I don't know what was in those cocktails but Patrick couldn't remember anything either and –'

'Grace . . .'

'Yes, all right. He seemed to get upset when I said we couldn't strike Selina off the list of suspects without confirming her alibi. He asked if he was a suspect because he didn't have an alibi.'

'What did you say?'

'I said I didn't suspect him but he guessed that you did

and he said we weren't doing a good job and that he wanted us off the case.'

'Not doing a good . . . the cheek of him,' Kitt said, crossing her arms. The pair sat in silence for a moment. 'And you've known this since this morning? Had me traipse up to Durham from York after a long shift at the library?'

'I'm sorry. I wasn't trying to inconvenience you,' Grace said, pushing her fingers into an awkward steeple. 'I just, I didn't want this to be the end of the case. I need to find justice for Jodie. If we give up it's just going to haunt me. It feels like we're the only ones who can help her and if we give up we'll have failed her, or something.'

'I know that feeling,' Kitt said, her voice a little calmer.

'I was going to tell you what Patrick said, I just thought it best that we question Selina first so you could pass any information to the police before we close down the operation completely.'

'We're doing nothing of the sort. Not doing a good job indeed. Wait till he hears that we've cracked the case in the space of a week. That'll show him,' said Kitt.

'We . . . we have?'

'Weren't you paying attention to what was happening in there? Selina is without a doubt involved in Jodie's expulsion and likely her disappearance.'

'Really? I agree she was hostile at times but you're really that sure that she's the culprit?'

'As sure as I can be at this stage. She mentioned she

dabbled in drugs. She admitted she had secrets she needed to keep. She doesn't have an alibi, she practically threatened me not to take it any further by referencing her lawyers, and don't even get me started on that little chat about proving she's got guts.'

'You think she . . . made Jodie disappear just to prove she could, or something?'

'I don't know but I do know that a thrill-seeker with that amount of money will always look for bigger thrills and if they're hungry enough for the rush, legalities don't concern them too much. I don't want to dismiss her claim that she was abused by her father outright and, in fact, her father's abuse may actually be a causal factor here; it could have triggered her to lash out in some terrible way. But there's still a chance she's told us some convoluted version of the truth rather than the pure truth. That this talk about her sexuality is a smoke screen for the secret society, or something even bigger.'

'So you think she's saying she fought with Jodie about her sexuality when really it wasn't about that at all?'

'Exactly. Selina's got her secrets. We may not know all of them. Jodie could have uncovered something we don't yet know about. When it became clear that Jodie had dirt on her and she was going to tell the world about it, Selina might have taken it as an opportunity to experience a once in a lifetime thrill. The thrill of committing the perfect murder.'

'But then why keep the photo of Jodie in her bottom

drawer if she murdered her? Wouldn't you get rid of all the evidence?'

'It depends how much she enjoyed it,' said Kitt. 'Killers often keep mementos. If she really was going to do it just the once she perhaps wanted something to remember it by.'

'I suppose that could be the case,' said Grace with a little shiver. Why anyone would want to remember an act as profane as kidnap or murder was beyond her. All this discussion about memory, however, got her thinking about the gap in hers. 'What happened to me last night, after I hid in Selina's wardrobe? I really can't remember anything much at all.'

'If you want a report on what you did at the party, I'm probably not the best person to ask. I lost coms with you about ten minutes after you left Selina's bedroom,' said Kitt. 'I heard you engaging in some small talk with a few other party guests and accept another drink. But that was it. After that, nothing.'

'Nothing?' said Grace. 'I'm so sorry, you must have been worried.'

'I would have been, if it hadn't been for this,' said Kitt, pressing a button on her phone and handing it to Grace.

Frowning, Grace accepted the phone and listened to an automated female voice. *'You have one new voicemail, received at twenty-two forty-one on Thursday, twenty-second of October.'* The robotic voice disappeared and was replaced by Grace's. Or at least, a version of Grace's voice. She seemed to be slurring quite heavily and she was talking a lot more slowly than usual. *'I've got three missed calls from you, Kitt, I know why. It's because you love me. Now, now, now, don't deny it. It's all right to admit it because I love you too. I love your love for books. I love your trilby hat and I love your black cat.'* There was a pause. *'Ha! Hat and cat rhyme! I never noticed that before.'* There was a shuffling sound and then a long beep sounded out. Grace ended the call.

'Let me get this straight. From that message, you thought everything was OK with me?'

'Well, you were alive, at least, which was my primary concern. I was going to give it another fifteen minutes and then knock on the door to say I was your Uber driver. But it wasn't necessary. You and Patrick stumbled out about ten minutes later and after some serious honking of the horn you both made your way over to the car.'

'Why don't I remember?' said Grace. 'Even if I drank loads I should be able to recall some bits and pieces.'

'Wait a minute,' said Kitt. 'You said Patrick didn't remember anything either?'

'No, it's funny, actually, because he says he usually remembers everything when he gets drunk.'

'You were behaving especially over the top when you got back to the car. But I just assumed the drink had hit you. Patrick was also in extremely high spirits but he seemed a little bit more with it than you did. He said he would walk you to your door but given how out of it you were I wasn't going to leave you alone with him, so I watched until you were inside and then he walked away. I waited until he was out of sight before starting up the car and setting off back to York.'

'Wait, you mean Patrick left?' said Grace, shaking her head. 'But when I woke up this morning he was in my room.'

'All I can think is that he must have come back after I left,' said Kitt.

'Why?' said Grace.

'I have no idea,' said Kitt. 'Have you looked at your text messages to him last night? Did you text him and ask him to come back?'

'No, I haven't,' said Grace, swiping the screen on her phone and scrolling. 'No, the last message on here is me giving him the details of the party.'

'And, when you woke up this morning was everything . . . OK? I mean, there were no signs that he'd taken advantage?'

'No,' said Grace. 'No way. We were both fully clothed and both having difficulty remembering the night before.'

Kitt's breath caught in her throat. 'Were any of the drinks you had last night left unattended at any point?'

'Uh . . . probably . . .' said Grace. 'I downed my first one pretty quick and don't remember much after that.'

'So someone could have slipped something in your drink when you were distracted?'

'I . . . suppose so. Do you really think someone would do that?'

'I'm sorry to say, it happens a lot, especially at student

parties. Of course, there's always the possibility that Selina drugged you. She did get those first drinks made up specially for you at the bar. She could have put anything in them,' said Kitt.

'Why would she do that?'

'You know I was suspicious of her motives for inviting you to that party. What if she drugged you so she could get the truth about why you approached her in the academy bathroom? And if she did you wouldn't remember?'

'You think she suspected Patrick was in on it as well and drugged him too?' said Grace.

'The fact that neither of you can remember much of anything does suggest that there was more than just alcohol in those drinks.'

'I hadn't even thought of that,' said Grace. 'But, drugging someone, that's a really big deal. Do you honestly think she'd do that?'

Kitt shrugged. 'Given her attitude during that interview I can't say for sure what she's capable of.'

TWENTY

Cynthia and Patrick Howard took a seat apiece on a table at the Sniffing Distance Bar and Restaurant. A chalk board by the door explained it had adopted this somewhat peculiar name because it stood on the cobbled street of Owengate just 'sniffing distance' from Durham Castle and Cathedral. Off the top of her head, Grace could think of about twenty other more appealing names for a bar in such a picturesque setting but decided just to be grateful that the owners hadn't gone with 'spitting distance'. Not an image anyone really needs from a venue that is trying to sell them food and drink. That said, the views from inside, even this late in the evening when the slender arched windows and blocky battlements of the castle were illuminated only by the glow of street lights and floodlights, were well worth ignoring the establishment's dubious choice of name.

Patrick looked at Grace as he sat down at the table. She expected to see anger in his brown eyes but she saw only softness in them, and maybe a hint of remorse. Did he regret the argument they had this morning? Or was he just able to stay detached because he knew their short-lived partnership was over? For some reason she had a hard time reading him. Maybe that was part of his appeal.

'Thank you so much for meeting us here,' Kitt said to the Howards once they were both seated. 'Even when an investigation's cut short it's important to do a proper debriefing.'

Kitt had ordered a bottle of wine for the table and Cynthia, without any prompting, helped herself. 'Let's just get on with it,' she said. 'This is not exactly my idea of a fun Friday evening and frankly, from the sound of things, I think you've put my son through enough already without putting him through any more.'

'I'm sorry you feel that way,' Kitt said.

'Don't deflect this onto me,' said Cynthia. 'Do you have any idea what this kid has been through in the past year? He's only twenty. He's not supposed to have to deal with stuff like this at his age. And you two were supposed to make things better, not worse.'

'Mum,' said Patrick. 'Calm down. It's done now.'

'The last thing we wanted to do was make the ordeal any worse for either of you than it already has been,' said Kitt. 'We understand you don't want us on the case any more, but I thought you should know that we think we've uncovered the culprit and we're going to pass all information about them on to the police for further investigation.'

Patrick's face froze. He stared at Kitt and then at Grace, as if searching her face would reveal the identity of whoever made Jodie disappear.

'You've really found them?' said Cynthia. 'You're not just clutching at straws because we've taken you off the case? You'd better not raise our hopes like this unless you can make good on your word.'

'Without forensic evidence there is no absolute certainty, I'm afraid. But there's enough circumstantial evidence against one of our suspects to warrant further investigation,' said Kitt.

'Who? Who is it?' said Cynthia.

'Following our conversation with Selina Grant it seems safe to say that she had some involvement with Jodie's disappearance. It's even possible that she was behind the whole thing.'

'Selina Grant? Humphrey Grant's daughter?' said Cynthia with a frown. 'So her falling-out with Jodie *did* have something to do with what happened. What have you found?'

'As I say, nothing concrete, but we think with the police's resources they could find more. She's admitted not only to dabbling with drugs but she also said she'd tried to tempt Jodie into taking them.'

'That doesn't really prove anything though,' said Patrick. 'It's not like drugs are uncommon among the super-rich, or for freshers to try and convince other freshers to live a little.'

'Agreed, but that's not all,' Kitt said. 'She made me very aware of how powerful and expensive her lawyers were in a way that suggested she was trying to scare me off the case. To my mind, that's not something an innocent person would do.'

'No, but it is something a millionaire might do as a force of habit. They probably have their lawyers on speed dial,' said Patrick.

'I agree, but in this instance there was something very peculiar about her manner,' said Kitt. 'There's also the matter of Selina's account of the fight she had with Jodie. It differs from the official report taken by the academy.'

'But isn't it obvious that she altered that to conceal her sexuality from the academy? If you're trying to keep something like that a secret, putting it on official record is probably not a good idea,' said Patrick.

'Again, point taken,' said Kitt. 'But there's also a chance that she's just using that as an excuse to feed us a different story. She said she was bisexual, rather than identifying as gay. We don't know for sure that she's telling the truth about having feelings for Jodie. If she did harbour feelings for Patrick then she may have tried to get rid of Jodie.'

'But she didn't even contact me after Jodie disappeared,' said Patrick.

'I know, but that could have been because something went wrong. I can't, for instance, think that it was part of Selina's plan for Jodie to call into a student radio station and essentially disappear live on air. But even if the story about the feelings she had for Jodie is true, it's clear that Selina has more than one secret to hide, one of which would undoubtedly result in her losing her family fortune.'

'We know that Jodie was about to expose a secret about an influential person at the academy,' said Grace. 'If she was going to reveal the fact that Selina was in charge of a secret society, that would be the end of Selina's tenure. The society would definitely get rid of someone who had managed to make their existence public knowledge in a matter of weeks when they've kept themselves a secret for decades. And assuming there are influential gains to being part of said society, she probably wanted to avoid that.

'So whatever secret she's hiding, she stood to lose a lot if Jodie exposed her. Selina's got secrets to hide that could cost her big. And that's what we're looking for in a suspect here.'

'Your theory works up to a point but there is one major flaw in your thinking,' said Patrick.

'What's that?' said Kitt.

'If it was about Selina's sexuality, Jodie wouldn't do a thing like that,' said Patrick. 'She wouldn't out someone publicly for her own gain.'

'I know it's hard to hear, love,' Cynthia said, stroking Patrick's arm. 'But Jodie getting into a fight with this girl was very out of character for her. For whatever reason, she must have been really angry about something. It sounds as though Selina was blasé about her involvement with drugs, there may have been more to their relationship than Selina is letting on or than Jodie ever told you. And if something did go wrong, well, we're all human. Jodie might have wanted payback. I'm not saying it was like her, but neither was disappearing the way she did. Something is going on here and from the sound of things Selina Grant knows what it is.'

'There is also the possibility that she didn't do it out of spite at all,' said Grace. 'She might have thought she was doing Selina a favour. Maybe she wasn't really outing her, but her father. Exposing his outdated attitudes would be a terrible blow, publicity-wise. Perhaps she was going to reveal the way Selina was treated. Or, should we say, mistreated.'

'I hadn't thought of that,' said Kitt. 'His daughter's online presence came up squeaky clean but we could do some more digging into Humphrey Grant. If what Selina says is true and he's capable of abusing his own child there may be other less savoury things about him that point to his involvement. We could certainly take a look, find out if he's got any indiscretions we should know about. If Selina tipped him off that Jodie was likely to expose them, he may have taken matters into his own hands.'

'I'm not being funny, but I hope we're not up against someone as powerful as that,' said Cynthia, taking a sip from her glass of wine. Grace couldn't help but notice the 'we' in that sentence. It seemed her initial hostility towards them was fading now that they'd offered up a suspect other than her son. 'With his amount of money who knows what he could orchestrate?'

'Certainly, getting some drugs planted in Jodie's locker would be no problem at all,' said Kitt.

'You're right,' said Cynthia. 'And who knows what else he could pull off if he really wanted to?'

'That's settled then,' said Kitt. 'I'm going to report all this to Halloran and to DI Thompson down at Durham police station.'

'You needn't bother coming down to the police station,' said a deep voice.

'DI Thompson?' Kitt said, turning to face the officer in surprise. 'What's going on?'

Grace also turned to take a look at DI Thompson, whom, up until this point, she had only heard about second-hand through Kitt. He was dressed in a long black winter coat and was holding a pair of handcuffs. His moustache twitched as he talked.

'I'm afraid we're here for Mr Howard.'

'For Patrick? Why?' said Cynthia. 'And how did you even know he was here? You're not still watching him a year after what happened to Jodie? You've no case against him, and you know it.'

'We tracked his phone here,' said DI Thompson, his expression grave.

Grace looked over at Patrick. He looked pale, faint almost, and was breathing heavily.

'Patrick Howard, you are under arrest on suspicion of the murder of Jodie Perkins,' DI Thompson said, before continuing to caution his suspect.

'This is ridiculous,' said Cynthia. 'Patrick didn't kill Jodie. He wouldn't. What evidence do you think you have?'

'A witness has come forward, madam. He saw Jodie down by the river just before the attack, with Mr Howard. He was the last person to see her alive,' DI Thompson explained.

'What witness?' said Cynthia. 'Who is it?'

'I'm afraid I can't disclose that, Ms Howard.'

'There's . . . been some kind of mistake. There must have been,' Cynthia said, panic really setting into her voice now.

'No, Mum, there hasn't,' Patrick said, looking at Cynthia with those big sorrowful eyes. 'I did it. I killed Jodie.'

TWENTY-ONE

'What are you talking about?' Cynthia said. 'Don't you say that. No, you didn't. You wouldn't do that.'

'I did, Mum. It's obvious, isn't it? I can't remember a thing about the night Jodie disappeared. But ever since, I've been having these . . . flashes. Like memories resurfacing or something. And I can see myself with my hands around Jodie's neck, strangling her. And now a witness has come forward saying I was the last person to see her alive? It's the only thing that makes sense. The case is closed.' Patrick stood and turned his back to DI Thompson, holding his hands out to be cuffed.

'If you're going to come willingly, sir, there's no need for that,' said DI Thompson. Grace could hear the disbelief in Thompson's voice at how readily Patrick was admitting to murdering his fiancée, and for her part she couldn't speak for the shock she was experiencing. All this time Kitt had harboured reservations about Patrick and all this time Grace

206

had defended him. Her gut instinct was to side with Cynthia and say that Patrick just wasn't capable of this kind of cruelty. Sure, she hadn't known him long but his manner was that of a gentleman. He'd got defensive that morning but even then he wasn't gruff and had seemed more wounded than angry. If he'd had memories of hurting Jodie resurface, however, and a witness had seen him with Jodie before he disappeared, what other explanation was there?

'I'm sorry,' Patrick said to Grace and Kitt. 'I hired you because I hoped you'd prove my suspicions wrong but I should have been honest. I did try and confess to you last night.'

'That's why you went back to Grace's dorm room,' said Kitt, putting together that piece of the puzzle. 'You were drunk enough to tell the whole truth.'

'Yeah, I guess I was. I didn't remember at first – clearly drank way too much at Selina's party – but today bits and pieces have been coming back to me. You didn't invite me in to discuss the case, Grace. I came back intending to tell you I thought I was the one who did it. But you weren't very with it, and then I started to feel really funny and must have passed out. By the time I woke up this morning I'd bottled it, that's why I got so defensive.'

Grace shook her head. 'I don't know what to say.'

What was there to say? If Patrick was a murderer as he professed to be, he clearly didn't remember even doing it to Jodie. He didn't remember last night either when Grace had slept in the same bed as him. She shuddered to think what a lucky escape she might have had. What if last night he hadn't passed out but had turned violent? She probably wouldn't be here right now. She'd be like Jodie, lost for real and never found.

Grace looked over at Cynthia. The word crestfallen didn't cover it. Her eyes had hollowed out and her face had become drawn. She shook her head, just gently, refusing to accept that her son could do a thing like this.

'DI Thompson,' Kitt said. 'Before you take Patrick away, you should know that I have reason to believe that Selina Grant drugged both Patrick and Grace at the party they attended last night. Neither of them have a particularly good memory of the night after a certain point.'

'What does this have to do with the disappearance of Jodie Perkins?' said Thompson.

'If Patrick can't remember much about the night of Jodie's disappearance, there's a chance she drugged him then too. And maybe has a part in all this,' Kitt clarified.

'Oh yes,' said Grace. 'Patrick, this morning you said that you'd only felt like this once before. Was it the night of Jodie's disappearance?'

'Yeah, I had the same groggy, slightly sickly feeling and my memory was . . . well, I woke up not remembering anything when the police came to call.'

'Do you have any evidence to support this accusation against Selina Grant?' said Thompson.

'I've got the notes from my interview with her and she has a framed picture of Jodie in the bottom drawer of her walk-in wardrobe.'

'That's . . . a start but it's not enough. There's lots of reasons why someone might keep a framed photograph of a deceased friend, even if they'd had a falling-out.'

'Agreed, I know the photograph alone isn't enough but we didn't get the chance to do a proper search of her room. There might be more we didn't uncover. Anyway, I can submit what we do have to you in a statement.'

Thompson nodded. 'If the information pans out we might be able to get a warrant to search Ms Grant's property but we'd have to be pretty sure of ourselves before going at a family like the Grants.'

'Given what Kitt and Grace were saying just before you arrived, it's obvious she's got something to do with all this and may even be the one behind it,' said Cynthia. 'Certainly that makes a lot more sense than my Patrick being a killer. And what about the fact that he might have been drugged?'

'We can conduct a drugs test,' said DI Thompson, 'but if the party was last night that means it's already been more than twelve hours and as such it might not show anything. A lot of the substances used to spike drinks at parties are out of the system very quickly. It makes it hard to catch. Which of course is why they use them.'

'Well, you could at least try,' Cynthia said. 'And in the meantime, Patrick, don't say a word until our lawyer arrives.

There's more to this than meets the eye and I'm going to find out what.'

'Come along, son,' said DI Thompson, nodding towards the exit.

'Can I come with you?' said Cynthia.

'It's probably not for the best, madam,' said Thompson. 'You won't be able to see your son while he's in custody and the chairs in the waiting room aren't the most comfortable.'

'I want word the moment he's released so I can come and collect him,' said Cynthia. She stood, gave him a kiss on the cheek. 'Patrick, look at me.' Patrick obliged. 'You're not a killer. We're going to find out what's going on here. OK?'

Patrick nodded but it was clear he didn't really believe what Cynthia was saying; that no matter what she said he was convinced of his own guilt.

'If there's any news, you'll receive a call from the station,' said Thompson, before turning and leading Patrick out of the bar.

Kitt, Cynthia and Grace looked on as Patrick slowly disappeared in the crowds.

Cynthia stepped around the table and slumped back into her seat. Then, without warning, she reached across the table and grabbed Grace and Kitt's arms. 'I know I'm his mother and that means my opinion is hardly unbiased but Patrick didn't do this. I don't care how much it costs; someone is setting him up and I need you to find out who.'

There was a moment's silence but when Kitt spoke again

her voice was kind, gentle. 'Cynthia, I know this is a difficult time but I'm afraid all I can promise you is that I'll continue the investigation. In doing so, I might well be able to rule out your son as a suspect, but I want you to be prepared. If I continue digging on this, there's a chance I'll find more evidence of your son's involvement. Are you sure you want me to keep going?'

'Yes,' said Cynthia. 'You do your job. It's OK for you to dig. He's a good boy, my son. He didn't do this. And I know if you keep investigating, you'll prove his innocence, I'm sure of it.'

'What I can't understand,' said Grace, 'is why a witness is only coming forward now. It's been a year and I know the police put out a fresh appeal when they reopened the case but what's that witness been doing? Just sitting on that information while Jodie's been missing presumed dead? Who would do that?'

'That's what I'd like to know,' said Cynthia. 'It doesn't make any sense.'

'Unless you were either too scared to come forward, or were bribed not to come forward,' said Kitt. 'I don't know who the witness is but I think I know someone who might.'

'Who?' Grace and Cynthia said in unison.

'Bertrand Hobbs,' said Kitt.

'Oh, yes!' Grace said. 'He should be back from his trip tonight.'

'Who's Bertrand Hobbs?' said Cynthia.

'The DJ at the student radio station who took Jodie's call the night she disappeared.'

'Oh,' said Cynthia. 'Why would he know anything about the witness?'

'He's a journalism student and a woman who calls into his show disappears for ever, what are the odds of him not trying to follow that up himself? Do some digging and see if he can crack the case. It's basically a story on a plate – if you can crack it,' said Kitt.

'So you think he might have done some investigating, got close to something and backed off?' asked Grace.

'It's a possibility, and of course if it was the Grant family he got too close to then we know they would have been able to offer him an incentive to stay quiet – he may even have blackmailed them for keeping his silence,' said Kitt.

'I'll try emailing the student radio station and see if we can set up a meeting with him tomorrow,' said Grace. 'I'll say I'm interested in following in his career footsteps, or something.'

'Well, call me as soon as you've talked to him,' Cynthia said, standing up from her seat.

'It won't be until tomorrow at the earliest now, I'm afraid,' said Kitt. 'We'll need to track him down and arrange a meeting with him.'

'That's fine, just as quick as you can. I've got to get my lawyer on the phone and see what he can do with Patrick. Honestly, a third-year community justice student and he stands there and confesses to murder in front of a police officer and three witnesses – you do wonder sometimes if academies like Venerable Bede's are worth the tuition fees.'

Kitt and Grace offered Cynthia a weak smile as she scurried out of the pub, mobile in hand.

'So,' Grace said, looking at Kitt. 'Wanna get drunk?'

TWENTY-TWO

Kitt and Grace sat on a wall near Durham train station. From there they could see every spire, crenellation and bell tower illuminated by the city's street lights. Grace was sitting cross-legged and clutching a bottle of gin she'd purchased from a nearby off licence. Was it a good idea to drink the night after you suspected you'd been drugged? Just then, Grace didn't much care. She needed something after that scene she'd just witnessed. The fresh air between the bar and here had done her some good but the gin was much better at taking the edge off the fact that three days ago she'd locked lips with a murderer – or at least someone who thought himself a murderer. Not to mention the fact that she'd shared a bed with him last night.

Kitt was hanging her legs off the side of the wall – since Patrick's confession back at the pub, she'd had the good form not to say 'I told you so.'

'How could I be so stupid?' Grace said, tears threatening

as she took another gulp of the gin, which she wasn't used to and stung the back of her throat.

'You're not stupid,' said Kitt. 'Believing the best in other people is never stupid. If they break your trust that's on them.'

Grace shook her head and took another gulp of gin.

'Easy with that, easy,' Kitt said, taking the bottle off Grace and then having a quick nip herself before putting the cap back on.

'I suppose you could expect nothing better from a girl as lost as I am. Not a clue what I'm doing, really. I get the feeling I'm supposed to have it all figured out by now and I can't even tell the difference between a good guy and a bad guy,' said Grace.

Kitt chuckled. 'Have it all figured out at twenty-two? Chance would be a fine thing. If you manage it do give me a call and tell me all the answers.'

'What are you talking about?' said Grace. 'You always have the answers. That's your whole . . . thing. And one of the reasons it's comforting to hang out with you.'

'I may seem like I know what to do all the time, but if you think about it I tell you I don't know the answer quite a bit. Especially during investigations when there are so many variables.'

'I suppose that's true,' said Grace. 'I never really noticed it before. I just think of you as someone who knows every-thing.'

'Nobody knows everything,' said Kitt. 'I've read a formid-able number of books, it's true. And I've studied hard enough to be a respected academic but, as Halloran's always so fond of telling me, there's a whole world out there that has nothing to do with books.'

'So, you don't have everything figured out?'

'I don't believe anybody really does,' said Kitt. 'All we can ever do is our best in the moment. You trusted somebody who perhaps didn't deserve your trust. We've all done it and we'll likely all do it again.'

Grace nodded. If what Kitt was saying was true and other people also had difficulty finding their way in life then maybe there was hope for her after all.

'The look on his mother's face when the police took him away,' Grace said, putting her head in her hands. 'She's the one I really feel for. She must be heartbroken.'

'We don't know if there's anything to be heartbroken about yet,' said Kitt. 'Just because he doesn't remember that night doesn't mean that he was the culprit.'

'What about the flashes he talked about, the memories?'

'Grace, Patrick has been through a prolonged trauma. I'm not sure if his mind is as trustworthy as he'd like to believe right now. He's no doubt suffering tremendous guilt over the disappearance of Jodie, especially if he's secretly believed all this time that he's somehow responsible – his mind could be playing tricks on him.'

'It's kind of you to float that theory, especially as you've thought all along that he might have had something to do with it.'

'I've kept him on the suspect list, yes. But from his demeanour when he was arrested it seems he genuinely doesn't remember anything from that evening.'

'Does that make it any less likely that he did it?'

'It's not so much his lack of memory I'm dubious about but the drugging. If a person is drugged it usually makes them happier, more mellow. The idea that someone as measured as he appears would commit an act of violence under the influence of drugs seems unlikely. The real question is, who might have drugged Patrick? If he was at home they would have had to get inside his house somehow.

'Which suggests that it was either someone he knew or a professional who knew what they were doing.'

'Whoever they are, they are likely to be the ones really behind Jodie's disappearance,' said Grace.

'Yes, even though Thompson is reluctant to go after the Grants I still think that they're the most likely people to be able to pull something like this off. Selina's attitude this afternoon was nothing short of blasé. If you ask me, she thinks she's untouchable and she's the only one to have a clear motive.'

'Selina has been pretty nice to me considering I'm a total stranger so I was reluctant to believe she was really behind it all before, but her being behind it, or her father being behind it, makes a lot more sense than Patrick being the guilty one. Especially given I can't remember much from Selina's party.'

'Well, there is still a possibility that Selina isn't acting alone and that Patrick had some part to play,' said Kitt. 'He could have been lying about the drugs that were found in Jodie's locker, for example. Maybe they belonged to him or Selina.'

'Patrick lied to us about his suspicions that he'd had something to do with Jodie's disappearance and seemed to conveniently forget about Jodie and Selina's spat, it's not unthinkable that he might lie about that too.'

'Again, though, it doesn't really fit with the way he handed himself over to Thompson. If he was going to con-fess to murder, confessing to selling drugs would be a minor concern by comparison,' said Kitt.

'So where does that leave us?'

'With no choice but to pursue the only person we know for sure has access to drugs.'

'Selina,' said Grace. 'She didn't say what kind of drugs she dabbled in so for all we know she does have access to stuff that blanks your memory.'

'If so, Selina could have drugged Patrick on the night Jodie disappeared to keep him out of the way while she did . . . whatever she was going to do . . . to Jodie, and then she drugged both of you last night with something gentler, something that would keep you awake, lucid, but remove your inhibitions.'

'And our memory.'

'She may even have drugged Jodie the night that she disappeared, to make her more pliable and then used the anaesthetic on her,' Kitt said, thinking. 'On the audio recording she screamed out but then her voice was muffled. We didn't know what could make her scream like that besides a weapon coming towards her but if she was being forced to take unknown substances or had a rag soaked with some kind of ether put over her face, I would imagine that would be just as scary – if not more so – than a knife.'

'So what do we do?'

'Selina still doesn't know you're working with me. When I talked to her, she wasn't going to be drawn about whether the secret society exists but given how she's taken you under her wing a bit, she might tell you. There is a possibility that the secret society is somehow at the centre of this mess.

'If you arrange another meeting with her, you might be able to trick her into revealing some sensitive information. Maybe you could pretend you've heard about it and want to join up?'

'I guess it couldn't hurt to try,' said Grace. 'It would look pretty suspicious if I just broke all contact with her right after you'd had your chat with her and anyway, for all we know, we might need to continue the undercover work to get some kind of confession out of her.'

'I agree, let's use your friendship with her to find out

more and in the meantime, we need to get hold of Bertrand Hobbs.'

'Yes, I wish we'd been able to talk to him sooner.'

'Well, he was on the radio at the time of Jodie's disappearance, so he definitely wasn't the one to make her disappear – at least not physically – but there was that twenty minute window where he was playing songs during which he could have tipped someone off or could have organized something with an accomplice. We can't rule anything out.'

'I agree. With all the secrecy at play here, something tells me a budding journalist like him must know more about all this than he's been letting on.'

TWENTY-THREE

Through the medium of some drink-fuelled text messages to Selina late on Friday night, Grace was able to organize a morning walk with their prime suspect along the river into town. Their route took them past the outhouse where they'd found the fibres, the limestone residue the owner couldn't account for and the rags doused in anaesthetic. As they walked by, Grace did her best not to look at the building directly. It wasn't just the fact that she didn't want Selina to guess they were on to her, she also couldn't look at the building without imagining what might have played out there the night Jodie disappeared. Instead, Grace looked for signs of discomfort or edginess in Selina's demeanour. But she didn't even pause for breath in her monologue about the preparations she'd been making in readiness for her trek through the Catskills.

Though Kitt had been adamant that they should stay in contact over radio, Grace insisted that, given the nature of the meeting, it was too much of a risk. It was thus agreed that Kitt would surveil from a safe distance and Grace would fill her in on the conversation afterwards.

'Your bodyguard is hanging quite a way back today,' Grace said as they started to cross over Framwellgate Bridge, which had spanned the River Wear since the fifteenth century. Up ahead was the arresting view of Durham Castle, which, as one would expect from the Norman motte and bailey design, was elevated on the hill in such a way that it dominated the city skyline. The impressive view took Grace's mind off the fact that they were being followed and watched at every turn. She had got a closer look at Selina's bodyguard when they first met up near campus and there was definitely something about him that unsettled her. Maybe it was how sharp and swift his movements were. Combined with his strength, Grace was sure he was very efficient at his job. This should have made her feel safer but somehow it didn't.

'I told him that we wanted to talk girl stuff,' said Selina with a sly smile.

'When really you are, like, going to initiate me into a top secret society?' Grace said, making her eyes look as big and naive-looking as possible.

'Shhh, keep it down,' Selina said, with a little chuckle. 'Your first pointer is that you're going to have to be a lot more discreet. Like texting me about the society last night, you'll notice I didn't address your questions directly in the text message.'

'No, you just asked me to meet you here.'

'And if this conversation doesn't go the way I'd like it to, I'll deny we even spoke about the society. I'll say I told you there was no such thing as the society. And on that note, you're not wearing a wire, are you?'

'A . . . wire?' Grace repeated, while at once being grateful she'd said no to the radio. Was Selina going to make her strip or pat her down or something?

She gave Grace a long hard stare. 'I think it's important to check these things. Especially after I saw this.' Selina pulled her phone out of her pocket and swiped the screen. She brought up a video and then turned the phone so Grace could watch it. The video was of Grace and Kitt sitting in the cafeteria at Venerable Bede's. The footage had been taken right before Grace had approached Selina in the ladies toilets.

Grace's eyes widened as she watched. Had Selina known about their undercover operation this whole time? Had she been watching them? And recording them?

'Where did you get this?'

'My bodyguard wears a bodycam. My dad makes us review the tapes once every week.'

'Oh. So you didn't know . . .'

'That you were stabbing me in the back until earlier this morning? That's right.'

'I am not doing this to stab you in the back, Selina,' Grace said. If even half the things Selina had told Patrick the night of the party were true, Grace would feel terrible for adding to her trust issues.

'Then what is going on?'

Grace explained the whys and wherefores of her decision to try and befriend Selina in an undercover capacity. To her credit, Selina listened without interruption, even though you didn't have to be her best friend to notice the hurt look in her eyes.

'So you see, the goal was always to establish your alibi for Jodie's disappearance at which point we could move forward with the investigation.'

'And now you know I don't have an alibi?' said Selina, raising an eyebrow.

'Nothing immediate happens,' Grace said. 'It just means that we can't remove you from the suspect list. We keep chasing down leads to do with the case, and assuming no evidence surfaces that links you to Jodie's disappearance –'

'Which it won't because, unlike some people, I know how to be a friend.'

'Then that's the end of the story. If there's no evidence there's no case, it's as simple as that.'

'You know what the sad thing is?' said Selina. 'If you had made a proper appointment with my father to see me, I would have put some money into the investigation myself. Now that I know you went behind my back like this, I don't want to ever see you sniffing around me or my family again.'

Selina made to walk off but Grace caught her arm. She

did it as casually as she could so as not to arouse the protective instincts of her bodyguard, who after reviewing the
footage with Selina must be watching her even more closely
than he was before. Assuming Selina had told her bodyguard who Grace was, of course. After having her cover
blown, the last thing she needed was a physical blow adding
into the mix.

'I will let you storm off. As you have every right to do, but
before you do, I need to ask you something. I know I don't
have any right to ask you for anything but something happened to me at your party the other night. Something bad.'

Selina frowned. 'What do you mean? Did someone hurt
you or something?'

'I . . . don't think so. Not in the physical sense, but you
might remember I said I was a bit out of sorts the day after.
It was actually quite a great deal worse than that. I couldn't
remember anything. Well, nowt much. The whole night was
a bit of a blank. I don't drink often – thanks again to my
parents – but I've never had a reaction like that to alcohol.'

'You were . . . in higher spirits than I expected,' Selina
said, a smirk crossing her lips in spite of her previous upset.

'What do you mean?'

'Well, I wasn't going to say anything – I'm not one for
rubbing people's faces in their drunken antics as long as
they're not hurting anyone but . . .'

'Oh my God, what did I do?' Grace said, cringing.

'Towards the end of the evening you streamed "Thong

Song" on your phone, climbed up on the kitchen counter and used it as a dance stage.'

Out of nowhere, something flashed in Grace's mind. An image of a crowd of people clapping and cheering. She was somewhere elevated, like the kind of height one might achieve by standing on a kitchen counter. She got a sense of her movements. Gyrating would be the only appropriate verb. And somewhere nearby, like she was hearing it from underwater or something, she could hear the husky vocals of Sisqo.

'Oh no,' she said, covering her eyes with her hands. 'Not again.'

'Again?' Selina said. 'You mean that wasn't a very special performance for just us?'

'I don't think I've ever danced on a kitchen worktop before but I have woken up on a few morning-afters following a lot of booze and found that I've inexplicably downloaded "Thong Song" at around the three a.m. mark.'

'How many times exactly have you drunkenly down-loaded that track?'

'This will make seven,' Grace admitted. 'Do you know what happened to me after that?'

'Nothing. Like I said, I could see you'd had enough so I sent you home.'

'The thing is,' said Grace, 'I wasn't just reacting to alcohol. Something else was going on with me that night and that's why I can't remember everything.'

'Like what? Oh, you don't think someone slipped some-thing in your drink?'

'I don't think it, I know it,' said Grace. 'I bought one of those rapid drug tests off the internet and I got a positive result.' This was yet another blatant lie but her bridges were burned with Selina so she might as well go for broke. There was no test but Grace was hoping that calling Selina's bluff would pay off.

'Oh my God, what did you test positive for?'

'I don't know,' Grace said, 'the test only offers an indica-tion. You have to wait forty-eight hours to find out what drug was in your system. 'Did you notice anyone acting oddly at the party?'

'Besides you, I knew everyone at that party pretty well. I can't believe that anyone would – Oh no.'

'What?'

'OK. Usually I'm super-vigilant at my parties because I just want people to have a good time and part of that is making sure things don't get out of hand. Some people walk into the house of a millionaire's daughter and think anything goes so you have to be mindful.'

'But, something happened? Something unusual?'

'Probably not unusual for your average house party but unusual for one of mine. I had to ask this bloke to leave because I didn't recognize him. I only let people I've invited in so it was a surprise to see someone I didn't recognize. When I asked who invited him, he said he'd delivered some food someone had ordered. I assumed whoever placed the order had had a phone call from him when he was outside and buzzed him in while I was otherwise distracted. He left without any trouble once I explained it was a private party. I didn't think much of it at the time because there was some food sitting on the counter in the kitchen – though now I think of it nobody had touched it. Maybe, for some reason, he'd used that as a cover to get into the party and he was up to no good, spiking people's drinks. Certainly, nobody else who was there would've done that. They know if I caught them they'd never be invited back.'

'What did this guy look like? Can you describe him?'

'Not very memorable. Short buzz cut. Quite chunky. Still had his coat on.'

'What colour was the coat?'

'Black – why?'

'I know you said you wouldn't help us but if you cared about Jodie at all you will turn your CCTV footage from two nights ago over to the police.'

'Why?'

'I can't be certain, but I think the man you talked to might have taken Jodie.'

TWENTY-FOUR

Kitt and Grace settled down in the seating area outside the Castle View Café on Silver Street. Grace and Selina had parted ways about half an hour ago and when she'd caught up with Kitt it had been decided they would stop for a pot of tea to talk over all that Selina had divulged.

Grace would have preferred to make some tea back at the dorm room. Largely because it was beyond entertaining to watch Kitt brew Lady Grey in the floral teapot and teacups she'd transported from York especially for that purpose. The fact that Kitt had brought along her own china was amusing enough but it was even more comical to watch her do this to the backdrop of her Marilyn Manson poster. Kitt, however, was determined that she was parched and couldn't wait until they got back to the dorm for a pot of tea. Consequently they'd managed to find what seemed to be the last spare table in the centre of Durham. As it was a busy Saturday, people were zipping all around and a few street performers were trying to draw the crowds to their corner of the main square in order to relieve them of their spare change.

'So, what can you tell me?' said Kitt, as soon as the waitress delivered their drinks.

Grace held the hot chocolate to her lips, inhaled the sugary goodness and then took a quick sip before responding. 'The first thing you should know is that my cover is blown with Selina.'

'What?' said Kitt. 'How? And why didn't you tell me that straight away?'

'I thought it safer to deliver that news when you had a calming cup of tea in your hand,' said Grace. 'Her bodyguard has a bodycam. He snapped us in the cafeteria.'

'So she's known this whole time?'

'No, just since this morning when they reviewed the footage but she was pretty upset about it.'

'I'll bet she was,' said Kitt. 'With no alibi and all the possible reasons Jodie could have been a threat to her she's still our top suspect.'

'I don't think she will be for long,' said Grace.

'How so?'

'Patrick's mysterious man in black seemed to have gate-crashed Selina's party. She caught some guy in a black coat at the party without an invite and ejected him. She reckons if anyone spiked our drinks it's him.'

'Hm, if I hadn't watched Patrick get arrested last night, I

might have taken their mutual blaming of events on a "man in black" as a sign they were somehow working together. But Patrick just gave himself up to DI Thompson, and I don't believe he'd do that if he was trying to escape justice. Unless this is all part of some bigger plan they've hatched I don't yet understand.'

'We shouldn't have to take her word for it for much longer,' said Grace. 'She's got CCTV outside her house, remember? With a bit of luck she's caught him on camera. The only problem is that she's so angry about the way we've gone behind her back she says she's not going to help the investigation. I tried to convince her to hand the footage to the police but she was really hurt, so I'm not sure what she's going to do.'

'If she's got any sense she'll hand it over straight away and get herself off the hook. The context of Jodie's disappearance, the radio show and the secret makes me suspect that he is hired by whoever it was Jodie was trying to expose. His appearance at Selina's house is strange though. I wonder if he might work for her father?' said Kitt.

'Selina's father has already got one man following her around whenever she's out of the house, it's not a stretch to believe he might hire another one,' said Grace. She'd only had a small taste of what it felt like to have your every move watched by someone during her walk with Selina and it was even more intrusive than she'd imagined it to be.

'Not a stretch at all. Especially if, as you suggested, he

knew Jodie was going to tell the world about how he abused his daughter when she came out to him. People would rightly boycott his business over something like that,' said Kitt. 'That said, I did some research while I was hovering around keeping an eye on you this morning and there's no immediate warning signs that he's into anything underhand – at least not from his online presence.'

'Yeah, I've been thinking – there's also the fact that something like that would be big enough for Jodie to take it somewhere more high profile than a student radio station.'

'Hm. I suppose you're right about that.'

'If you're right about Bertrand Hobbs being paid off though, then he could have paid any number of people to keep his dealings quiet. I imagine someone with his amount of money could make almost any problem go away. And for all we know Jodie could've been one of them.'

'Maybe Jodie took it to other outlets and, just like the police, they were either too scared of what Grant might do with his high-powered lawyers when they had no proof or they'd been paid off to ignore anything relating to the family.'

'But they would have had Selina's testimony as proof.'

'Sadly, the testimony of a victim in these cases doesn't hold the water it should. And we don't actually know if Selina would have been willing to testify against her father and call out his abuse. For many reasons other than money, she may have been too fearful.'

'If that's true, Jodie might have tried the late night student radio show as a last ditch effort to expose him. She wouldn't tell Bertrand who the secret was about. Maybe because she thought he wouldn't run the segment if he knew.'

'With someone like Humphrey Grant, unless we talk to him in person or find a way to snoop around his house we're probably not going to get to the truth,' said Kitt.

'There's always a chance that our good friend Randy will spill his guts,' said Grace. 'He's agreed to meet us in a bit, by the way. Around two thirty, if you're free?'

'Mal's working until three thirty. He's planning to come up to Durham but it'll be at least half four before he gets here so I'm sure we can get Randy's interview out the way before teatime.'

'And if he knows something about this witness, maybe we can work out why they waited a year before implicating Patrick,' said Grace.

'That is an odd detail,' said Kitt. 'And it's the only hard evidence they have against Patrick. The rest is circumstantial – lack of evidence; lack of alibi.'

'Is it too crazy to imagine that Selina's family might have paid someone to act as a witness?'

'You know, I don't think it is,' said Kitt. 'This witness, whoever they are, has only come forward because of the recent police appeal. What if the police reopening this case rattled the Grants? They escaped interrogation the first time

233

round but perhaps they were concerned they wouldn't be so lucky again.'

'So, to take the police off on a different track, they hire a witness who conveniently points the finger at the person the police always suspect first: the boyfriend.'

'Thompson wants me to go down to the station this evening once he's questioned Patrick, to make a statement. I'll be sure to include this theory in the report. Though I wish I had more than a theory. Here's hoping Bertrand is feeling talkative.'

'Well, he is a radio host, I hear talking is kind of their thing.'

'Very droll.'

'I'm sure we could come up with a plan to make him a bit more open,' said Grace, looking at her watch. 'We'll need to set off soon if we want to make it back to the radio station on campus in time. Shall we leave in a minute and see what we can come up with on the way?'

'Sounds like a plan,' said Kitt, before drinking what was left of her cup of tea.

Grace picked up her bag, which had been hung on the back of her chair. She was about to sling it over her shoulder when she noticed something strange. The zip was open and something she didn't recognize was poking out. A brown envelope.

'What's this?' she said, carefully pulling the envelope out of her bag.

'Where's that come from?' said Kitt.

'I have no idea. I just found it.'

'Is it from Selina, perhaps? Maybe she stuck it in there? Maybe she wanted to tell you something that she couldn't say out loud?'

'No, it can't be that, I opened my bag on the way to meet you to get my phone out. The envelope wasn't there then so it's definitely not from Selina.'

'Oh lordy,' said Kitt. 'Has someone just stuck it in your bag while we've been sitting here? That's a bit of a creepy thought.'

'Maybe, but I'm always careful about zipping up my bag. How would they manage it without us noticing? They'd have to be very sly about it.'

'You're right. With the position we were sitting in, if someone had done something like that I'm sure I would've seen them,' said Kitt. 'Unless they did it while I was ordering the drinks . . .'

'I suppose they could have done that. I was busy looking at my phone . . . I was looking Randy up online to see if I could drag up any useful information before we interviewed him, so was engrossed in that.'

'Maybe we'll know more when we open it, eh? You'll have to be careful, mind. Whatever's in there might be evidence. Here, use these just in case,' said Kitt, pulling a couple of pairs of plastic gloves from her pocket. She put one pair on herself and offered the other to Grace.

Once Grace had the gloves on, she gently opened the envelope and unfolded a piece of cream notepaper. She was silent for a moment as she scanned down the page reading words she couldn't quite believe, and then her eyes widened as she looked at the signature at the bottom.

'Oh my God. It can't be.'

'What? What is it?' Kitt said, stepping around the table to try and get a look.

Grace handed her the note and sat back down. Her whole body felt like lead. She could barely believe what she was about to say: 'It's a letter . . . from Jodie.'

TWENTY-FIVE

'I can't believe it,' said Kitt. 'This . . . is unreal.'

'Here, let me read it again, I only skimmed it the first time,' said Grace. 'I need to take another look if I'm going to believe it.'

'Just be careful, hold it by the sides. One way or another we're going to need to turn this over to the police and the first thing they'll do is check it for fingerprints. We don't want to destroy evidence.'

Kitt handed the letter back and Grace took care to follow her instructions. If this letter was evidence that Jodie was still alive she didn't want to do anything that might jeopardize verifying that fact. If Jodie was alive then Patrick couldn't have killed her and the police would have to release him. She started to read again and this time Grace took pains to slowly digest every word.

Dear Grace,

I'm sorry I couldn't come to see you in person but if you want to disappear, you have to make it stick. The only reason I'm writing to you now is because I heard on the news that Patrick has been arrested in connection with my disappearance. I always knew when I disappeared that there'd be questions for him and the worst thing about this whole mess is how it must have impacted the lives of the people I love. But I knew the police wouldn't have any evidence on Patrick so I didn't think there would be any consequences. I thought he'd get over me and that would be the end of it.

I don't know what they think they've got on him now, but I'm writing this letter, in my own handwriting, to clear his name. To let the world know once and for all that I disappeared because I had to, not because Patrick did something unforgivable to me. He would never hurt me. Anyone who knows him would know that.

The only person in all this who has done something unforgivable, besides me, is Selina Grant. I knew about that stupid secret society she was running and it was obvious they were doing more than just doing silly stunts behind their parents' backs. Selina had a bit too much to drink and let slip a couple of times that there was some kind of drugs ring going on within the society and I told her if she didn't stop I would go public with what I knew.

The next thing I knew some drugs had been planted in my

locker and Berkeley wouldn't hear a word against Selina, even after she'd admitted to starting a fight with me a couple of weeks before I disappeared. I couldn't go to Patrick about what I knew because it was obviously dangerous information and I didn't want to drag him into something that at the time I was scared might cost him his life. It was a small miracle it didn't cost me mine.

It was Selina who abducted me mid-radio appearance. She drugged me and when I came to she'd tied me up somewhere – I still have no idea where – and told me that if I didn't disappear for good, she was going to kill me. It didn't feel like I had any other choice at the time, so I disappeared.

I thought the police would figure out Selina's involvement but she must have covered her tracks too well; either that or they're too scared to take on the daughter of a millionaire. I've stayed quiet all this time because I was scared Selina would catch up with me, she's got the resources. She told me if I ever tried to come back people I loved would get hurt and then she'd come after me. But when I heard Patrick had been arrested, I knew I had to do something.

I can only hope Selina's people won't trace this letter and that it's enough to get Patrick released. He really was the best boyfriend, a bit too good for the likes of me if truth be told. I don't think I'll ever be able to risk returning to the north-east again but at least this note will bring him some comfort. At least now he'll know that I'm still alive and making my way as best I can. I hope he can forgive my silence and know that, the way I left things, it was to protect him.

I know when he reads this letter he'll want to try and find me but even if the police did eventually apprehend Selina for what she did to me, I can't trust that she won't have someone waiting to finish what she started. So please, encourage him to let me go. It's for the best.

When you see him, please tell him I'll always love him.

Jodie

Tears threatened in Grace's eyes and she swallowed hard, trying to hold them back. She looked over at Kitt and could see she, too, was working hard not to break down. At least it was now clear that this letter wasn't from Selina. She'd have no reason to pass on a letter that directly incriminated her.

'I don't know whether to cry out of happiness that she's still alive or out of sadness for all she must have gone through in the last year,' Grace said at last, shaking her head.

'I'm facing the same dilemma,' said Kitt.

'Can you even start to imagine what that must have been like for her? Knowing she would never see her friends and family again, that they would all think she was dead.'

'It doesn't bear thinking about. I'm doing all I can to distract myself by seeing if the pieces of this story really fit.'

'What do you mean?'

'We need to verify this really is Jodie's handwriting, for a start. There are one or two phrases in there, I'm not sure I'd expect them from a nineteen-year-old girl. "Apprehend

Selina" for example, would someone around your age more likely just say "catch"?'

'I guess.' Grace nodded, again struggling with the threat of tears. She hadn't even thought about the fact that the letter could be a forgery. To have the relief that Jodie was still alive dangled and then snatched away sickened her. Who would do that? An enemy of Selina, perhaps? Someone who wanted to see her framed? Less than an hour ago, Selina had sworn blind to Grace that she didn't have anything to do with Jodie's disappearance. Maybe this was a message from someone who was more in the know. A message to say they shouldn't let Selina off the hook so easily.

'Patrick would be best placed to verify it,' said Kitt.

'Yes, but I don't think the police are allowing him visitors just now. They wouldn't even let his mum go with him. Oh . . . but maybe Cynthia could tell us if it's Jodie's handwriting?'

'Maybe, but I'm not quite ready to show her this letter. If it is a forgery then I don't want to raise their hopes about finding Jodie alive and then dash them. Remember, for her it's not just about Jodie being alive, it's about her son not going down for her murder. We've got to be really sure before we give her any hope that we can clear his name.'

'So what should we do?'

'Still contact Cynthia, but maybe go in with a different tack. Ask her if she's got anything with Jodie's handwriting on it and get her to send you a picture on your phone. Say we need a sample on file. You don't need to go into any more detail than that. She wants us to do all we can to free Patrick so she's probably not going to question our methods.'

'All right,' Grace said, pulling her phone out of her coat pocket. She sent the request to Cynthia and then looked back at Kitt. 'It might just be wishful thinking but it seems to me that the story does fit though, you know. Patrick was drugged on the night of Jodie's murder and then we were drugged at Selina's party. She was probably trying to get information out of us and who knows, maybe she did. We could have said anything to her, we wouldn't remember.'

'Drugs has been a common theme running through this whole investigation. It's probably what Selina and Jodie really fought about in the cafeteria.'

'If that's true then why did Jodie go along with Selina's story about her liking Patrick?'

'We don't know that she did.'

'You're right . . . we never saw her written statement,' said Grace. 'And who is Regina Berkeley more likely to believe: her favourite millionaire or a scholarship student?'

'Exactly. Mal often says that when an investigation takes you back to the same spot it's not usually by coincidence. If she was running some kind of drugs ring at Venerable Bede's it would have been lucrative, and remember Selina said she wanted to find a way to become financially independent.'

'Oh my God, you're right,' said Grace. 'I hadn't made that connection. Selina wants to become financially independent to get out from her father's control and she decides selling drugs on campus is the quickest way to do it.'

'If this secret society is as shady as it sounds then the drugs ring might already have been established. All the hard work was done and Selina just took the reins.'

'And if that's true,' said Grace, 'and Jodie threatened to expose the drugs ring, Selina would have been well placed to plant drugs in Jodie's locker.'

'In that case, maybe the man in black does exist, but he's not working for Humphrey Grant, he's working for Selina and she's just feigning innocence. Certainly it would be too risky for her to do her own dirty work and anyway, she wouldn't have been able to take Jodie down and get her to that outhouse on her own.'

'So she hires some anonymous crony, the way rich people do. He plants the drugs on Jodie and when she doesn't just leave quietly they realize they have to take things a step further. He drugs Patrick so he can't help her and follows Jodie down to the river after she tries to go to him.'

'When it becomes clear that Jodie is going to expose Selina's darkest secret to the entire academy and confirm the existence of the Scarlet Stocking Society, the man in black realizes he has to act then.'

'Though, Jodie did seem to recognize whoever attacked her so maybe Selina was there?'

'Possibly, or maybe somebody else associated with Selina that Jodie also knew.'

'And like you said, they had to get her out of sight fast.'

'As the abduction happened live on air, they'd know the police would be on their way. They had to find somewhere to hide out until the coast was clear.'

'So they drugged her.'

'And that place they took her to – the place where she didn't know where she was – that was probably the out-house.'

'That's where they threatened her.'

'But when they let her go, wouldn't she see where she was?'

'They probably drugged her again or blindfolded her and dropped her off somewhere random. Made sure she left town.'

'So she couldn't even say goodbye to Patrick.'

'This all links up logically,' said Kitt. 'Selina has been telling us half-truths all along. Denying she knew anything about the drugs when really she was the one who put them there.'

'It would certainly take her a lot longer to find ways of monetizing that YouTube channel than it would to sell drugs to rich kids,' said Grace. 'The problem is, she's been careful, and we don't have any hard evidence against Selina. The police won't go after her unless they're sure.'

'We've still got our interview with Randy, that might reveal something. If we get enough circumstantial evidence we might be able to trick her into confessing and record it. I –'

Grace's phone beeped. 'Sorry. It's Cynthia, she's been digging through some drawers and found an old birthday card Jodie gave her a couple of years back. Look at this.' Grace picked up the letter and held her phone next to it so Kitt could make the same side-by-side comparison she just had. 'It's the same – the handwriting's the same.'

'My God,' said Kitt. 'Jodie's really alive.'

TWENTY-SIX

'You ladies comfortable?' Bertrand Hobbs said as he settled them on the sofa in the waiting room next to the radio booth at Castle Rock FM. Through the glass, they could see another host wearing headphones and talking a mile a minute into the microphone about a climate change protest that was due to happen on campus the following week.

'Very comfortable, thank you,' Kitt said, though her expression indicated otherwise. She was staring down her nose at the sofa, which was upholstered in brown corduroy. It looked to be from the 1970s by its design and Grace couldn't help but wonder what awful stains and general grubby behaviour that particular shade of brown was hiding. Don't ask, don't tell. If she wasn't careful that was going to become her new life motto.

'Thanks so much for agreeing to talk to us,' said Grace. She was keen to move this conversation on as quickly as possible and not just because she wanted to minimize the

246

time she had to sit on this scummy sofa. After the discovery of Jodie's letter, Kitt had put a phone call in to Durham police station. They were supposed to take the letter there directly but as it was almost time to meet Bertrand they'd agreed to make a quick stop off on the way and see if they could uncover anything else to add to Kitt's statement. If Bertrand did have some grand insight about the events that took place a year ago, such as some evidence of a drugs ring operating out of Venerable Bede's, it was worth twenty minutes to collect the information and pass it all on to the police in one go.

'Hey, I'm always happy to meet fans of the show. Especially those interested in following in the footsteps of the Hobbster.' As he said this, Randy pointed a thumb at his chest lest there was any confusion about who the 'Hobbster' was. Randy's manner was far from the only distracting thing about him. For some strange reason he'd opted to wear a pair of gold loafers to this meeting. Despite the weather outside being rather crisp he'd unbuttoned his white shirt quite some way, revealing rather more of his hairy chest than Grace was happy to see. On top of that he had ten or so gold bangles on each arm that jangled every time he gesticulated. Staying focused on the words coming out of his mouth was thus going to prove quite the challenge.

'Oh yes,' said Grace, noticing, now that she was up close with this guy, just how much gel he had in his hair. He'd sculpted it into a quiff that looked just as cheesy as he was acting. 'I hadn't thought about radio as a career path before but since I started listening to your show I've been inspired. The campus station seems like a great starting place.'

'Right on. It's not an easy job,' Randy said, 'but it is rewarding.'

'Oh, I'm very sure you make it look a lot easier than it really is,' said Grace. 'I'm surprised you haven't won some kind of award, actually.'

'I'm not sure I'm quite at award-winning level yet,' said Randy.

'You're far too modest,' said Grace even though she highly doubted modesty was at the top of the list of Randy's best qualities. 'I've been hearing a lot about your show, particularly how professionally you handled that awful incident when the student disappeared.'

Randy's grin dropped a bit. 'Yeah, that was a ride I wasn't expecting. But that's the thing about live radio – you never know what's going to happen, you always have to be prepared. People say that, and you think it's a cliché until something like that happens.'

'Some listeners who heard it said that the whole thing sounded staged, like you knew what was going to be happen, can you believe that?' Kitt said.

'Professional jealousy. When you do a good job you can always expect it. People talking rubbish like that just demonstrates how much I believe in the motto: the show must go on . . . Who said that, exactly?'

'There's no consensus about who exactly used that phrase first,' said Kitt. 'But generally speaking it's thought to have originated in circuses in the 1800s. It was used as a sort of motto amongst the performers; if an animal wouldn't behave or someone broke an arm during the trapeze act they were encouraged to keep going, hence: the show must go on.'

Bertrand and Grace looked at Kitt in silence for a moment.

'That's . . . fascinating but actually I meant who said that the call between me and Jodie sounded staged?' said Randy.

'Oh,' Kitt said, the brightness in her expression dimming. 'Yes, that . . . that does make more sense.'

'I can't remember, actually, it was just some first year mouthing off during a freshers' event. I never saw him again,' said Grace. 'I confess I did listen to a recording of the show.'

'Oh really, and how'd you get your hands on that?'

'An admiring fan has her ways,' Grace said with a coy smile. 'After I heard about what happened I wanted to hear how a true master manages that kind of situation. It was awful to listen to, I can't believe how calmly you handled it. Cutting to a song like that. No wonder people thought it was staged. You handled it like a pro.'

'To be honest, I'm lucky I was able to put on such an act. I don't want to give you the impression we took that kind of event in our stride. Behind the scenes we tried to re-establish the call with Jodie and when we couldn't we dialled

999 right away. We gave the police Jodie's number but by that point the phone must have been in the river because it wasn't showing a live signal. They tracked its last location and arrived down at the river less than an hour later. But it was raining like crazy that night and so the story we got was that any evidence might have been lost.'

'Nothing short of tragic,' said Kitt.

'No argument from me,' said Grace, leaning closer to Bertrand and even stooping to batting her eyelashes. 'Though I have to admit, when I listened to the recording, I was curious about something.'

'And what was that, exactly?' Randy said with a leer.

'Well, I'm sorry if you find this a bit morbid but I couldn't help but wonder if you knew what the secret was – the secret Jodie was going to tell you on air?'

'Nothing wrong with healthy curiosity up to a point,' said Randy. 'But no, she wouldn't give it up. I tried every trick I knew to get her to tell me in advance but for some reason she insisted it had to be live on air. Afterwards, I realized it was because she had something so big she couldn't risk telling me beforehand, in case – maybe she thought she was being followed or that someone was listening in. I don't know. But what happened that night was messed up.'

'Agreed,' said Kitt. 'But, I have a feeling an intrepid reporter like you wouldn't just leave a story like that alone. Surely you must have done a bit of digging. If Jodie could uncover the secret on her own then someone with your research credentials would surely have no problem at all following in her footsteps.'

'What, so I could disappear too? No thanks,' said Randy. 'Some journalists won't stop until they get the story, no matter what it costs them, but here's a word of advice: it's good to be alive. Even if it means you don't get the big break you were hoping for. Sometimes, you've got to know when to leave well enough alone.'

Well, wasn't that an interesting philosophy? Grace couldn't help but wonder if Randy was speaking from personal experience. Had he got close to something, close to a big break, and been forced to back off by Selina?

'That makes sense,' said Grace. 'I am generally a fan of being alive. But if you didn't investigate it, then I'll bet that a seasoned media star like yourself had some kind of hunch about who the secret involved, right?'

Randy took a deep breath and looked at Kitt and Grace for a long moment. 'Can't help but notice that we've been talking for nearly ten minutes and eight of them have focused on Jodie's disappearance. You're not really inter-ested in getting into radio, are you?'

'What was it that gave us away?' said Grace with a sigh.

'Referring to a student DJ as a seasoned media star is a push even for my ego. What are you doing poking around Jodie's disappearance?' said Randy.

'We've been hired to investigate it,' said Kitt. 'Our clients want the truth about what happened to Jodie and we're very close to finding the person responsible but we need some confirmation of our hunches.'

Randy shook his head. 'I told the police all this a year ago. I don't know anything about it and even if I did, like I said, blabbing about it is probably going to guarantee that I disappear just like Jodie did. And that wouldn't exactly be a positive next step in my otherwise bright future, now, would it?'

'I understand,' said Kitt. 'But we're talking about the disappearance and possible murder of a young woman. It's a matter of justice.'

'These are all things I don't want to get mixed up in. I come to work, I do the show, I go home. I'm not some justice warrior bent on ending himself early.'

'Even if your help in solving such a high profile case might lead to some national media appearances?' said Grace.

Randy looked between Kitt and Grace for a moment, weighing up the offer. 'All I could offer you is hypotheticals.'

'All right,' said Kitt. 'Hypothetically, a radio host would need to at least ensure that the target of the secret was newsworthy enough to run on their show, right? A secret about the drinking antics of first-year students, for example, wouldn't be worth their time.'

'Hypothetically, yes,' Randy said. 'The host in question would want to make sure that the person the secret was about was worth the risk of letting someone on air without actually knowing what they're going to say.'

'So who would such a secret have to involve to warrant air time . . . you know, hypothetically?'

'In my opinion, it would need to be a senior faculty member. Maybe even the most senior faculty member, hypothetically.'

Randy looked at Kitt and Grace hard and nodded. Confirming their unspoken assumptions.

All the air left Grace's lungs. Berkeley. Randy was pointing them at the dean. Could that be true? Had she really been involved in this all along? The very first person they'd spoken to – after Patrick. She'd acted very strangely when they interviewed her but Selina's motive was so much stronger than anything Grace could think of for Berkeley. Unless . . . was Berkeley also in on the drugs ring? Everything about her gave the impression of a strict school ma'am who wouldn't tolerate any nonsense, but maybe that was just an act. Maybe she was in cahoots with Selina, creaming money off the top for turning a blind eye. If that was the case and Jodie was going to expose her that would definitely be the end of her career. More than that, she'd likely end up in jail. Judges didn't look too fondly on people who corrupted young and impressionable students for their own monetary gain.

'Well, thank you. That is a very interesting hypothesis, Mr Hobbs,' said Kitt.

'No problem. I think until further notice, though, it's best that you don't mention this conversation to anyone.'

'Except the police,' said Kitt. 'We are expected to pass information on to them that has a chance of opening new avenues up in the case. But I don't have to say who I heard it from until they've got concrete evidence.'

'All right,' Randy said with a nod. 'And if they do get evidence and if this hypothesis turns out to be true and you find out who was behind Jodie's disappearance, be sure to push some media appearances my way, just as a courtesy for my consultation.'

'I'm sure, if your theory ends up being correct, then that can be arranged,' Kitt said.

Grace's phone buzzed.

Apologizing, she swiped the screen.

'Oh my God,' she said, looking over at Kitt. 'It's a text from Cynthia. The police are going to release Patrick. Selina's been arrested. According to Cynthia, they've found hard forensic evidence that suggests she killed Jodie.'

'We need to get down to the station right away. I've no doubt Selina has played her part in this but from the sound of things she's not the only one.'

TWENTY-SEVEN

When Kitt and Grace exited Durham police station an hour later, Patrick had been released and was standing on the steps. As soon as Grace saw him, her step quickened. After a night in a police cell he looked tousled and vulnerable. The sharp October breeze ruffled his long dark hair and caused him to huddle in his coat. Grace approached, frowning into his eyes. There was an awkward moment where they stood a foot or so apart but then instinct took over and she leaned in to give him a hug.

'Are you all right?' she said, wrapping her arms tighter around him as he did the same.

'Not really,' said Patrick. 'But I'm hoping at some point I will be. Mum not here?'

'I got a text from her to say she'd already set off from Chester-le-Street and would meet us at Berkeley's house up in Heddon-on-the-Wall,' said Kitt.

Patrick frowned. 'Berkeley's house? Why are we going there?'

'I'll . . . explain on the way,' said Grace. 'A lot's happened while you've been inside.'

'You make it sound like I've been locked up for twenty years, not eighteen hours,' Patrick said.

'In some ways it feels like a lot longer than eighteen hours,' Grace said. 'Do you know the deal with Selina? What they found that's so incriminating? And what happened to your star witness?'

'The witness thing was really weird. According to DI Thompson, initially his story was that he was out of the country when the first appeal happened a year ago. He left for a job in Sweden the day after Jodie disappeared but apparently that story didn't totally check out and under a bit of pressure he confessed he was paid by someone to come forward. They're trying to track down who it was now.'

'We already suspected that the Grant family might have paid someone off to distract police attention from them and focus it on you,' said Kitt. 'From all the information we've collected, and the fact that the police now seem to have hard evidence against her, it looks as though Selina really is the culprit – or one of them.'

'If it is the Grant family, it's doubtful the police will find a link between them and the payment. People that rich have the resources to cover their tracks,' said Patrick.

'But if the witness folded and the police have found something they can charge Selina with, I guess this means there isn't any evidence against you after all?' Grace said, brightening.

'No, but that doesn't bring me much peace of mind. The drug test didn't show anything in my system but sitting in custody I had time to think over what you said about Selina drugging us. I don't know how she would have pulled it off a year ago when I was in my own house for the evening, but the feelings I had on Thursday night . . . they weren't just similar to the way I felt on the night of Jodie's disappearance, they were identical.'

'But if she's responsible for drugging you, then that surely means you're not to blame for what happened to Jodie?' said Grace.

'It depends on if she managed to get me to do something when I was under the influence of the drugs. Those flashes of strangling Jodie have to be coming from somewhere. For all I know I'm remembering something she put me up to. She said she suffered abuse herself, maybe she's repeating the pattern and abusing others.'

'Now the police have her in custody with what must be undeniable evidence, I'm sure the truth will come to light soon enough,' said Kitt. 'And as for any involvement you may have had, the thing is, Patrick, even if you did do something untoward that night, you weren't in your right mind. You were under the influence of an unknown substance and the person who administered it. So long as we can find some proof of that, a court wouldn't hold you responsible.'

'Well, we don't know that there's any proof out there. A year on. At any rate, it doesn't stop me feeling responsible,' Patrick said, running a hand through his hair.

'I wonder what the police found in Selina's house,' said Grace. 'I thought they weren't convinced they should go after Selina head-on anyway. Did they change their mind?'

'In a way,' said Patrick. 'When Thompson found out the person who said they saw me by the river had been paid off, he knew the Grants would have the resources to do that. He couldn't go at them head-on, exactly. He went to the academy and had Selina's locker searched. I don't know what, but they found incriminating material and then got a warrant to search her house where they apparently found even more to tie her to Jodie's disappearance.'

'Did the police mention anything else?' asked Kitt.

'No . . . why?'

Grace and Kitt exchanged a look.

'What? What is it?'

'I'm about to tell you something but it's important you do your best not to let it get your hopes up too much,' said Grace. 'Do you promise?'

Patrick nodded. 'All right.'

'This afternoon, I found an envelope in my handbag. I had no idea where it came from, somebody must have slipped it in there, but in the envelope was a letter and it was written and signed by Jodie.'

'You mean, she wrote it and she's . . . alive?'

'We don't know, we . . . hope so,' said Kitt. 'But it's important not to get your hopes up too far. We asked your mother to send us a sample of Jodie's handwriting and when she did the handwriting was a match.'

'Was there a date on the letter?'

'No,' said Kitt. 'And that's why we have to be cautious about making any rash assumptions about Jodie. The letter of course could be genuine but there's also a chance that Jodie was forced to write it under duress, or that it is a forgery. The police are doing some DNA testing on it to find out more.'

'What did the letter say, exactly?'

'That Selina was behind her disappearance. And that you definitely had no part in it,' said Grace.

Patrick took a deep breath. 'I'm going back in there to ask if I can read it. Maybe she's put some clue in there that only I can decipher that will tell me where she is.'

'If they let you read it, and given you're a suspect they probably won't, that's probably not the best use of your time right now,' said Kitt. 'Even if you could find Jodie from that letter and she is still alive, it wouldn't be safe for you to go after her until everyone who was involved in her disappearance has been brought to justice.'

'But, they've already got hard evidence against Selina. Even if she gets bailed they'll make her wear a tracking device.'

'She might not be the only one involved in what happened to Jodie,' said Grace.

'There's a lot of evidence pointing at Selina but there's one more loose end to tie up that might unravel this whole case,' said Kitt.

'What's that?' Patrick asked.

'Bertrand Hobbs implied that the secret Jodie was going to expose was about Dean Berkeley.'

'Not Selina?'

'Bertrand didn't even mention her. He suggested Berkeley straight away – well, after a little persuasion,' said Grace.

'So, you think Selina and Berkeley are somehow in it together?'

'We need to talk to her directly and find out. If that is the case, they may have conspired to frame you, and hired that witness to come forward. We think Berkeley planted those drugs because Jodie was going to expose a drugs ring she and Selina were in on.'

'I can't believe it,' said Patrick. 'Berkeley's so strict. The idea that she'd turn a blind eye to drugs trafficking, let alone partake in it, doesn't ring true.'

'Well, appearances can be deceiving and we need to be sure,' said Kitt. 'Mal's already running Berkeley's financial records now as a favour and he'll be on his way to us shortly. She was the one who sent the letter to Jodie about her expulsion. It's also possible that Berkeley's behind the whole thing and she could have forged the letter from Jodie to make sure Selina took the fall for whatever plan they hatched.'

'But the birthday card Cynthia sent – the handwriting was a match,' said Grace.

'If Berkeley got Selina to write a statement about the fight they had, you can guarantee she did the same to Jodie. She could have used the handwriting in that statement as a model and copied the style into the letter.'

'But it's really difficult to copy someone's handwriting that carefully,' said Patrick. 'And if it was Berkeley, why not just let me take the fall?'

'I – I don't know,' said Kitt. 'It's easy to paint people as monsters in situations like these but maybe something just went wrong and they didn't mean to do whatever they did to Jodie. Maybe she's grown a conscience?'

'Or maybe, like you say, she wanted to pin it all on Selina Grant for some reason we don't yet know about,' said Grace. 'Her job and her reputation are at stake here. That's a lot to lose.

'All I do know is when we get to Berkeley's house, I'm not going to stop asking questions until she tells me the truth. Regardless of what's really going on here, she obviously withheld a huge amount of information when we interviewed her the first time round. It's cost us time and money, and worst of all it has delayed us getting justice for Jodie. I won't let her get away with that again.'

'Have you told the police about Berkeley?' said Patrick.

'Yes,' said Kitt. 'But they think they've got their suspect and an off-the-record insinuation from a student DJ doesn't really count as a development.'

'Fair point,' said Patrick.

'Like any other suspect, we need to have something concrete and indisputable before they can act on it. Once we have at least a confession from Berkeley as to how she's mixed up in all this, I'll come back here to the nick with what I have.'

'Since when do you say "nick"? Halloran's rubbing off on you,' said Grace. Then, on seeing Kitt's unimpressed glare, added: 'Sorry, that sounded better in my head.'

'It's only a fifteen or twenty minute drive to Berkeley's house at Heddon-on-the-Wall so we'll hopefully have something concrete soon enough,' said Kitt. 'I said I would check it out with Mal in tow which is why he's also agreed to meet us at Berkeley's.'

'Well, it won't hurt to have a trained police officer in the room,' said Grace. 'He might just command enough authority to make even Berkeley think twice about lying.'

'Here's hoping,' said Kitt. 'Though if he gets there first you can guarantee he'll go in without us and we'll miss Berkeley's big confession. I love him but he's not a man known for his patience in matters like these, so we'd best get going.'

TWENTY-EIGHT

On any other day, on any other errand, Grace would have found the quaint village of Heddon-on-the-Wall nothing short of heart-warming. Situated a mere nine miles outside the bustle of Newcastle city centre, the village was home to a significant section of Hadrian's Wall; a seventy-three mile dividing line forged of rock that stood in ancient times. In order to break up the uneasy silence during the car ride here, Kitt had dispensed some facts about the village that she deemed of historical and cultural importance. Neither the fact that the village was located on the ruins of an old Roman fort, nor the revelation that the name 'Heddon' translated as 'hill where the heather grew', however, was romantic enough to distract Grace from the fact that they were likely heading into a bitter showdown with Dean Berkeley over her possible involvement in the disappearance of one of her own students.

Kitt parked Halloran's Fiat in the small cul-de-sac. There

HELEN COX

was no sign of his police vehicle so it looked as though they'd arrived first. Climbing out of the car, they made their way towards the driveway for 134 Akenside Crescent.

The crescent was deserted.

Dusk was approaching so everyone was likely inside starting to put the tea on. Very sensible. Much more sensible than putting pressure on a corrupt academy dean to confess their crimes. Despite her small frame, Berkeley was intimidating enough when she had the upper hand. Who knew what she'd do when she was backed into a corner? The only sound Grace was aware of was her own breathing and the crunch of her trainers on gravel. She looked down at the small white pebbles and her breath caught in her throat.

'Kitt,' Grace said.

'What is it?'

'The gravel. I think it's limestone.'

Kitt looked down with a start. 'I think you're right.'

'Why does that matter?' asked Patrick.

'Limestone powder was found in the outhouse where the attackers kept and likely drugged Jodie,' said Grace.

'If Berkeley was involved in Jodie's disappearance she might have transferred the powder off her shoes or clothes,' said Kitt. 'We're going to need to be very careful here. The evidence is mounting against her. We should be OK because we outnumber her but, above all, we need to keep her calm.'

Slowly, the trio kept walking up the path, until Kitt stopped abruptly and held Grace and Patrick back with her arms.

'What's – Oh . . .' Grace said as she noticed the same thing Kitt had.

The front door was ajar.

'That can't be good,' said Grace.

'Agreed. Maybe we should wait for DI Halloran,' Patrick said. 'Going in there doesn't seem like the best plan right now.'

'I don't think we can do that,' Kitt said. 'We're assuming Berkeley is the culprit but there's also a chance that she might be in trouble in there. That someone has come after her. Just stay behind me and if I tell you to run, run and bang on the doors of the nearby houses. Anything to get some more witnesses to the scene as soon as you can.'

Grace swallowed hard as they walked the last few steps up to the door. Kitt prodded it with a gloved finger and it swung open.

Kitt waited a moment, listening. For signs of a struggle perhaps?

'Dean Berkeley,' she called out. 'It's Kitt Hartley. Are you in?'

Kitt stepped over the threshold. Patrick and Grace followed after her.

A dog started barking and all three of them jumped. The barking was coming from one of the rooms further down the passage. By the depth of the bark it was clear it was a big dog and Grace didn't relish the thought of grappling with a ferocious hound on top of everything else. Kitt, a card-carrying cat person, slowed her pace but didn't stop.

'Dean Berkeley?' Kitt repeated again as she glanced into the living room before moving on through the passage towards the barking mutt.

'Dean Ber—' As Kitt peered into the dining room her words cut off.

Taking a deep breath, Grace followed Kitt into the room to see Berkeley lying pale and wide-eyed on the jade carpet. The dog, that Grace had feared would be a snarling Rottweiler, was in fact an over-stuffed basset hound. The poor thing was standing over his late owner, sounding the alarm. On closer inspection, Grace could see a dark stain near Berkeley's head and a ring of red around her neck. Grace noticed a knife in Berkeley's hand, also stained red.

'Oh my God,' Grace said, whipping away from the sight and turning to Patrick who was standing just behind her. She looked up at him and he down at her. That mournful look, that she knew so well now, flared in his eyes.

'Is she . . .' Patrick started, unable to finish.

'She's dead,' Kitt said and then addressing the dog added, 'Easy now, fella.'

Collecting herself, Grace turned back to face the scene in the room. Kitt was crouching near the body and giving the dog a little pat on the head. He began to whine.

'Either she died by suicide or someone wants it to look that way,' said Kitt.

'How can we know for sure?' asked Grace.

'We can't. It's impossible to say anything for sure until the pathologist has been to the scene. But finding the door left open like that is a bit suspicious. Whoever it was wants us to believe that Berkeley slit her own throat and bashed her head as she fell to the ground. But that seems a very graphic way to off yourself when there's probably a car in the garage. Carbon monoxide poisoning is comparably less painful.'

'Nothing like a cosy chat about methods of suicide,' said Grace.

'Sorry,' Kitt said. 'No way to avoid it, I'm afraid.'

'Maybe she left the door open on purpose in the hope that someone would find her quicker?' said Patrick. 'She might have been able to accept death but not the idea of her body lying here undiscovered. Maybe it was a way of signalling something was wrong.'

'Maybe.' Kitt took her phone out of her pocket and started to dial. 'Either way, we've got to be careful not to touch anything – Grace, what did I just say?'

'Sorry,' Grace said, pulling her hand away from a piece of paper sitting on the dining room table. 'I only touched the sides of it. I was very careful.'

'What is it?'

'A note, printed off her computer, I think.'

'Another note. We seem to be getting a lot of these lately. What does this one say?' Kitt said, standing and moving over to the table so she could get a look at the piece of paper.

In silence, Grace, Kitt and Patrick read the last words of Dean Regina Berkeley:

I'm so sorry for the pain I've caused. I know I can never make up for it. As I can't undo the things I did or live with them, ending things here seems the only rational choice left to me. Up until a year ago, I had a good life so I've got to be grateful for that. Since I'm not going to be around to face the consequences, I may as well tell you everything that led me here.

If you haven't already arrested Selina Grant by the time you read this, you need to do that right away. She was the one who pressured me to frame and expel Jodie after she learnt her secret. Jodie confronted me and taped my confession and was going to expose what I'd done. I couldn't bear the thought of losing my job, my house, my reputation. So I killed her.

I still can't believe I did it. Even seeing those words in black and white doesn't make it feel true. It feels like reading about someone else's life. But I did do it. I hit her over the head with my Leaders in Education award and didn't stop until she was gone. I threw the weapon into the lake at the academy.

This was all so unnecessary. If Jodie had just left all this alone, if she'd just left the academy as she was instructed to do, we could all have been saved so much pain. Now, like her, I'll pay the ultimate price.

Patrick's eyes narrowed. 'I thought Jodie's letter said that Selina had kidnapped her but left her alive?'

'It did,' said Grace. 'This is a completely different version of events. And it's not very specific. Berkeley talks about

Jodie finding out about Selina's secret but it doesn't say what that secret is.'

'Also,' said Kitt, 'that dog is very well cared for. Pretty well loved by the cut of him and there's no mention of who should care for him after she's gone.'

'That . . . is a bit weird,' said Grace. 'I don't know what her living arrangements are but if the dog's her only companion you'd think there'd be some mention in there.'

'There's no matching the handwriting on a printed note either,' said Kitt. 'We already know that Selina has more than one secret she wants to hide, so if Berkeley did write this the only way we'd get to the bottom of which secret she was talking about was if Selina confessed.'

'And that doesn't seem very likely. I get the feeling that even with all the evidence against her, her lawyers will encourage her to plead not guilty while they search for some kind of loophole,' said Patrick.

'I suppose the one thing the police could verify is the murder weapon. She says she threw it in the academy lake. If the police dredge it and find nothing then we know this letter is a fake,' said Grace.

'Maybe; finding something in a lake like that can be time-consuming because of all the sediment at the bottom,' said Kitt. 'The police might search for weeks and not find anything.'

'If this letter is real,' said Patrick, 'then that would mean that someone else forged the other letter and that Jodie's . . . really dead.'

'Before we leap to any assumptions we need to know more. We could be looking at a few different possibilities,' said Kitt. 'Yes, one of them is that Jodie didn't write the letter and that it was forged by someone who is yet to be identified. But there's also a chance that the person who killed Berkeley doesn't know about Jodie's letter and just wrote something to frame Berkeley, not realizing that another letter, allegedly from Jodie, was already with the police.'

'So there's still hope?' said Patrick. 'That she's alive, I mean?'

Kitt nodded. 'There is some, but it comes with a caveat, I'm afraid. The fact that we've received two notes in the space of the same day does suggest that they came from the same person. What I'm still trying to figure out is who that person is and which, if either, of the two different versions of this story is the truth?'

TWENTY-NINE

Halloran strode into the living room and closed the door behind him. He'd arrived half an hour ago, just after DC Chalmers who had been dispatched from Durham station after Kitt had called in about the discovery of Berkeley's body.

DC Chalmers was a gentle-spoken Asian lady who had politely insisted that they all wait in the living room for DI Halloran to arrive. Kitt had put up a bit of resistance about this, wanting, as ever, to be at the forefront of the investigation, but ultimately acquiesced when it became clear DC Chalmers was simply too courteous to be argued with.

For her part, Grace had been quite relieved to be moved to another part of the house. Of all the things she'd expected to find at Berkeley's house, somehow her corpse hadn't been one of them and she didn't welcome the prospect of being in the same room as the dead body any longer than she had to be.

'All right, pet,' Halloran said, putting his arms around Kitt. Grace averted her gaze to give them a bit of privacy and focused on Patrick. She had been rubbing the top of his back on and off for the past half hour, trying to comfort him over the fact that they were still in limbo about whether Jodie was dead or alive, but he hadn't said much. The basset hound, who according to his collar was called Roxy – and thus was a she, not a he – sat on Patrick's lap and looked sorrowfully about the room. The poor thing must have watched the whole scene play out. She looked up at Halloran and then put her head back down to her paws.

'What's the verdict then?' said Kitt. 'Is it what it looks like or is there more to it?'

'We've ruled out suicide, but it's a pretty good attempt at faking one,' said Halloran.

'How can you tell that it isn't a suicide?' said Grace, not really sure she wanted the answer. Whenever Kitt had been involved with investigations like this in the past, she had always felt left out when she missed some big excitement. Today she'd learnt not all excitement was the kind you wanted to invite. Every time she closed her eyes she saw Berkeley's staring back at her, cold and empty. Maybe some people would think she had brought it on herself, especially if she was involved in some kind of drugs ring with Selina Grant. But Grace couldn't bring herself to think that way. There were more lasting forms of justice for people like Berkeley than killing them.

'It's a silly little thing that gave it away. The knife in her hand is the wrong way round,' said Halloran. 'If she lifted it to her own throat in the position it's in, then her skin would meet with the blunt side. As she couldn't have rearranged the knife in her own hand after she died, it's clear that somebody else did.'

'But, why would someone take the pains to make it look like Berkeley offed herself, writing a lengthy note implicating her, and then make a mistake like that?' said Kitt. 'Seems like if you're going to go to all that trouble, you'd pay attention to detail.'

'I suspect this lass had a little something to do with it,' Halloran said, rubbing Roxy's head. She sniffed his hand for a moment as if trying to suss Halloran out and then, seemingly deciding he wasn't a threat, nuzzled into him for some more fuss. 'You said she was barking when you came in. The odds are she started when the attacker was here and they were concerned they were going to get caught.'

'If that's the case, she's lucky to be alive,' said Kitt. 'I can't think someone who's willing to off Dean Berkeley would think twice about putting an end to the dog, too, if they got in the way.'

Patrick, as though out of instinct, cuddled the dog closer. Grace reached out and stroked Roxy's soft ears. She didn't want to think about a person ending anyone's life, let alone a defenceless animal.

'I'm sorry to say, there is a chance they didn't leave the dog out of mercy but because they ran out of time to do anything about it,' said Halloran.

'What do you mean?' said Grace.

'I mean, Berkeley has not been dead very long. Which means you must have found her pretty quickly after the attack took place. Possibly a matter of minutes.'

'Mal, you're not suggesting . . . the killer could have still been here when we arrived?'

'Oh my God,' Grace said, shuddering. 'Tell me that's not true or I'm never going to be able to sleep again.'

'There is a chance that they heard you enter and left through the back door before you could see them.'

'Good God,' said Kitt, raising a hand to her chest. 'That's a reminder not to do any door-to-door investigating on my own. The only reason they probably didn't come at us is because we were in a group.'

'There's a reason why the police make house calls in pairs, you know,' said Halloran.

'Wait a minute,' said Grace. 'If Selina's in custody right now then she couldn't be responsible for Berkeley's death, could she?'

'Not directly,' said Halloran. 'But people like that don't do their own dirty work. She will have an accomplice, or at the very least a gun for hire.'

'But she would have had to arrange it before she was arrested,' said Grace. 'Is that likely?'

'The likelihood is, Selina had some kind of contingency in place in case she was arrested and went to prison. If they are a professional, the odds of us finding any DNA evidence on Berkeley's body are slim. Those kinds of individuals know what they're doing and are very tricky to catch.'

'But the note on Berkeley's table implicated Selina anyway,' said Kitt. 'Why would she order Berkeley killed and then implicate herself in the note?'

'The note implicates her as someone who "pressured" Berkeley to expel a student. This is underhand behaviour but a private academy's dealings are their own. It's not a legal matter. The note makes it clear that Berkeley took matters into her own hands, independently of any pressure Selina may have applied. Thus, Selina's lawyers might argue that Selina was framed by Berkeley before her crisis of conscience and suicide, and that's how evidence showed up at her home and locker.'

'Do you know exactly what kind of evidence they found to incriminate Selina?' Kitt asked.

'Apparently, bottles of chloroform and GHB.'

'Does that outright prove she had something to do with Jodie's disappearance?' said Grace.

'Given the discovery of those rags at the outhouse it goes a long way, but there's more,' said Halloran. He looked at Patrick before speaking again. 'The cardigan you said Jodie was wearing the day she disappeared. They found it in Selina's wardrobe. And it was speckled with blood.'

'Is it Jodie's blood?' said Patrick.

'We haven't confirmed it yet,' Halloran said. 'But I'm afraid, given that it's her garment and she's been missing for some time, we suspect so.'

'Wait, whereabouts did they find the cardigan in Selina's wardrobe?' said Grace.

'I'm not sure. Is it important?' said Halloran.

'It might be,' said Grace. 'I've been in that wardrobe, remember? At Selina's party I spent a fair amount of time rooting around. I didn't see the cardigan and I was actively looking for incriminating stuff. I knew what colours the fibres were but I didn't notice a cardigan of that colour. That seems unlikely, doesn't it?'

'Maybe you were too flustered to notice it,' said Kitt. 'Doing that kind of snooping does tend to get the adrenalin going and you didn't know exactly what you were looking for.'

'Maybe,' said Grace, biting her lip.

'What? What is it?' said Kitt.

'It's just that the notes we received had conflicting information in them but both implicated Selina. And now this cardigan turns up that I saw no sign of when I searched her property. Halloran said Selina's lawyers might argue she's a scapegoat for somebody, maybe they'd be right. Or, given the conflicting information, maybe more than one somebody?'

'How would that even work?' said Halloran. 'Why would more than one person be trying to frame Selina?'

'I don't know,' Grace admitted. 'But I do know one thing: with Selina currently in custody there's still at least one killer still out there.'

THIRTY

There was a moment's silence while everyone in the room digested Grace's comment. It was the buzzing of Halloran's mobile that at last broke the quiet.

'Banks,' Halloran said, as he answered the call from his partner back in York. 'What do you know?' There was a pause. 'Oh really? When? Well, that's a break. Yes, all right. Thanks.'

Halloran hung up the phone and stood thoughtfully for a moment.

'Well, don't keep us in suspense, Mal. Howay, out with it.'

'I apologize for taking a moment to think,' Halloran said.

'I suppose you're forgiven,' Kitt said with a small smile.

'Very magnanimous. I asked Banks to do a bit more digging into Berkeley's finances for us and it looks increasingly as though she did have something to do with Jodie's disappearance.'

'But I thought the police already looked into her finances and didn't find anything,' said Grace.

'When they looked it wouldn't have seemed like anything out of the ordinary and Berkeley could probably have easily explained it away. She was receiving cash payments into her account but they weren't large. They were between £500 and £1000. The first one was made two months before Jodie disappeared. There was a pause after that, presumably while she was under investigation by the police. They resumed three months after Jodie's disappearance and stopped about six months later. The payments totalled £10,000.'

'Well, that pretty much confirms that that suicide note isn't worth the paper it was printed on,' said Grace.

'You're right,' said Kitt. 'Selina and Jodie hadn't even met a month before she disappeared so if that payment does relate to Jodie's disappearance, it doesn't corroborate the idea that Selina put pressure on Berkeley or bribed her in some way to expel Jodie. In fact, it pretty much dashes most of the details in Berkeley's alleged suicide note.'

'Ten thousand pounds though,' said Grace. 'That might be enough to bribe a person to expel a student, but to make them disappear or kill them? I imagine the asking price would be much higher.'

'You might be right on that score but that's not the end of the story,' said Halloran. 'The money paid to Berkeley was deposited in cash through the same ATM machine and we've got a snap of the guy who deposited it from the security camera.'

'Even from three months ago?' said Kitt.

'Financial institutions tend to keep their security footage for longer because of issues like money laundering. Most operations like that are going on a lot longer before they're stopped. Banks has sent me a copy of the picture. This could be a picture of the person who made Jodie disappear.'

Halloran swiped his phone screen and tapped the message. 'Yep. Looks to me like your mysterious man in black isn't a figment of your imagination after all.'

Halloran turned his phone screen to Patrick.

'Oh my God,' he said, frowning. 'That's him, and without the sunglasses I recognize him now. He worked for my mum. Years ago. He was her head of security at her furniture factory.'

'It also fits the description of the man Selina caught at her party. She's probably got video footage of him accessing the property, hopefully she's handed it to DI Thompson by now.'

'Did this man lose his job when your mum became a lady of leisure?' Kitt asked. 'Maybe he's never got over losing his job and is trying to find ways of tormenting you and your family.'

'Although that doesn't really account for the death of Berkeley,' said Grace.

Patrick shook his head. 'She let him go long before she retired. But there may be something in your theory. She didn't say anything outright but she hinted once or twice that he was intense, you know. I think he might have overstepped with her a couple of times.'

279

'Overstepped in what way?' asked Halloran.

'I don't know, I just got the impression that something went down between them. I was only young at the time so I knew if I asked I wouldn't get any straight answers.'

'Do you know his name or any other details about him?' said Halloran.

'It was so long ago. But I think his last name was Marks. Mr Marks. Though I could be misremembering. I'm sorry, I don't remember anything else.'

'That's all right. We'll question your mum as soon as possible and I'll send that name to Banks and see if it brings up any leads.'

'Wait . . . if this guy's involved with this and he's got some kind of grudge against Mum, she could be in danger – or worse,' said Patrick. 'He killed Berkeley, and she could be next.'

'Do you know where your mother is now?' Halloran said, a note of urgency in his voice.

'Last I heard she was on her way here but even with traffic it doesn't take that long to get here from Chester-le-Street. She should already be here.'

Frantically, Patrick whipped out his phone and dialled.

'Put her on speaker, will you?' said Halloran. 'If there's anything important going on at the other end of that line we need to hear it too. She's probably not in danger but if she is we might get some clues from listening in.'

Patrick obliged. The phone rang out in the otherwise

silent living room. Then there was a scratching sound as the call connected.

'Mum, where are you?'

'I'm still on my way to Berkeley's, love. Terrible traffic,' Cynthia's voice rang out.

Patrick's posture visibly relaxed. 'Thank God you're all right.'

'Why wouldn't I be?'

'It's Dean Berkeley, Mum. She's . . . she's dead.'

'Dead? Oh my God, wh-what happened?' said Cynthia. 'I thought Selina Grant had been arrested. Did her people get to Berkeley somehow?'

'You probably don't want all the gory details, to be honest, but we came to her house to question her over Jodie's disappearance and found her dead.'

'My poor lad. That must have been so horrible for you. Wrongfully arrested for murder and now this. I'll be with you very soon. I'm just another twenty minutes away.'

But even as she said this there was a strange, high-pitched buzzing sound in the background.

'Mum, what's that noise?' said Patrick.

'A siren passing by.'

But then a familiar but robotic voice said: 'This station is Tynemouth. This train is for all stations to Northumberland airport.'

Patrick's frown deepened. His voice shook as he spoke. 'Mum, why are you on the airport train?'

There was no sound at the other end of the call. Kitt, Halloran and Grace all exchanged a frown.

'Mum? Answer me. Why are you on that train?'

'I . . .'

'Mum?'

'I'm . . . so sorry, Patrick. It wasn't supposed to end like this.'

With that the line went dead.

THIRTY-ONE

'I know what you're all thinking,' Patrick said as the sirens on Halloran's police car wailed out all around them.

Roxy, who was still sitting on Patrick's lap, had let out the occasional discontented groan, but otherwise nobody else had said much at all since it became clear that a man who used to work for Cynthia Howard had been the one to pay off Berkeley. Not to mention the fact that Patrick's subsequent phone call to his mother had revealed her to be on her way to Northumberland airport, seemingly in a bid to make some kind of getaway.

'We don't know the full story yet,' Grace said, trying to convince herself that was the case even though it seemed pretty obvious to anyone that Cynthia had known what happened to Jodie all along, and likely had some hand in it. That said, there were still definitely some pieces of the jigsaw that didn't fit, as far as Grace could figure them, so maybe there was some strange and unexpected explanation.

But then, why hadn't Cynthia just explained what was going on down the phone? When her son was desperately holding on for answers? The only conclusion Grace could come to was that Cynthia had done some things she was ashamed of and couldn't bring herself to confess them to her son.

'No, but one way or another you think Mum's been up to no good,' Patrick said.

'If you can't think of any motive she'd have for wanting to get Jodie out of the picture, then there's probably a reasonable explanation,' said Kitt, eyeing Patrick in the rear-view mirror.

Patrick shrugged. 'Nothing that would be worth all this.'

'So . . . there was something?' Grace said, as gently as she could. Patrick had been through an incredible amount in the last twenty-four hours, never mind the last year, and the last thing he needed right now was accusations. More than anything, Grace didn't want him to feel alone in this. No matter what his mother had done.

'I suppose, looking back, she . . . never really warmed to Jodie. Once or twice Jodie mentioned that she had been off-hand with her. I always challenged her about it when she did, and after a few times she seemed to back off. She would've preferred me to marry another rich kid. But it was just typical protective mother stuff – nobody ever being good enough for their son. Nothing more than that. It's not the kind of thing that makes you go out and abduct someone and make them disappear. Surely everyone here can agree that is not proportional behaviour?'

'Certainly, your mother's never given any indication that she would make an overreaction like that,' Kitt conceded. 'But can you remember how she reacted to your engagement to Jodie?' Grace noticed that Kitt was doing all she could to keep her voice soft, just as she had a moment ago. Talking to Patrick just then felt like trying to talk someone down off a ledge. She got the feeling he was on the brink of a major meltdown, and given the circumstances, who could blame him? The best thing they could do was try and keep him calm.

'She, well, she wasn't happy at first. But then, I don't know, she seemed to accept it,' said Patrick. 'She was talking about taking Jodie out shopping for a dress and started sending her links to venues and caterers. She really got into the spirit of it. I thought she'd just got over her initial concern.'

'Roughly how long were you and Jodie engaged before she disappeared?' asked Halloran, as he indicated for the airport turn-off.

'Let's see. We went to Berlin in late July. Proposed by the Spree. I remember the sky was such a deep blue, it made the river look bluer than usual. We couldn't find anywhere selling champagne so we bought ice creams to celebrate.'

'Sounds very romantic,' said Grace.

'It does that, and late July . . . that would mean you

proposed just over two months before Jodie disappeared,' said Kitt.

Grace pressed her lips together. Two months. So that's why Halloran had asked Patrick about the time frame. Could that really be a coincidence? Patrick gets engaged and then the dean, who heads up the academy Jodie is due to start studying with, receives a cash payment as a fee for expelling her on false grounds. Surely, even though it was the last thing he wanted to believe, Patrick could see that the sequence of events didn't reflect well on his mother?

Patrick swallowed hard. 'You think Mum changed her attitude about the engagement because she was paying off Berkeley to expel Jodie? To what, try and break us up?'

'It's a possibility that you shouldn't dismiss,' said Kitt. 'I'm not saying that your mother meant any real harm. She likely would have done it from the perspective of a caring parent looking out for her son. You were very young to be engaged, in most people's eyes, you said it yourself. Your mother might have just thought she was protecting you from a mistake you'd later come to regret. But if that is what she did, I think we can agree that something has gone terribly wrong.'

Patrick nodded. 'At the absolute extreme, I suppose I can imagine a moment of motherly insanity where she could've tried to pay off Berkeley but all the other stuff – Jodie's disappearance, Berkeley's death – Mum just wouldn't get involved in something like that. She's not . . . like that.'

'We all want to believe the best and we'll know soon enough what's been going on,' said Halloran as he pulled the car up in the closest space to the airport entrance and switched off the sirens. Up ahead the terminal building loomed in the darkness. The green illuminated signage somehow had an eerie look about it. Grace had always found airports strange non-spaces. A sort of place between places where everything was in flux and nothing was steady or certain. Now she had one more reason not to be fond of them. Whatever happened in the next half hour, the news was unlikely to be good.

'If she was at Tynemouth when she rang, she won't quite have arrived here yet,' said Halloran, snapping Grace out of her thoughts. 'We should be able to head her off before she goes through security. We've got the airport police looking out for her on the other side just in case. To be clear, you are here for lookout purposes only. If you see the subject, do not approach her. Kitt, did you hear that?'

'I'm sure I don't know why you're singling me out,' said Kitt.

Halloran stared hard at her.

'Yes, all right, message received.'

'Patrick, I know she's your mother but the no-contact rule includes you. We can't take any risks until we know what's really going on here. It's going to be tempting to approach if you see her so are you sure you wouldn't rather wait in the car for this?'

Patrick shook his head. 'I can't just sit here while you all go in. I said I'd see this investigation through, no matter where it went, and that's what I'm going to do. She's my mum. If something serious goes down I need to be there.'

Halloran nodded, unbuckled his seatbelt and opened the car door. Patrick opened the door at his side and unravelled Roxy's lead. Apparently Patrick and Roxy were not going to be easily separated. Grace wondered if perhaps she'd make a good guard dog if they stumbled into jeopardy, or even help them sniff out the criminals? As Grace watched the pudgy pooch waddle its way around just outside the car door, however, all such hopes evaporated. Well, at least she'd be soothing company for Patrick in what was likely to be a difficult time.

Grace slid out of the car herself and noticed her hands were shaking. She shoved them into her pockets before anyone else could notice, did her best to steady them and tried to make a possible list of all the explanations in her head for everything that had happened, besides the most obvious: that Patrick's mother was a conspirator in a double murder.

THIRTY-TWO

Grace and Kitt were first to the airport entrance. Yanking open the door, they dashed in, followed closely by Halloran and Patrick, with Roxy in tow.

On entering, Grace wasn't sure how they had any hope of finding Cynthia given the sheer number of people zooming about. After a quick scan of the crowds, however, Halloran strode towards a uniformed airport security officer and flashed his badge. 'DI Halloran from York police station. We've phoned through already about Cynthia Howard who is under suspicion of several serious crimes. Her passport has been flagged and her photograph circulated. Can you radio through and find out if she's being detained anywhere? It'd make my job a lot easier if you've already picked her up.'

The officer, seemingly unimpressed by Halloran's subtle attempt at lightening the mood, nodded without dispensing any pleasantries and then spoke straight into his radio. 'Come in, control.'

'*You've reached control, over,*' said a woman's voice on the other end of the line.

'Can you check if a Cynthia Howard is in custody. Apparently we've got her flagged on the system already.'

There was a moment of scratchy silence before the reply came through. '*Nobody in custody, slow night.*'

'All right, thanks,' said Halloran. 'I'm going to take a look around for her. I might need your assistance, depending on how things go.'

'I'll be here,' the officer said.

Halloran half-smiled. It was clear Halloran wasn't any more impressed by the officer's attitude than the officer was by Halloran. 'If she's not in custody already, that means she shouldn't get further than the check-in desk, if we don't find her first. Fan out. We need to get a good look along these check-in queues so . . . what's that look for?'

'Does everyone else hear "Buttons" by the Pussycat Dolls accompanied by faint screaming?' Kitt said, her nose crinkling.

They all frowned and then turned towards the source of the noise. A small corner of the departures lounge had been screened off. There was a woman standing outside the area with a collection tin, which she was rattling intermittently.

'Oh aye, some young men from the check-in desks are doing a striptease for Cancer Research,' said the officer, much more animated than he was when Halloran was trying to get information out of him about a potential flight risk.

'They're over there right now tearing off Velcro pilot uni-forms. I was asked to take part but declined. Didn't want to make those young 'uns feel bad.'

Grace looked at the man and hoped her disgust at the mere thought of him taking his clothes off didn't show too much. It wasn't anything particularly physical about him – though she suspected the greasy layer of sweat didn't stop at his neckline – it was more the attitude that put her off. Usually people with that level of arrogance had a patented unsexy dance move they thought they could pull off when everyone else knew they couldn't.

'I wonder if Cynthia is hiding out in there,' Kitt said, pointing over at the screened-off area. 'Can't hurt to take a quick look just to be sure.'

'Oh no you don't,' said Halloran with a note of amuse-ment in his voice. 'If anyone's going to poke their head in there it will be me and it will be brief.'

'But isn't Kitt more qualified? She does have a personal experience in stripping,' said Grace. She knew they didn't have time for banter but when was she ever going to get an opportunity like this to casually drop into conversation that Kitt had been caught streaking across the academy football pitch?

'What's this?' said Halloran, looking Kitt up and down.

'Oh, ignore her, will you?' Kitt said with a dismissive wave. 'And Grace, for goodness' sake, give over. Finding Cynthia is our priority, not making silly jokes.'

'I know, I know,' said Grace.

'Right,' said Halloran, still looking a little bit unsettled by Grace's joke but clearly deciding there were bigger matters to attend to. 'Start taking a look up and down these queues, I'll just verify that she isn't hiding in that charity event. You could help us with the search as well, if you want,' Halloran said, addressing the officer.

'Suppose I could,' he replied.

Halloran turned and started walking away but as he did so Grace heard him mutter under his breath, 'Don't do us any favours, will you, mate? There's only a bloody murderer on the loose.'

Grace smiled to herself at Halloran's dig but her smile soon vanished as she, Patrick and Kitt made plans to split up. They selected a couple of check-in queues apiece and set off on their search for Cynthia. The plan was to regroup as soon as they'd finished their surveillance of everyone in line.

To begin with, Grace started looking for a blonde woman but then wondered if Cynthia would use some kind of wig or other disguise to try and go undetected. That would present a problem if she was using her own passport, and that's when she realized that the passport checks Halloran had set up might be useless. Cynthia wasn't as rich as Selina Grant but she wasn't poor either. She probably had the money to secure a fake passport if she needed to and Grace couldn't believe that Cynthia had just made the decision on the spot to make a run for Northumberland airport. The likelihood was this had been on her last-resort list for some time. Grace's heart quickened as she suddenly understood how imperative it was that they find Cynthia before she passed through airport security.

Looking along the row, Grace passed numerous families, one or two with an exhausted-looking mother holding a child who had fallen asleep on their shoulder. There were several men in suits, likely flying back home after some kind of business meeting, and given that it was Saturday night, Grace could only assume they were workaholics. Who's flying around having business meetings on a weekend? But none of the people in the first queue, from the young woman listening to her music so loud that everyone within five metres of her could feel the beat, to an elderly tanned couple probably heading off for some winter sun, were Cynthia.

Sighing, Grace moved onto the next, taking the time to look carefully at each face she passed. She reasoned it wouldn't seem too weird to the people in the queue. They probably just thought she was looking for family members or perhaps a boyfriend she was flying out with. With every face, however, came disappointment. Grace was almost at the end of her second queue and was on the brink of heading back to regroup and see if the others had had any luck when all of a sudden someone grabbed her arm and she felt something sharp jab into her side.

'If you so much as squeak I'll stab you where you stand,' said a deep, gravelly voice. Grace glanced down at the hand that held her and saw the sleeve of a black coat.

The man in black.

He'd found her.

'If she's here, she won't be alone,' said another voice. A woman's voice, Cynthia's.

'Who've you got with you?' the man in black muttered.

'Nobody,' said Grace, wishing her voice wasn't wavering quite so much.

'You're lying.' The knife dug deeper into Grace's side and though she tried to shuffle away the man's grip held her in place. If he pressed any harder he was going to break skin for sure. 'Tell me who else is here, or I'll gut you.'

Grace would have thought she'd be a lot braver in a situation like this one. She liked adventure. Got a kick out of being impulsive. But right now all she could think about was Berkeley's body, lying with her throat cut on her dining room floor. Grace couldn't be sure but she would wager that was the man in black's handiwork. She believed him when he said he would gut her and as Randy Hobbs would say, being alive is a good thing. In a small, resigned voice Grace replied, 'Kitt and Halloran are here.'

'The copper,' said the man in black, gruffly.

'Patrick's here too,' Grace said, keeping her breathing shallow to avoid the prick of the knife tip. The man in black must have been camouflaging it under his coat somehow,

as nobody around them was paying any attention whatsoever to what was going on. 'He's worried about you, Cynthia.
His first thought when he found Berkeley was for your
safety. He just wants to see you. To talk to you. To try and
understand.'

There was a moment of silence before the man in black's
rough response. 'If she's brought the whole gang with her
the odds of us leaving on a plane are slim. We'll have to
move to plan B.' He pushed Grace forward. 'Start moving
towards the exit and act natural. If you do anything to raise
the alarm, that's the end of you.'

Swallowing hard, Grace did as she was told and started
moving towards the exit. With every step she could feel
the knife in her side. Was this what happened to Jodie? she
wondered as tears filled her eyes. Did the drugging only
come later? Had the man in black marched her down the
river path like this and then killed her the first chance he
had? The very thought that she could suffer the same fate
as Jodie, lost without a trace, made Grace sick to her
stomach.

She needed to find a way out of this, but couldn't think
of one. Kitt and Halloran would hear her if she screamed
out, she was sure of it, but would they be quick enough to
come to her aid before the man in black put an end to her?
She might not know exactly what she wanted to do with
her life yet but she would like to be around long enough to
feel out a few options. There was other stuff too. Stuff she'd

been planning to do once she had the basics of home and work in order. She wanted to see the sunset over the Golden Gate Bridge; to sail to Iceland and marvel at the Northern Lights; and to fall in love. Properly fall in love with someone who meant it when they kissed you. She guessed Jodie must have had those plans too, before they were cut short.

The sound of a dog barking jolted her out of her thoughts.

'Grace?'

She heard Patrick's voice calling but didn't dare turn to face him. The man in black dug the knife in harder, prompting her to move faster.

'Grace! Mum!' Patrick shouted. It was clear from the ragged nature of the call that he was running after them. Roxy was going nuts. Probably because she recognized the man in black from her earlier encounter with him back at Berkeley's house.

'Stop that man,' came Halloran's thundering call, audible even over the many conversations people were having. 'Stop them!' he called again, just as the man in black hustled Grace out of the door and into the airport car park.

The October chill hit her the second she was outside, though she wasn't sure if she'd already been shaking.

'Get your legs moving,' said the man in black, lapsing into a run. 'If you want to still be here tomorrow you'll move faster than that.'

In less than a minute they stopped next to a green Honda Civic. 'Get in,' the man snapped.

'Don't bother getting in, Grace, they're not taking you anywhere,' said Halloran's voice. There was a mere split second of relief before the man in black whipped round and the next thing Grace felt was a knife at her throat.

THIRTY-THREE

Wide-eyed, Grace stared at the circle of faces surrounding her. Kitt, Halloran and Patrick were all frozen to the spot. They were joined by their reluctant ally, the airport officer from earlier who, given the serious expression on his face, was rather wishing he'd taken Halloran a bit more seriously. Roxy was still barking incessantly; clearly she wasn't going to be content until she'd barked herself hoarse.

The depth of Halloran's frown confirmed to Grace what she suspected when she'd first felt metal graze her skin: that the man in black had angled the knife in such a way that one swift, sudden movement would be all it took to end her.

'This whole thing is over,' said Halloran. 'Airport police have been alerted and back-up is on its way. We can see the vehicle you're planning to get away in so tracking you down will be no problem. You've already got blood on your hands, I wouldn't make it any worse for yourself by hurting anyone else if I were you.'

'Well, you're not me,' said the man in black. 'We're leaving and if any of you even think of coming after us I will slit her throat in a moment.'

Grace felt the blade start to push harder against her skin and cried out. She wasn't ready to die. She couldn't die, not like this. Not when she was on terrible terms with her whole family. If she died and they never settled the argument, they'd never forgive themselves. An image of her mother's face formed in Grace's mind. Out of nowhere she could see her mother teaching her how to count on the abacus. And taking a zillion photographs on her phone when she graduated from the Vale of York University. All of a sudden, all she could think about was how proud her mother was of her. How much she wanted the best for her, even if she had a funny way of showing it. If she could just talk to her one last time, she could tell her that.

'And then what?' said Kitt. 'If you kill Grace – her name's Grace, by the way, and she's a mere twenty-two years old – then you'll have no leverage and the police will come after you anyway. Is it really worth cutting yet another life short when there's no escaping the inevitable?'

'We'll be long gone by then.'

'It's no good, Quentin,' said Cynthia. 'We're not going to get away. Not this time.'

'Shut up,' Quentin snarled. 'If you hadn't let that stupid little bitch record your confession, none of this would have happened in the first place and I wouldn't have to clean up your mess.'

'Don't you dare try and pin this on me,' Cynthia said, outraged. 'You're the one who kidnapped her.'

'And you're the one who killed her!' Quentin spat.

Seizing the moment while Quentin was distracted by Cynthia's unexpected verbal attack, Grace gripped his arm with all her might and started pushing the knife away.

'Don't you dare, you little . . .' but it was too late. On seeing Grace was momentarily out of immediate peril, Halloran dived towards Quentin and grabbed his knife arm. There was a struggle, but between them, Halloran and Grace managed to relieve Quentin of his knife. Now unarmed, Quentin started to lash out with his fists. Halloran deflected the punches and delivered two of his own to Quentin's face. He didn't go down but the hits were strong enough to disorientate him, and Halloran took the opportunity to restrain him.

'You can give me a hand anytime,' Halloran said to the airport officer.

'Oh, right, aye,' he said, walking over and helping Halloran with the cuffs.

Grace stepped back from the fray, panting hard, knife in hand.

'I'll take that,' Kitt said, pulling a plastic bag from her satchel and dropping the knife inside.

No sooner had Halloran and the officer restrained Quentin than Patrick called out.

'Mum! No!'

Cynthia was trying to make a run for it in the kerfuffle.

How she thought she was going to get away on foot was beyond Grace but it seemed there was no logic left. Only desperation. Patrick caught her in just a few moments, grabbed her by the arms and shook her. 'Did you kill Jodie?'

'Patrick, don't, I —'

'Did you? Did you kill her?'

'Yes! But I didn't mean to. She was dead in an instant. She didn't suffer. I —'

'How could you? Why did you do this?'

'She wasn't good enough for you. You weren't supposed to be with her. She was . . . poor and badly dressed and . . . a mechanic. I couldn't just let you settle for that. You were far too young to get married. You were making a mistake. But . . . she wasn't supposed to die. She was never supposed to die.'

'Shut up!' Patrick shouted back at her, before staggering backward as though he'd been punched in the face.

Halloran looked the airport officer up and down.

'Here, think you can look after this one?' He nodded at two more officers walking towards them from the main entrance. 'It looks as though your colleagues have finally roused so they'll be able to help you. I'll be back to caution him once I've secured the other one.'

Grace watched as Halloran strode over to Cynthia.

'Will handcuffs be necessary?'

Cynthia looked at Patrick and then back at Halloran; slowly, she shook her head.

'Cynthia Howard, you are under arrest for the murder of Jodie Perkins and conspiracy to murder Regina Berkeley,' Halloran said, starting the caution speech that had become familiar to Grace over the time Kitt had started investigating murders. There was a strange relief in hearing it. Though often coupled with an unspeakable sadness about the fact that somebody had taken it upon themselves to end the life of another, it also meant that the culprit had been found. That the killing was over and justice would hopefully be served.

Halloran began to lead Cynthia back towards Quentin, who he then proceeded to caution. Glancing over, Grace noticed Patrick was looking unsteady on his feet. She went over to him.

'Patrick – are you . . .'

But before Grace could even finish her question, before he could verbally respond, Patrick fell to his knees on the uneven tarmac and pushed his head against Grace's tummy.

'She's gone,' he began to sob. 'She's really gone. I'm never going to see her again.'

Not knowing what else to say and at once understanding that nothing she could say would bring Jodie back to life or undo his mother's betrayal, Grace did the only thing she could think of. She stroked Patrick's dark hair and pressed his head close to her, as though that alone would be enough to shield him from any further pain.

THIRTY-FOUR

Grace sat out on the twelfth floor balcony of the Ryedale Hotel in York, overlooking the Ouse. Glancing inside, through the glass door she'd left ajar, she checked to see Patrick was still wrapped up in bed, sleeping. Satisfied that he hadn't stirred, she opened her laptop and dialled into a Zoom call. Within moments, a familiar face flashed up on the screen.

'Hi, Selina,' Grace said, her voice wavering. 'How are you?'

Grace had been surprised when Selina had sent her a text message asking for a video call. After what had passed between them before she was taken into police custody, Grace didn't think she would ever get to speak to her again.

'I'm . . . better. Glad the whole Jodie affair has been put to rest,' she said with a small smile.

'I'm with you on that,' said Grace. 'But I am sorry that to get to the truth I had to deceive you. People probably look

303

at you and just see the money you have but you've got a lot going on that they don't know about and it was never my intention to add to that. Me and Kitt, we just wanted to get to the truth.'

'I know,' said Selina. 'I can't pretend I wasn't angry when I found out but if it weren't for you and Kitt I might have gone down for Jodie's disappearance, and possibly her murder. The police had all that evidence against me, more than enough to convict, and if you hadn't found out what was really going on, well, I'm not even sure the family law-yers could have got me out of that one.'

'So . . . you forgive us?'

'Let's say, I think the good deed cancels out the bad.'

Grace nodded. She couldn't expect full forgiveness from Selina, she knew that. The poor woman not only had to hide who she truly was but had been abused by a family member because of it. Her trust was understandably hard to win and although she and Kitt had had the best of intentions, some-times you don't get to the truth without some fallout.

'If there's ever anything I can do to help you win that financial independence you were talking about,' said Grace, 'please let me know. I don't want to think of you stuck in this situation for ever.'

'I will,' she said. 'How's Patrick?'

Grace glanced back to the hotel room to check he couldn't hear the conversation but he was still buried beneath a thick duvet.

'I don't know,' she said. 'It's a lot. Things have come out about his mother, and the man she was working with – Quentin.'

'I did read something online, about them working together at her company years ago and being responsible for an employee's death?'

Grace took a deep breath, suddenly feeling quite sick. Though that letter from Jodie had been a forgery by Cynthia, there was one ring of truth to it. The worst thing about this whole mess, aside from the bitter truth that Jodie was truly gone, was the impact it had had, and would continue to have, on the people Jodie loved. Halloran had gone with DI Thompson to break the news to Jodie's parents. They were understandably devastated to at last receive final confirmation that their daughter would never be coming home. Grace could only hope that by uncovering the truth they had granted them some closure on the matter. They would be able to conduct a funeral and though they would never move on from a loss like that, they could give Jodie a proper farewell.

As for Patrick, it had been bad enough for him that his mother and Quentin's misdeeds went back years, but for it all to be made public so that the world could judge them – and him – was even worse.

'Yes, there was some accident around the sawmill in Cynthia's furniture factory that should never happened. It was negligence on both Quentin and Cynthia's part but they covered it up and said all the safety measures had been in place but the employee hadn't taken the proper precautions. They parted ways professionally soon after but have of course been at each other's mercy ever since. Cynthia told Quentin if he didn't help her with the situation she was facing with Jodie then she would turn them in to the police over the accident that happened years ago.'

Selina shook her head. 'Poor Patrick, to find all of this out about your mum must be . . . unbearable.'

'I've largely kept him off the internet, to be honest. I'm feeding him information in small nuggets so he has some hope of . . . metabolizing them. But it's a disturbingly tangled web. We could barely make out which way was up when we were trying to untangle it, to be honest. Which is part of why we went to the lengths we did with our undercover work.'

'Well, I handed the CCTV footage over to the police that shows Quentin on the premises on the night of the party, so they've got evidence that he had opportunity to plant Jodie's things in my house . . . though I try not to think about that too much. The idea of that cardigan, covered in blood, just hanging there in my wardrobe . . . I watched them carry out the search. It was right at the back. I never would have found it on my own. It must have been hanging there since the party. And I had no idea . . .'

Grace's eyes filled with tears. She could barely bring herself to think about it either. When all this began she had some naive hope that there was a chance they would find Jodie alive. More than anything, she'd wanted to be able to bring a lost daughter back home. And now, even though they had caught the killers, there was no hope of that. It was a bitter pill to swallow and a fact that would prey on Grace's mind for some time.

'Oh, sorry,' said Selina, wiping a tear away. 'I've set myself off. It's just not fair, you know. She had her whole life ahead of her and it happens to so many young women.'

'I know,' Grace said with a sniff, while wondering if there was something she could do about the injustice. Though she hadn't told Kitt yet, she'd already made the decision that she wasn't going to continue on the library studies course at Venerable Bede's. After all that had happened, she just . . . couldn't. And she hadn't been able to save Jodie, but maybe if she chose some other walk of life there were other people she could help.

'I suppose it's just a reminder to live life to the full while we can,' said Selina, slicing through Grace's thoughts.

'I think you've already got that covered, haven't you?' said Grace, trying to lighten the mood after their emotional moment. 'I don't think I've known anyone as keen on death-defying feats as you.'

'Maybe, but I like to think there are other ways to feel alive besides jumping out of an aeroplane.'

'So do I, because you'll never catch me doing that!'

The pair chuckled.

'What time is it?' Patrick called from the bedroom, just loud enough for Grace to hear.

'Patrick's awake,' Grace said, 'I'd best sign off for now.'

'All right.'

'But, Selina? I may not be your new best friend any more, especially after everything that's happened, but stay in touch, won't you?'

'It's a deal,' Selina said, offering a small smile before ending the Zoom call.

THIRTY-FIVE

Grace turned from her seat on the balcony to see Patrick rubbing his eyes and squinting towards the light shining through the door. Slowly, she closed the laptop and went inside.

'It's nearly half twelve. I need to go and meet Kitt shortly,' she said.

Patrick's only response was to open his arms to her, inviting her back into the warmth after her spell out in the crisp October day.

She gladly accepted the invitation and stretched out on the bed.

Patrick wrapped his arms around her and laid his head on her tummy. It had been three days since his mother had admitted to murdering Jodie in the car park at Northumberland airport, and for most of those three days he hadn't left his bed.

Understandably, he hadn't wanted to go back to Durham

with everything so raw. Neither did he want to be alone. Grace was grateful for that last part. There was only so much trauma one person could take and she preferred to be with him so she could keep watch, make sure he didn't overthink anything, and most importantly didn't get to a point where he was struggling to find reasons why he should keep on living.

Though not aesthetically dissimilar to Durham, Patrick decided that York was just about far enough away from all that had happened and so booked himself into the Ryedale Hotel for the next week. He had slept for most of the three days, eating only when Grace really pushed the matter. He just lay there and let Grace hold him while he cried.

'Thank you,' he said, as she stroked his hair. 'For letting me . . . for holding me like this.'

'Yeah,' Grace said, 'because holding hot, tortured boys is a real hardship. How will I ever cope?'

He lifted his head so that his chin rested on her tummy and looked up at her. She couldn't be entirely certain but she thought she could see the ghost of a smile on his face. That was a start.

'Is Kitt going to update on you on the case when you see her?'

'Probably,' Grace said. 'Although she was being a bit funny on the phone. She seemed sort of weirdly excited . . . giddy almost. Which is not a word I thought I'd ever use to describe her.'

'No. Me neither. I've only met her a handful of times but she doesn't strike me as the giddy type.' He paused before speaking again. 'You already know more than you've told me, don't you? About what Mum did.'

'Every girl has her secrets.'

'Grace . . .'

'Oh, all right. Nothing gets past you . . . or my parents, or Kitt for that matter. It seems I am doomed to be surrounded by people who know my tells.'

A small light shone in Patrick's eyes at her protest but the light disappeared again in an instant.

'I need to know.'

Grace pursed her lips. 'When I was on the phone to Kitt yesterday, she did update me on a few things that have come to light, yes.'

'Tell me.'

'Are you sure you're ready to hear? Couldn't it wait till I get back from seeing Kitt? So I can be here.'

'I can handle it.'

Grace took a deep breath. Where to start? 'Well, the main riddle that's been solved is what happened with Berkeley. From what your mother said, she took the bribe to expel Jodie just fine but when Jodie disappeared, she suspected what Cynthia must have done and threatened to go to the police. Your mum told her she had someone watching her and if she did that she would frame Berkeley for all that'd happened and make sure she suffered the same fate as Jodie . . .'

'Go on . . .' said Patrick. 'I need to know what she did. Everything.'

'All right. Berkeley kept quiet about what happened to Jodie, fearing for her life, not to mention the fact that if she told the authorities it would come to light that she'd accepted the bribe. But when the police launched another appeal for information, she saw an opportunity and paid someone to say they saw you down at the river with Jodie right before she disappeared.'

'Wait. Why me? Why not Mum? If Berkeley knew who did it, why did she implicate me?'

'Quentin got a full confession out of Berkeley before he offed her so he could decide what the next move should be, and according to him she didn't want your mother to be able to link the paid witness to her. If Berkeley had bribed a witness to step forward and point the finger at your mum it would have led straight to her. But not so much if the witness claimed you were the culprit. She reasoned that if your mum bribed her to protect your future then you were important to her. Berkeley thought that by implicating you, your mother might be forced to come forward and admit her crime.'

Patrick let out a long, heavy breath. 'Did Mum write the letter from Jodie?'

Grace nodded. 'The police found CCTV footage of Quentin in the Silver Street area the day I found the letter. Selina also handed her CCTV footage to the police when she was in custody. He must have gone to Selina's to plant evidence at her house and dropped the note in my bag a couple of days later when I wasn't looking. Your mum tried to match the handwriting as best she could and came close but it didn't test positive for Jodie's DNA, and on close inspection there were some small but noticeable differences in the handwriting.'

Patrick winced, and rubbed the side of his head. 'Jodie paid with her life for being with me,' he said. 'With her life.'

'You cannot look at all that's happened that way, OK?' said Grace. 'You had no idea that your mother was capable of any of this. None of us did. You are not to blame.'

Patrick nodded but then frowned. 'The story didn't match Berkeley's suicide note though. If Mum and Quentin were behind both, wouldn't they try and make the stories match?'

'Your mum didn't realize that Berkeley was behind the paid witness when she wrote the first letter. She only wrote it in an attempt to get you released from custody. When she and Quentin figured out Berkeley was behind it, they went after her and wrote another letter in the hope of confusing the police and throwing them further off the track. Quentin stole the award Berkeley mentioned from her house and planted it in the lake at the academy on his way to meet your mum.'

Patrick was silent for a few moments before speaking again. 'Are you sure they did it, and they're not just protecting me somehow? I had those flashes, remember? I saw myself with my hands around Jodie's neck. I couldn't remember anything that happened but I saw it. I saw myself hurting her. I — '

'Shhhh,' Grace soothed. 'The evidence clears you of any wrongdoing without a shadow of a doubt. Those flashes were probably not memories. They were probably a symptom of PTSD.'

'I hope you're right. This is all such a mess,' Patrick said, sitting up and pushing his hair out of his face. 'Is there anything else I should know?'

'Not yet, but after my meeting with Kitt there might be more.'

Patrick nodded. 'You won't be long?'

'I shouldn't think so. Kitt's on her lunchbreak and her manager is, shall we say, a little bit on the strict side. Roxy will keep you company while I'm gone.'

At the mention of her name the basset hound in the corner raised her head and looked over at them. When it became clear that Berkeley didn't have a next of kin and Roxy would be taking a trip to the pound, Patrick had adopted the mutt on the spot.

Easing herself up, Grace walked over to the dog and with some considerable effort just about managed to pick her up before carrying her back to the bed. 'Here you go, Roxy's cuddles are almost as good as mine.'

'What about her kisses?' Patrick said. There was no glint in his eye, no smirk on his lips, but, given the most he'd managed for the last few days was a few monosyllabic phrases, she knew his joke was a big step forward.

'You tell me,' Grace said with a smile as she pulled her coat on.

'Hey,' Patrick said, grabbing her hand. 'I'm sorry I can't, you know, offer you anything right now.'

Grace shook her head and frowned as though the mere idea of him offering her anything more than friendship was lunacy – which, after everything that had happened, it was. 'That's OK, I didn't ask you for anything.'

He smiled and started to stroke Roxy who was nuzzling him for some fuss. Grace moved towards the door. 'I'll be back in about an hour, don't miss me too much,' she said, before stepping out into the corridor. She pressed the button for the lift and was down to the ground floor in no time. As she exited the building she realized there was a call she should make on the way to meet Kitt at the Minster. Pulling her phone out of her pocket she dialled and felt a nervous clench in her stomach as it rang. After a minute the call connected.

'Mum? It's Grace,' she said as she walked along the riverside making the most of the autumnal sunlight.

THIRTY-SIX

'Everything all right?' said Kitt as Grace ended the call with her mum and joined her on the bench in front of the Minster.

'Yeah, just had to call home, you know, let them know I was doing all right.'

Kitt nodded. 'I'd imagine everything that's happened in the last week or so has put your disagreement in perspective.'

'Er, yeah. Just a bit.'

'How's Patrick doing?'

'Still trying to sleep it all off, I think. Certainly, sleep has been a major theme.'

'And you're being his nurse Nightingale?' said Kitt, her look a bit too knowing for Grace's liking.

'You've seen *The English Patient* one too many times if you think there's any funny business going on,' Grace replied. Though secretly she couldn't deny that, since the showdown at Northumberland airport three days ago, all she'd wanted to do was hold Patrick close and kiss away his pain, she recognized that this wasn't an appropriate response to dealing with the level of grief he was experiencing. Just now she'd have to make do with the holding him close part, and then perhaps after six months of rigorous therapy, if he still enjoyed her company, she would let him take her out for a milkshake and see where things went from there. In the meantime, all she could do was help him get through the unthinkable challenges that lay ahead as best she could.

'I'm probably the only person on the planet who hasn't seen the film. I have read the book though.'

'Why am I not surprised?'

Kitt raised her eyebrows. 'Reading the Booker Prize long list is a minimum stipulation for someone in my walk of life. Besides, the romance was particularly—'

'Enough about *The English Patient*, eh?' said Grace. 'I need details. What's going on with Jodie's case? Did Cynthia give up the whereabouts of Jodie's body, or what?'

Grace wasn't trying to be rude but the location of Jodie's body was, as far as she knew, the only detail the police hadn't got out of Cynthia. She'd admitted to tasking Quentin to plant the drugs in Jodie's locker and to drug Patrick while he slept in his room – using the spare key Patrick had trusted her with – so he wouldn't wake up until it was all too late. Quentin had also drugged their drinks at Selina's party so he could plant the evidence at Selina's house without being recognized by either of them. Although Patrick had asked for updates on everything to do with the case, Grace thought drip-feeding the information was probably for the best. There was so much to talk through, so many sordid details, she feared giving it all to him at once would be too much, despite his protests to the contrary.

The police had dredged the lake at the academy and found Berkeley's Leaders in Education award but Cynthia had soon confessed that this wasn't the murder weapon at all – simply an attempt to frame Berkeley for Jodie's death. Despite all of these unsavoury confessions, the whereabouts of Jodie's body had not been forthcoming.

Kitt bristled at the interruption, as she always did when one of her lengthy book monologues was in some way derailed, but she soon recovered herself and offered a slight nod in response to Grace's prior question. 'Halloran reckons it's going to hit the news tonight so you'd probably better keep the TV and radio off, and warn Patrick that it's best he avoids the internet, at least for this evening. It turns out that Jodie's final resting place was far closer to home than Patrick could ever have realized. Cynthia had made sure the body would never be discovered by a random dog walker out in the woods by burying Jodie beneath her own garage and then getting Quentin to cement over it.'

'How did she manage that without the neighbours noticing?'

'Well, it was inside the garage so I suppose she must have

parked her car somewhere else, got Quentin to transport the equipment late at night while nobody was looking and then closed the garage doors so nobody would see what they were up to.'

'You mean, every time Patrick's been home to visit his mum in the past year, Jodie's body has been . . . pretty much under his feet?' Grace pressed a hand against her tummy. Was she going to throw up? It sure felt like it. She took in a deep breath and slowly let it out, doing all she could not to think about Jodie's body slowly decaying while Cynthia went to lunches with well-to-do-friends and cooked Sunday dinner for her son.

'I'm afraid so. Cynthia tasked Quentin with hiding a few things that might come in useful for framing other people should they ever get desperate, like Jodie's cardigan, and he went back to the outhouse to plant the limestone from Berkeley's drive too.'

Grace shook her head in disbelief. 'How the hell is Patrick ever going to get over all this? Move forward . . .'

'With the help of his friends he'll hopefully be able to move forward the same way any of us do when something terrible happens: one step and one breath at a time,' said Kitt.

'I know,' said Grace. 'But even that's painful at first. I just can't believe the way this all played out. What the hell was she thinking?'

'The whole thing redefines the word "disgusting",' said

Kitt. 'Cynthia still claims she didn't mean to kill Jodie. She just wanted her to surrender the recording of her confessing she'd bribed Berkeley. When it became obvious she wouldn't, she rang Quentin. Pressured him using their previous indiscretion as leverage. He kidnapped Jodie and held her in a drugged state in that outhouse for two days until he was certain the coast was clear.'

'So even if the police checked traffic cameras for the night of Jodie's disappearance, they wouldn't see Quentin's car,' said Grace.

'Right, and he'd taken another precaution. He'd used masking tape to alter the registration plate.'

'He really thought this through.'

'Yes,' said Kitt. 'Well, it wasn't the first time either of them had had to cover their tracks so I'm sorry to say they've both had practice at it. But still, there were some things Cynthia couldn't have expected. She has admitted that behind Patrick's back she would often make cruel comments to Jodie and make it clear she wasn't welcome in the family, so as soon as Jodie received the expulsion letter, she knew that Cynthia had had some hand in it.'

'So, she tried to get the truth out of Berkeley? Berkeley did say that Jodie had barged into her office.'

'That's right, but when Berkeley wouldn't engage and had her removed by security, Jodie went to Cynthia direct and tried to reason with her. She tried to explain how much this was all going to hurt Patrick, and begged her to reverse whatever influence she'd exerted. That's when Cynthia told Jodie what she'd done.'

'And Jodie was, what? Recording the conversation for collateral?'

'It would seem so. She was smart enough to wait until she'd left the house before calling Cynthia back and playing the recording to her. She tried again to get Cynthia to retract the bribe and get her reinstated at the academy, otherwise she was going to go to Patrick with the tape.'

'But Cynthia wouldn't budge?'

Kitt shook her head. 'She told Jodie if she went to Patrick's house, she'd regret it. She had made sure Quentin was following her that morning. After Jodie paid Cynthia a visit and then revealed she had a recording of them, Cynthia told Quentin to pick up Jodie's trail to try and bribe her to hand over the recording, and if that didn't work, go to Patrick's house, drug him, and intercept Jodie if she dared to show up.'

'Is that why she showed up at Patrick's so late?' said Grace. 'She thought it was too risky going round to his any earlier than that.'

'We think so. Patrick did say he had a whole bunch of missed calls and cryptic voicemails from her. She'd clearly tried to call him and let him know she needed to talk to him several times. She probably didn't want to go to his house, in case Cynthia made good on her threat. But she was running out of options. Cynthia knew Jodie had an incriminating recording that could ruin her reputation – not to mention the relationship she had with her son – and Jodie probably feared that Cynthia would go to extreme lengths to keep it under wraps.'

'And she was right,' Grace said with a sigh. 'So when she couldn't get hold of Patrick and she thought Cynthia was coming after her, she resorted to calling the radio station?'

'Yes. Quentin confessed he planned to abduct her. They knew she'd go to Patrick's sooner or later so Quentin snuck in using Cynthia's spare key and drugged the drink on the desk when Patrick was in the bathroom so he would pass out and wouldn't be involved in any of what was about to unfold.'

Grace shuddered. The idea of Quentin creeping around your house without your knowledge was a scary thought indeed. 'So, he waited outside Patrick's house for Jodie to show up?'

'His plan was to take her unawares but he made a noise as he approached and gave himself away. Jodie didn't stop to look at what was making the noise; clearly on edge, she just made a run for it. While she was running, in some desperation, that's when she must have come up with the idea to call the radio station and out Cynthia. She may even have planned to play the recording she'd taken live on air when Randy called her back down by the river.'

'So, when Jodie recognized her attacker, that was Quentin, and she recognized him from when he tried to bribe her?'

'Yes, he tried to pay her off earlier in the evening in the

hope that would be the end of the matter. But she wouldn't hear him out.'

'And the ssssssss sound. Jodie was trying to say Cynthia.'

'I think so,' said Kitt. 'If she'd got another few syllables out Berkeley would still be with us and Cynthia would have been apprehended much sooner. In fact, if Randy had put her on air even a little bit sooner, poor Jodie would still be alive.'

'So, after the outhouse, Quentin took Jodie to Cynthia's house?'

'Yes. Quentin missed his opportunity to stop Jodie before she called the radio station and that phone call meant the police were alerted to the fact that something was going on.'

'By the time Quentin took Jodie to Cynthia's house there must have been a full-scale police investigation in operation focusing on her disappearance.'

'Correct, so they both knew they were in trouble and had to find a way of dealing with the mess they'd created.'

'So, what? Cynthia just panicked and killed her?'

'Not quite. They tried to reason with Jodie first. They tried to get her to agree to a story about her falling into the river and waking up unconscious further downstream. They said that if she went along with their story and deleted the recording of Cynthia confessing to bribing Berkeley, they could just all forget about this and move on.'

'But Jodie was better than that and wouldn't give in.'

'Yes. Cynthia started to really panic about what Patrick

would think about her; she thought she'd lose him for good, so she and Jodie ended up getting into a struggle. Cynthia hit Jodie over the head with a vase, she fell backwards and cracked her head on the stone fireplace. And that was it. They kept her body hidden inside until nightfall and then buried her in the garage when they were sure the neighbours wouldn't be awake to notice anything.'

Grace shook her head. 'It's all so needless.'

'I know. We can't change what's happened in the past, I'm afraid, only bring the truth to light and try and find comfort in whatever justice is served.'

Tears started to slip down Grace's cheeks and she opened her mouth to speak a couple of times before actually managing to get the next sentence out. 'There's something I have to tell you.'

'I'm listening.'

'I'm sorry, I'm not dismissing what we've done all these years. I loved working at the library with you, helping people discover new things about the world and themselves. But I wanted you to be the first to know: I dropped out of the library studies course at the academy. Given the circumstances, the academy have agreed to refund the tuition fees.'

Kitt looked at Grace for a long moment. 'I already know you dropped out of the academy, Grace. The acting dean is an old friend of mine. I called to discuss Lowenthal with her, and to make sure you and Patrick were granted the appropriate compassionate leave from your studies after all that had happened. That's when she told me you'd left the course.'

'Oh . . . I'm sorry you found out like that, I had to. I just . . . I can't do that any more. If I had my choice of anything I could do just for the sake of being happy I'd be a librarian. It's not an easy job but it's so rewarding. Working with you in the women's studies section is the happiest I've ever been. That's why I applied for the course at the academy.'

'But . . .' Kitt prompted.

'But when things like this are happening, I think I need to do more than just look after my own happiness. I need to be out there doing something to make sure that nobody else ends up like Jodie.'

'You don't have to apologize to me. I can't blame you for deciding you don't want to stay there for another three years after all that's happened in the first six weeks. And seeing what happened to Jodie, it's understandable that you'd want to choose a slightly different track. Have you made any decisions about what you might do next?'

Grace jerked her head to one side. 'You sound like Mum. I only dropped out two days ago. Give me a chance, eh?'

Kitt smiled. 'What if I don't want to give you a chance? What if I want to make you an offer before someone else snaps you up?'

Grace frowned and dried her tears. 'What kind of an offer?'

Smiling, Kitt pulled a black rectangular box out of her satchel and handed it to Grace.

'What's this?'

'Open it and see.'

'It's not Gwyneth Paltrow's head, is it?'

'Why would it be Gwyneth Paltrow's head? It's much too small for that, for a start.'

Grace suddenly got a flash of how Kitt felt whenever she didn't get one of her many book references. 'Never mind.'

She gave the box a dubious look and lifted the lid, wondering if something vile or startling was going to leap out at her. After all the pranks she had played on Kitt over the last three years of working together, she understood revenge was well overdue, but surely now was not the time? Thankfully, it seemed, her friend and former boss wasn't in a vengeful mood.

Inside the box, Grace found a stack of business cards. They had her name printed on them and an address for a small office space that, by the postcode, looked as though it was situated just outside the city walls, just beyond Walmgate Bar. The most striking and exciting element, however, was the business name written in embossed gold font at the top of the card.

'Hartley and Edwards Investigations,' Grace said, barely able to believe her eyes. 'Are you serious?'

'I'm very serious. What else would you expect from a prim librarian?' Kitt said, with a twinkle in her eyes.

Grace had the decency to look shamefaced for a split second but then excitement overtook her again. 'What's the deal? Will I be your assistant?'

'To begin with, but with training I expect you to become a full partner in the business. That is, if you're interested.'

'Yes, of course I'm interested! Although,' Grace said, the cheeky smile returning to her face for the first time since she was held at knifepoint, 'if that does happen, we should probably change the business name to Edwards and Hartley – it's got a better ring to it, don't you agree?'

'No,' Kitt said, 'but if you feel strongly about it by the time you're qualified you can hand in your notice and form your own rival investigation agency.'

'I won't rule it out but it will take a lot more effort to play tricks and jokes on you so I'm not convinced it will pan out.'

Kitt chuckled and Grace joined in.

'Wait, does this mean you're giving up the library too? You can't leave that place. How will it survive without you?'

'Sometimes I think you don't know me at all. Of course I'm not going to give up the library. I'm like a stick of rock, chop me in half and I'd have librarian written all the way through. I'm just reducing to part-time hours – two days a week. Unlike some, I can't so easily kiss the thing I love most in the world goodbye.'

'Better not tell Halloran that,' Grace said with a giggle.

'I see you haven't lost your sense of humour through all this,' said Kitt.

'How could I when the half-year anniversary of Arch Streaking Day is a mere one hundred and seventy days away?'

Kitt sighed.

'Thanks for this. It's what I need right now.'

'I think that makes two of us,' Kitt said.

Grace leaned in and gave Kitt a hug and smiled as her friend returned the gesture. 'Want to see your new office then?' Kitt said.

'Oh yes!' Grace said, jumping up.

The pair of them set off in the direction of Walmgate. Despite Kitt's kind offer of employment, Grace still wasn't as sure as she wished she could be about what the future held. But wasn't that true for everyone when it came down to it? Nobody really knew what was around the next corner: whether their plans would come together, or, as in the case of Jodie, whether they'd be cut unexpectedly short. Perhaps the best thing to do was just to keep moving forward despite the not knowing, just like Kitt said, taking one step and one breath at a time.

ACKNOWLEDGEMENTS

Heartfelt thanks to Hazel Nicholson who continues to provide such wonderful feedback on police procedure for this series. Her observations usually throw a spanner in the works for my characters, which of course only leads to a more interesting story.

Thank you to my agent Joanna Swainson who is a truly nurturing presence in my writing career. Thank you also to Quercus Books for deciding to publish yet more instalments of the series and to my editor Stef Bierwerth whose comments and suggestions have undoubtedly helped this latest story to flourish.

Gratitude as ever to family and friends who do not hear from me for long spells when I'm on deadline for the latest book, but still have the good grace to pick up the phone to me when I eventually get time to call.

And thank you to my husband Jo, who so enthusiastically

endures so many countless conversations about my characters and the situations they manage to talk themselves into. Without such support, I'm not convinced these books would exist.